The Pleasure Device

Harwell Heirs Book 1

Regina Kammer

Viridium Press

Published by: Viridium Press, Friday Harbor, Washington
ISBN-13: (paperback) 978-0-9910166-3-1
ISBN-10: (paperback) 0-9910166-3-7
ISBN-13: (ebook) 978-0-9910166-4-8
ISBN-10: (ebook) 0-9910166-4-5

The Harwell Heirs

Victorian aristocracy has very strict rules concerning marital connections and familial obligations. But the Harwell heirs—Helena, Sophia, and Arthur—discover love doesn't always follow the rules. Scandalous affairs force these scions of society to choose between duty and desire, deference and destiny.

Book 1: *The Pleasure Device*

Book 2: *Disobedience By Design*

Book 3: *Where Destiny Plays*

Harwell Heirs Legacy Romances

Travel beyond England's shores for these stories featuring beloved secondary characters from the first three books of the series. The Legacy novels delve into the romances of the friends, family, and intimates of the extended Harwell family.

Book 4: *A Delicate Seduction*

Book 5: *Discovering Her Delight*

Book 6: *Their Noble Deceit*

Acknowledgments

Thank you to my family—especially my parents—and friends for their enthusiastic and continued encouragement, and to my colleagues for their advice, knowledge, and support. Most of all, thanks to my husband for his advice, patience, and love.

Dedication

To Chris Baty for making me believe I could write a novel, and to my husband for reading every word.

Chapter One

London, May 1879

"Observe, gentlemen, how our subject is in the flaccid, or un-aroused state."

Dr. Julius Christopher made note of the blasé tone of Dr. Waddington's voice, seemingly completely unaffected by the circumstances in which he was instructing his audience. As if he had a pretty girl lying on a table with her legs splayed open before him every day.

Not bloody likely. Julius stifled a chuckle. Waddington catered to a much older, and less agitated, clientele.

His host inelegantly manhandled the privates of the female subject. "We have brought before you a young woman of the laboring classes—"

The girl on the table rolled her pretty brown eyes.

"Suffering from the anxieties of her circumstances. Tending toward drink and belligerence—"

Julius noted the girl exhibited no signs of anxiety or alcoholism, just a little exasperation.

"Thusly unable to control her desires, her intercourse with her fellow man approaches a manner most uncivilized—"

Intercourse preceded by proper seduction is a social equalizer. Any woman can respond in a "manner most uncivilized".

"Her symptoms, therefore, are different from the symptoms of ladies of culture and breeding. More violent, frenzied, akin to madness. In other words base, like her class—"

Said the man violating the girl's genitalia.

"But a fine subject nonetheless—"

Because she's available and cheap.

"As this new remedy works the same on all women, regardless of class distinction."

There were scattered murmurs of skepticism and admiration amongst Julius' colleagues present.

"We have our brethren in France to thank for this new method of electro-therapy."

The murmurs were now tinged with incredulity and gratitude. Julius had figured the ever-industrious Americans would have been the ones to congratulate instead.

The girl stared blankly at the ornate ceiling of the small medical room, giving Julius a chance to observe her. Most likely Waddington—or his housekeeper, rather—had promised a meal, some clothes, perhaps even a fashionable hat. Whatever it was, seeing a doctor in his office was probably much better than what she usually had to do for food or drink. Although, as he studied her, he wondered if lying with her legs spread open, her feet in stirrups, her petticoats up to her waist, her arms strapped down at her sides, and at least a dozen men observing her was better than letting a drunken sod spend between her thighs in a dark alley.

"Let me show you the exact locus of stimulation," Waddington continued, inelegantly revealing the girl's clitoris with his thumb and index finger. "It is a nerve with direct connection to the brain." He touched the girl's forehead. "A current will pass along the track of this nerve." He traced the hypothetical path bisecting her torso. "Taking the place of nervous energy, producing a muscular contraction. By creating such a resolution in this area, we can calm the emotions."

"But Dr. Waddington," said Dr. Dodsworth in his typical high-pitched, shaky whine, "we can do this with our hands."

"Or with the pelvic douche," added Dr. Hargreaves, his accent ridiculously far above the professional classes.

"Yes, yes," agreed Waddington. "However, gentlemen, this device uses neither manual labor nor water pressure, but instead the most modern of energy sources." He lifted a black cloth covering a shiny, two-tiered cart, unveiling a curious machine, an engine of sorts, housed on the lower shelf. "It uses electricity."

There were murmurs of doubt and disbelief in the small theater.

Waddington took a long, thin cylindrical rod lying on the top tray of the cart next to him and held it up. "The device is connected to a dynamo-electric machine." He indicated the cord attached to the engine at the base of the cart. "No more digital fatigue, gentlemen, and no more mess with water."

Waddington indelicately smeared an oily substance on the girl's privates. She flinched.

"See how contact to the area already excites the subject?"

The girl closed her eyes. Probably in acquiescence rather than anticipation.

"Now, gentlemen, observe." Waddington reached for the engine. There was a sharp click, then a whirring sound. The rod in his hand began to oscillate.

He pressed the vibrating wand against the girl's "locus of stimulation".

The girl gasped in shock, her face registering utter surprise. She moaned and writhed, flailing against her bindings. Her pelvis jerked upward toward the vibrating wand as if wanting more, an action that elicited scattered cries of appreciation in the room.

Julius had to suppress a smile as her body lifted and tensed for several seconds before she screamed and crashed back down onto the table.

She opened her eyes, the reality of the drab room and its banal occupants causing her to blush. It was rather charming.

"*Et voilà*, gentlemen!" exclaimed the very gratified Dr. Waddington. "Mere seconds to achieve the hysterical paroxysm. Faster than any hand among you, and even faster than any other device you have available in your offices."

Julius smiled to himself. His colleague had absolutely no idea what he had just done to the very pretty young lass before them. But Julius knew, and the stiffness in his trousers was annoying evidence. For the last few years, he had wondered why the men of the medical profession had never made the connection between the ill-termed "hysterical paroxysm" and sexual culmination. It was simply bizarre and most unscientific.

"Dr. Waddington," he began, his voice tinged with the utmost of respect, "in your opinion is there any connection between what a woman feels in a state of sexual pleasure and what she feels when this procedure is performed upon her?"

There were muffled gasps of mortification in the room.

"My dear Dr. Christopher," said the hoary Waddington with authority, "we all know that a woman cannot possibly feel sexual pleasure in the absence of penetration."

There was, apparently, a consensus of agreement amongst those in attendance.

"Thank you, Doctor," replied Julius with sincere politeness. "Of course, I had forgotten that fact. You have presented to us a most useful treatment for hysteria. I think my colleagues will agree that this device will enable us to see so many more patients. And with the modern world changing as it does every day, we will have so many more patients to treat."

As his fellow doctors voiced their concurrence, Julius smiled along, satisfied in the knowledge that he could now procure a new toy from France with which to pleasure women, and, in effect, to elicit his own.

Telling one's valet to take the afternoon off was a pleasure more men should experience, Nicholas Ramsay mused as he relaxed in his steaming bath, looking forward to being undisturbed for hours. Undisturbed, yes, but continually occupied.

He had been in London for several weeks already, practically ignoring the mountain of books and papers he had brought back with him from the Edinburgh Medical School, a selection of which mocked him as they lay neatly stacked on the floor next to the tub. It was high time he undertook a serious review of current practices in family medicine.

He lifted his head from the curved rim and watched minuscule bubbles forming on his skin, floating along his thigh under the water. Gaseous exchange.

Respiration.

He let out a long exhale. His life was finally on course. He could breathe easy.

And much of it was due to his patron—and lover—Lady Foxley-Graham. Lavinia had helped him tremendously upon his return to Britain, reacquainting him with civilization, recommending him to Edinburgh, arranging a good set of rooms in London, insisting on finding him a position with another doctor before he struck out on his own. She was also rather resolute that he avail himself of the opportunities of the Season to garner a wife, "a fine young woman who will bolster you in your career, Nicky." Meaning not necessarily someone who was overly clever or very beautiful. Mere convivial matrimony.

Was it too much to ask for a true meeting of minds? Mutual physical desire?

He grunted and let his head rest on the cool porcelain, staring blankly at the lines of the varnished dark wood paneling truncated by a length of molding. Bath-time was the perfect time to take a respite from the dread of peacocking amongst the upper crust. He had left that life behind years ago and did not look forward to mingling with men and women of the *ton* who kept their sordid secrets well-hidden. It was bad enough he had his own blasted scandal to conceal.

He shifted his head to gaze up at the plaster ceiling before finding his wits and jolting his attention back to the pile of medical journals on the floor. His new life wasn't going to start with him pouting and pining about the past. No. He had a profession and the possibility of a wife with whom he would start a family, a new family, a proper family. And, to support that family in a manner befitting his station, he would have to be the best damn doctor in London.

He grabbed the first journal on his stack. "November '78," he grumbled. Already six months old and probably filled with news and notes he had by now gleaned some other way. He let out a sigh then methodically leafed through the pages.

The article on page twenty-six piqued his interest. "Clinical and Therapeutic Treatments of Hysteria". Hysteria "is a disease which affects the higher classes in a disproportionate degree" afflicting only the female of the species, but occurring more frequently in "unmarried women and those who are unhappily married". Causes included "sexual excesses…especially masturbation". Nicholas chuckled to himself. If all that were the case, then his own lover must certainly "suffer" the same ailment.

He read on. The women thus plagued took on any number of symptoms from paralysis of the limbs to convulsions to religious delusions. Nicholas had to admit that he was still rather new to the profession, but surely a disease that rendered a woman paralyzed was far different than one that rendered a woman delusional? He turned the page. The section on treatments included illustrations. His eyes widened.

Beside the various herbal and medicinal remedies, diet modifications, and cold showers, were the "localized" treatments to the patient's pelvic area. One engraving showed the "douche" therapy—a woman in a hip bath with a strong jet of water aimed between her legs. Another showed a physician massaging a female patient, his hand at her crotch.

Nicholas was incredulous. The doctor was stimulating the patient to orgasm. Even he, a neophyte, could see that.

He put the journal down and let his head relax against the back of the tub, wondering if he himself could perform such a treatment. He could, he supposed, but not without his cock growing to full stand as it had just by reading a damn medical journal.

He grabbed his erection.

Good God. He would probably spend in his trousers if he had to perform such a remedy.

Waves rippled across the top of the water as he distractedly played with his shaft.

Especially if his patient were a delicious ginger-haired girl with green eyes, gazing up at him in wonder, her face flushed, her chest heaving as his skillful fingers produced magnificent sensations previously unbeknownst to her.

Christ, the thought made him so very, utterly hard. His attention to his needy cock was in earnest now, turning ripples into rhythmic churning. It was probably because he hadn't fucked Lavinia or even masturbated for two days that his errant prick was behaving as such. Surely it wasn't reading about what the journal said was a normal medical procedure.

He watched as he pulled the prepuce over the glans, newly intrigued by the mundane yet stimulating act, fascinated that the pleasure he was bringing to himself was, while not considered thoroughly proper in men of his class, certainly tolerated as long as it did not become obsessive.

His movements became more determined and vigorous, sloshing bathwater up the sides of the tub.

It was rather unfair that the female sex was taught that such self-pleasuring was immoral and damaging. No wonder the result was a delusional disease.

A delusional disease suffered by most women of his class, women who would lie still under their husbands during the marital act, women who would flee in terror at the idea of orgiastic delight. Women who would never, ever touch themselves.

Christ! The thought almost made him flaccid until the image of the enraptured ginger-haired girl lolling and moaning under his ministrations strengthened his conviction that surely there was a woman who had discovered the joys of lubricious solitary satisfaction. A woman for whom physical pleasure elicited not shame, but such wondrous contentment as to provoke her to seek out sensual gratification.

He had to find that woman.

His hips bucked up, splashing water over the edge of the tub, as he groaned his satisfaction. He held on to his prick as he continued to spasm, jetting his semen into the water.

Yes, he exhaled, *it is a fine thing to spend an afternoon in private indulgence.*

Helena Phillips slowly pulled up her cambric nightdress under the sheets. She wanted to touch herself. No, that wasn't right. She *needed* to touch herself, a need so strong she couldn't wait to excuse herself after luncheon to go upstairs, pleading a headache, needing rest before the social obligations of the evening. The urge had never been so insistent. She had ignored the reasons until they had surged forth while she lingered in front of the cheval glass staring at her nude figure before dressing for bed.

The fate of the family rested upon her shoulders and she was nervous.

Not scared, no. It wasn't fear that rattled her, more like trepidation and dread. While she had been prepared for marriage all her life, and by fourteen knew it had to be to a titled man—an earl at the very least—the reality of it was settling in. She was being introduced to men at every turn, some attractive, some not so much, some old, some young, some interesting, some tedious. Of course, she had confidence in her desirability to the men of the aristocracy. Mama had assured her she was by far the most beautiful debutante in London that Season, and Papa had assured her his industrial fortune made her by far the wealthiest. But she didn't want a husband who wanted her for beauty and wealth. She wanted a husband who would be her best friend, who would ask her opinion, who would converse intelligently about the latest scientific discoveries, who would make her laugh.

When they heard such "nonsense", her parents would chastise her for daydreaming too much, for reading too much, for laughing aloud too much. They would complain she was far too clever and far too curious about the world around her for any duke or earl.

Helena worried she would end up with a man who was not curious about the world around her.

What if he wasn't very clever?

What if he wasn't very witty?

What if he was thoroughly boring?

Did she have to marry such a man? Make empty chitchat at breakfast? Pretend fondness at soirées? Keep her children silent when he was in his study?

Did she really have to share a bed with such a man?

Helena knew nothing of the marriage bed, but could tell not all husbands and wives shared the same level of satisfying intimate camaraderie as her parents. Some wives looked utterly frustrated.

If it came to that, Helena knew how to relieve her own frustrations. But what if her thoroughly boring husband forbade her to touch herself?

She knew it was wrong to touch herself. Well, no one had actually told her so. The mistresses at her finishing school avoided the subject. Besides, they were too busy telling her how to hold a cup and saucer or how to curtsy to a dance partner. But she had heard from some of her friends that to touch the area reserved for the husband was unchaste and he would know just as he would know if she were a virgin or not. Then there were the stories of girls who went mad from hysteria, a peculiar disease that only struck those who went against this moral code and touched themselves…there. The disease marked them for life as trollops and strumpets, no better than gin-soaked streetwalkers. And no gentleman, especially not a peer, would ever want to marry such a girl.

But when Helena had returned home to London, she slowly became aware that what she had overheard might be just myths and rumors. She found a book—quite a few, really—in her parents' library in an area reserved for special books, some of which were very, very old, their gilt edges and flourished scripts forbidden to her. But next to these fragile ancient volumes were books about people exploring each other's bodies and, she was most interested to see, sometimes their own bodies. The illustrations were quite delightful and remarkably instructive.

No one in the fascinating tales suffered from any disease. And, not only did the young men favor the young women who had unleashed their desires, the young women in the stories enjoyed all the pleasures they experienced very, very much.

That's when Helena decided to explore herself.

She had been clumsy at first, her trembling fingers feeling cold against the heated, moist flesh between her legs. Curiosity had led her to touch everything, every fold, every cleft, resisting the urge to put too many fingers inside herself as the books had warned such an action would divest her of her virginity. Her tentative ministrations continued for several nights as a very pleasant diversion before she fell asleep.

Then one night, after everyone in the house had gone to bed, she stayed up to read a book with a curiously misspelled title and a handful of rather poorly done illustrations, *The Bed-Fellows: Or, The Young Misses Manuel*. Every night, Lucy and Kate, the eponymous young misses, both about her own age, exchanged stories about their erotic experiences, becoming so aroused by each other's adventures that they began pleasuring each other, at which point Helena was so engrossed with the story that she simply stroked herself distractedly.

And that's when she found the spot.

A delicate caress with a slippery finger sent the most amazing jolt of pleasure from her head to her toes. She pushed the book away and turned onto her back, closing her eyes so she could concentrate on the nub under her fingertip and the sensual pleasure the tiny spot elicited. She rubbed lightly at first, discovering this produced a sensation of gentle waves surrounding her, like relaxing in a warm bath. She increased her motions and the pressure, finding this increased the thumping of her heart and the expiration of her breath, like running quite fast in a warm rain, water cascading on her bare skin, dripping from her hardened nipples aching with sensitivity. Her free hand grabbed a breast, kneading it with the same rhythm as her hand below. Running became climbing, up a mountain peak, to stand, arms wide, wanting, willing heated showers to deluge her in pleasure. She teetered for a moment, her breath catching, her body arching, before she fell into the abyss of sybaritic serenity below.

Helena opened her eyes, suddenly more aware of what she was seeing, her body more aware of the mattress beneath her, the soft sheets covering her, her mind more aware of the possibilities of life.

And knowing she could never, ever marry a man who considered any of that wrong.

CHAPTER TWO

Grace had been allotted a corner of the medical room to dress while the doctors drank port on the other side in celebration of their medical victory. Their chortles and toasts of praise for the extraordinary French machine were reminders of their presence, and of the fact that she had no screen, only a straight-back chair to hide behind while she pulled on her drawers. Of course, her sudden feelings of modesty were somewhat unwarranted given what had transpired moments before. But the room was grand, with its Oriental carpet, vast windows letting in cloud-soaked daylight, and intricately carved wood paneling. Surely they could have afforded her a dressing screen?

"And how are you feeling, my dear girl?"

She looked up at the concern-laden voice and was pleasantly surprised. The entire time, she hadn't noticed this particular gentleman when she really should have as he stood out like the queen at a debutante ball. He was younger than most of the men present—although still middle-aged—and far more handsome than any of them. Tall, lean, with a trim black goatee and moustache, a touch of gray at his temples, he angled over her and smiled. His brilliant blue eyes were hypnotizing.

"Hungry." What was she supposed to say?

"Is that your only coat?" He pointed to her moth-eaten green wool sacque sagging on the rack.

"No," she said sharply. "Me other one's at me country estate." She sat down too hastily on the hard chair but ignored the ache in her bottom as she pulled on a stocking.

The handsome man chuckled. It wasn't the reaction she had expected. She flushed in embarrassment.

"I'd reckon you would like another wrap, especially during the wintertime." His gaze wandered to the shabby bonnet perched on top of her coat. "And perhaps a hat as well?" His voice was kind, not mocking, but possibly a little too keen.

Grace tensed as she slipped on her other stocking. Was he offering to buy her clothes? By the look of his own attire, a fine-gauge wool suit tailored precisely for his lean form, he could afford to spend a bob or two on her. But what would she have to do to earn it? While what she just went through was astonishingly pleasurable, she wasn't sure she wanted to be on display like that ever again. And besides, the man's charismatic presence was making it very difficult for her to put her shoes on. He unnerved her. She wasn't sure if it was in a good way.

"Right now I only want me tea."

"Yes, of course, my dear," he soothed. "You may have your dinner in the kitchen, then when you are finished we can discuss my offer."

Offer? She glanced up. "What offer?"

"Why, I would like to buy you a new hat and coat for the chance to practice using this new device on you." He waved his hand to indicate the French pleasure machine.

Grace looked him in the eye. He seemed sincere. Still ... "I don't wanna buncha old men gawking at me."

"Oh, heavens, no. It will be just you and I, so I can become adept at using the technology as well as exploring its possibilities." It was said matter-of-factly. "Very private, I assure you."

Alone with this handsome gent? "Where do I go?"

"To my offices in Chelsea."

So far from the East End. She'd probably walk, but… "I'll need cab fare," she blurted.

"Of course, my dear." The handsome man reached into his frock pocket and pulled out a fine leather coin purse. He counted out six shillings. "Will this be enough?"

His smile was disarming. Grace could swear his blue eyes twinkled at her. "Yes sir." It was more than enough.

"Good, good." He put his purse away and pulled out a calling card. "This is where you will go. I hope to have the device installed tomorrow, so perhaps if you could come by Monday after luncheon? Around three in the afternoon?" He handed the card to her.

Grace looked at the card then back up at him. His lips twisted in concern. He must have noticed her defeated expression.

"Oh dear. You do know how to read, don't you?" His voice dripped with genuine sympathy, devoid of contempt.

"A bit." Grace swallowed the lump in her throat. She didn't want to appear unworthy of such a charming man.

"Well, my dear girl—what is your name?"

"Grace Danby, sir."

"Well, my dear Grace—what a lovely name, it suits you—"

"Thank you, sir." Grace blushed again.

"Why don't you remember this, then. I am Dr. Julius Christopher of 16A Chelsea Manor Street off the King's Road. If you've gone to Flood Walk you've gone too far."

Grace repeated what Dr. Christopher had told her. As he listened, his captivating smile sparked mini-fantasies in the back of Grace's mind.

And then he bent down and put his warm hand on her very cold one.

Grace practically jumped from the chair, but a gentle caress calmed her.

"I will see you Monday, Grace," he murmured in her ear. "I promise we will have much enjoyment from our little exercise, wouldn't you agree?" Dr. Christopher winked at her.

Grace watched intently as he glided across the fancy carpet to join his stodgy colleagues on the other side of the room. Monday couldn't come quickly enough.

"Christ, Lavinia! You vixen! Whatever are you doing?"

Nicholas was about to spend when his lover had decided to stop bouncing on his now painfully erect cock and just sit on top of him and smirk.

She narrowed her lovely amber eyes at him. "Say you'll escort me to Lord and Lady Wrexham's ball tonight and I'll continue." As a token of trust, she flexed her muscles, tightening temptingly around him.

So good, so good... "All right, all right, I'll take you to that blasted dance! Now just let me spend!"

"Very well, Nicky," Lavinia said coolly, as if she herself were neither involved nor interested in their physical union. She proceeded with her movements, riding his shaft excruciatingly slowly, increasing her rhythm far, far too languidly.

Nicholas sighed. He so needed the release. He closed his eyes, concentrating on the inevitable.

But Lavinia was an expert. She held him at the point just before bursting.

"And, you'll bring me roses beforehand."

Good God the woman was infuriating! "Yes, yes, Vinny, love. Anything!"

Lavinia smiled and slammed her body down onto his prick, then gripped him as she pulled up only to crash her hips against his once again.

It was all Nicholas needed. He howled his orgasm as he jetted his sperm inside the fair lady's cunt.

Lavinia laughed and rolled off him to stretch, sated, at his side.

Nicholas lay panting, his heartbeat slowing as he came down from his sensual height. "Why do I put up with you, Vinny, love?"

As she nuzzled against him, he knew exactly why. At forty-five, his lover had a body to rival any twenty-year-old's, plus the sexual skill to rival any whore's. She diligently maintained all the connections built up by her late husband, and now had the power to rival most men's as well.

"Because the Honorable Nicholas Atherley needs an entrée into Society."

Nicholas cringed. "Don't call me that," he said a little too curtly. "And don't you mean a re-entrée?"

"Yes, darling."

Lavinia got up to put on her silk dressing gown much to Nicholas' disappointment. He'd really rather have her naked at his side.

"You do have proper evening attire, don't you Nicky? Nothing too exotic?" Her rich brown hair flecked with gold and gray dazzled in the late-afternoon light as she walked past the window.

"I was thinking of an elaborately embroidered kaftan I picked up in 'Stamboul."

The shock on Lavinia's face was well worth the joke. She sneered at him the moment she realized he was having his fun with her.

"Darling," she said as she made a nest of pillows on her side of the bed, "this will be your first Season in seven years. It is very important you meet all the right people, make the right connections. I made a promise to your mother you would not end up in some squalid hell-hole in the East End, or, God forbid, some uncivilized viper's den in the colonies." She lay down, comfortably bolstered and sidled up to him.

"Thank you, Vinny," Nicholas said softly as he put his arm around her. He knew Lavinia felt the weight of that promise daily. Lavinia and his mother had been the best of friends.

"Louisa knew you would never return to the family home. But she also knew you wouldn't spend the rest of your life traipsing across the barren outlands of Asia. Before she died, we used to plot how she would be able to slip away to visit you in London without the earl knowing."

The casual reference to his mother's death chafed him. "'Murdered,' you mean. My mother did not merely die. She was murdered, Vinny."

Lavinia fussed needlessly with her robe. "Let's not talk about that now, Nicky," she said darkly.

He kissed her forehead. "Yes, love." Nicholas would do anything to satisfy his late mother's wishes. His only regret in life was that he had not been by her side at her deathbed. Instead, he had been in the mountains of Anatolia learning native and Muslim healing arts. It had been Lavinia who had written to tell him of her untimely death and who had assured him her last thoughts had been of him. In her memory, he took her maiden surname of Ramsay.

"Also," Lavinia continued cheerfully, poking him in the chest, "don't forget I promised that you would meet a pretty girl and settle down. That's one reason I'm making you go to the Wrexhams."

Nicholas put his face in his hands and groaned at the prospect. He rarely heard of marriage being a good idea for any of the parties involved. Lavinia's wasn't. His mother had only tolerated his drunk of a father because he was an earl and had given her two sons. "I'm dreading that, you know."

"I don't see why. You're handsome, charming, and witty. You even have a respectable income. You'll have admirers at your feet."

"All the talk about the latest fashions and who's marrying whom, it's just a varnish over self-doubt and fear, if not an outright expression of a poor intellect."

Lavinia laughed. "So you want a girl who speaks plainly."

"And who reads more than just ladies' magazines."

"And one who can recite *The Iliad* in Greek, I suppose?"

Nicholas flashed her a disapproving grimace. "I just want to be able to have an interesting conversation. That should not be too much to ask."

"There will be plenty of young ladies having their second or even third Season."

"For good reason, I expect," Nicholas grunted.

"Not always. Some are very pretty, rather clever too, just very shy. I've found that once they've resigned themselves to a life of spinsterhood, they gain confidence in their relations with the opposite sex. They no longer need to be careful about what they say or how they act. What you see is the true woman." She wrapped a lock of his hair around her finger. "Should make wife-hunting that much easier for you."

"Does that mean they'll be friendly in dark corners? I remember the last time I went through all of this, it seemed girls wouldn't even let you hold their hands."

"Rake!" she said with a swat. "Keep your hands off, and I mean it, Nicky. That's what I'm here for. You don't want to make any mistakes or else your career as a doctor may be ruined before it's even started."

"Yes, Lady Foxley-Graham, ma'am," baited Nicholas. He pulled her more closely to him and kissed her forehead again. "Will this mean I'll have to give you up?"

Lavinia snuggled more deeply against him at the thought of the inevitability. "Eventually, dear. And definitely after you are married. Well, for the first year or two."

"Hmm."

"But you may find someone you really like. You may fall in love, Nicky."

Nicholas found the idea unlikely. After traveling across Europe and the Near East for seven years, he had not once discovered love. Erotic experiences beyond his imagination, yes, but love, no. He was beginning to think that, at the advanced age of twenty-eight, he would never fall in love. And with Lavinia at his side, he was happy just as things were.

CHAPTER THREE

Helena tugged at her gloves, then traced the arabesque on the brocade of her silk skirt, then toyed with the fringe on her cashmere *sortie de bal*. And when the jostling carriage finally slowed to a jerky amble, she gripped the leather seat cushions for dear life.

"Helena, a lady does not fidget so," Mama scolded gently as they pulled up to Lord and Lady Wrexham's Mayfair residence. "You must calm yourself. A man does not want a girl who fiddles and twiddles. He wants a fine young woman who will attend to him without distraction."

"Yes Mama." Helena drew in a fortifying breath as she stepped down from the brougham and mounted the marble steps of the Neoclassical mansion. She fought back desperately against pangs of anxiety. The stakes were high. If she succeeded in a good match, her grandparents, the Marquess and Marchioness of Richmond, might not look upon her and Mama as the black sheep of the family.

Well, at the very least, Mama had intimated to her, they might have more respect for Helena. As far as the Marquess of Richmond was concerned, Mama was no longer his daughter—much less the Lady Sophia Harwell—after she had married Joseph Phillips, a commoner, and, even worse, an American.

At the top step, Helena sighed, preparing to meet her destiny.

"Sophie, you're looking radiant. And Helena, all grown up."

The familiar voice filled her with a glow of joy. "Uncle Arthur!"

Uncle Arthur, ever so dapper in his evening attire, stood next to a column with his arms open wide waiting for her to hug him. Helena knew she had to restrain herself in such a public place. Still, he was her favorite uncle, and she, his favorite niece, a private joke since neither had any more of such relations. He wrapped his arms around her and patted her politely, then turned to Mama and kissed her on both cheeks.

"I didn't expect you, Arthur."

"Ah, but 'Lord Petersham' must make an appearance every once in a while," he said with a smirk. "Otherwise the gossips of the ton might think me dead."

"And not throw eligible widows your way?" Mama teased. She and Uncle Arthur shared a wonderful rapport.

Uncle Arthur was terrifically handsome yet remained a confirmed bachelor, something having happened in his past that her parents just hinted at but would never actually discuss. Helena only knew that the lady in question had been beautiful and that it had happened a very long time ago, before she was born.

Uncle Arthur turned to her. "I received a letter from your father. He told me all about our business overseas."

"Oh?" Helena tried to be polite, but it was not quite what she wanted to hear.

"And that he sends his love."

She bit her lip in abashment. "Thank you." She smiled up at him. "Are we allowed to dance?"

"Together? I think not." He glanced at Mama. "I'm sure you'll have legions of suitors and I should not stand in their way." He winked. "I'll keep an eye on you, make sure none of the young men misbehave."

Like Mama and Papa did.

"Arthur, we must be going in now," Mama reminded him.

"Yes, of course." He hugged Helena once again and pressed his lips to her ear. "You'll know him when you meet him, Helena," he whispered. "Don't settle for anyone less."

Helena grinned, then quickly composed herself before she and Mama stood in line to enter the Wrexham mansion.

"Darling," Mama said softly with a proud smile, "you look beautiful."

"So do you, Mama." Helena thought she saw her blush. Even at thirty-seven, Mama was still a captivating beauty. Tonight, though, Helena sensed a touch of sadness, probably because they were alone. Papa was far too often in America for his business, and Helena knew Mama missed him desperately. Her parents had a very enviable connection, a deep intellectual, physical, and emotional bond.

"Mrs. Joseph Phillips and her daughter, Miss Helena Phillips." The footman's announcement when they had reached the front of the receiving line revived Helena to her surroundings. The entry hall buzzed with women in gowns the colors of pastels, smiling, laughing, seductively waving fans while gazing up at men of all sizes, shapes, and ages but each wearing black evening dress. The dull glow of gas lamps and candles made everyone a little more attractive than they probably actually were.

As Mama and Helena exchanged greetings with Lord and Lady Wrexham, a rather formidable older woman approached, wearing far too much lace and reeking of expensive French perfume.

"Oh my dear Sophie!" the lady exclaimed a bit too loudly. "Excuse me, my lord, Lady Wrexham, I simply must have a word with my friend Mrs. Phillips. You do not mind?"

Clearly her forthright manner was indulged by their hosts. Lord and Lady Wrexham said they certainly did not mind.

She grabbed Mama's arm affectionately before she spied Helena. "Oh my," she said with sudden and uncharacteristic delicacy. "This is your daughter, is it not? She is the very image of you." She exhaled a sigh of marvel and approbation.

"Thank you." Helena curtsied, then flushed with alarm knowing she must have done something terribly wrong. She had completely forgotten what one did when complimented.

"Charlotte," Mama acknowledged with a slight bow of her head. "Lady Banbury, this is my daughter Helena. She is just eighteen and is enjoying her first Season."

Helena knew exactly who Lady Banbury was, besides of course the wife of the Earl of Banbury. Mama had said Lady Banbury knew everybody who was anybody and everything about them, and it was a very good idea to get to know the countess and to do whatever she said.

"Oh my dear," exclaimed Lady Banbury taking Helena's arm. "I must introduce you around. Tell me, what have you done so far this year?"

Helena glanced quickly at Mama who nodded. "I've been presented to the queen."

"Of course you have. I remember when I was presented. Mind you, it was the same queen." Lady Banbury's high-pitched laugh put Helena a little more at ease.

"We've been to the Royal Academy exhibition," Helena continued.

"Ah." The countess nodded. "Their new president, Sir Frederic Leighton, is well represented."

"Yes," Mama agreed. "Someone compared his *Biondina* to Helena."

Lady Banbury inspected Helena with new interest. "Yes, I think so," she mused. "So my dear, I suppose you are here to find a husband—"

"Yes, ma'am." Helena cringed, realizing she had interrupted, and with the incorrect honorific.

"Good!" Lady Banbury seemed blissfully unaware of any faux pas. "Let me think of some fine young men." She looked around the ballroom, humming yeas and nays as she spotted various candidates.

With the brash countess at her side, Helena was herself emboldened to scan the room. The sights, the smells, the sounds were wondrous. The finery and the spectacle of the fashions, the glitter of jewelry and crystal in the dim light, the low indistinct hum of conversation and music—

It all vanished when she saw him.

He was tall, elegant in his evening attire, which fit perfectly on his athletic form. His hair was brown—no, something romantic like chestnut…no, something darker…maybe…mahogany. Yes, that's what it was, dark and sleek and smooth to the touch like gloved fingers sliding along a polished mahogany table. Or perhaps a rich dark frame highlighting the handsomest face she had ever seen, made even handsomer by his obviously affectionate rapport with the woman at his side. He was too far away to see his eyes, but Helena had a very wicked notion of those eyes gazing at her, twinkling with admiration and invitation. Brown. His eyes must be a chocolaty brown.

"Lady Banbury," Helena dared, "who is that tall man with brown hair standing next to the woman in pale blue?" His stunning companion was absolutely befitting of his own perfection, tall and slender, exquisite in her robin's-egg-blue sheath, her necklace dripping with amber beads that highlighted the golden brown of her hair and the orange flounce of her underskirts. Her gestures were practiced, controlled, suggesting she was older, more mature, probably not his wife.

Please don't let her be his wife.

Lady Banbury considered the question for a moment. "Yes, hmm, I don't know him well. His companion, Lady Foxley-Graham—she knows absolutely everybody, my dear," she buzzed as if to a confidante. "And has a penchant for moving young men up in Society. Which means he's quite probably in the professions." Lady Banbury glanced briefly at Mama. "I'm sure your mother is hoping for someone of higher rank."

Helena's heart shattered. It crumbled further when she took one more look at him, smiling and chatting, oblivious to the fact that he had already broken her heart simply by being a solicitor or an engineer. She tried to console herself that he must be a bore. Of course, deep down inside, she knew he wasn't. Lady Foxley-Graham was laughing too enthusiastically for him to be anything but fascinating. Helena reluctantly peeled her eyes away, tamping down fantasies of herself being fascinated by him in another way.

Sophia found her daughter's enthusiasm for the task of finding a husband encouraging, despite Helena's disappointment that the young man she was most interested in was deemed unacceptable. That Helena was undaunted by the formidable Lady Banbury was also heartening. Charlotte was a good ally.

"Oh!" Charlotte chirped in surprise. "Sophie, dear, see that man with the French beard?"

Sophia looked where Charlotte indicated. "The handsome one with a touch of gray?" It was the most polite thing she could say. The man was clearly far too old for her daughter, and she had been afraid that Society's matrons might suggest a middle-aged man as the most suitable match. He was, however, she had to admit, very attractive. Very attractive.

She sighed quietly. Living apart from her husband for months on end had prompted them to arrive at a unique arrangement. She indulged him his peccadillos, and he allowed her to have her own. Neither discussed the matter nor questioned the other. Unless there were *complications*.

And the devastatingly handsome man with the beard looked as if he could be complicated.

"Yes, yes." Charlotte gave her a queer look. "Oh no, my dear. Not for Helena," she lowered her voice, "for you."

Sophia choked back her utter shock. "Whatever do you mean?"

"I mean for those times you feel quite distressed and need some professional advice and care. That man is Dr. Julius Christopher. He works with all of Society's women to cure their complaints. From ennui to hysteria. All the modern ailments," she drawled, emphasizing the doctor's keenness for the contemporary. "I know you've been feeling morose with your husband gone for such long spells. I'll introduce you."

Before Sophia could protest, Charlotte had called the doctor over, and he complied with a confident nonchalance that set him apart from the frenetic buzzing of the ballroom. Even more handsome up close, he exuded a captivating warmth, and as he kissed Charlotte's hand with a bow, Sophia felt a flutter of envy. "Lady Banbury, how very wonderful to see you." His bass voice dripped charm. He flashed a raised brow at Sophia, revealing the most magnificent eyes. Cerulean. The color of abandon on a summer's day.

The fluttering spread to her belly.

"Dr. Christopher, likewise," Charlotte twittered with glee. "I would like to introduce my very dear friend, Mrs. Joseph Phillips, Lady Sophia."

Sophia offered her hand and the doctor took it gently, his practiced touch sending an electrifying thrill surging through her, his brilliant blue eyes boring into her perceptively, surely knowing how he was affecting her.

"My lady."

The low rumble of his voice resonated deliciously in her core.

"Please, Doctor, I am simply Mrs. Phillips." Sophia withdrew her hand reluctantly, then turned to Helena. "And this is my daughter, Miss Helena Phillips."

A spark of awe flickered across the doctor's face. Sophia knew Helena was beautiful, but sometimes forgot just how beautiful.

"Miss Phillips." Dr. Christopher merely offered a slight bow of his head. Anything more would have been presumptuous, of course. Sophia smiled sweetly at him and he returned a devastatingly tempting curl of his lips, inciting her heart to thrum loudly. For once, she was glad for the competing clamor of the ballroom.

"Dr. Christopher," Charlotte began, "I was just telling Sophie—Mrs. Phillips—how you offer your services to all the fine women of Mayfair."

"Thank you, my lady."

"We simply could not survive without you."

"Much gratitude, Lady Banbury." Dr. Christopher seemed to be quite humbled by the countess's effusions.

"And what, pray tell, are these services, doctor?" Sophia boldly inquired.

For a moment, Dr. Christopher looked sheepish. "I am a family doctor really, but I do seem to treat mostly mothers and wives. They spend so much time looking after others that they often forget their own needs."

Sophia's curiosity was piqued by the vague description. A momentary fantasy of the doctor fulfilling her needs flitted through her mind. "Such as?"

"Well, I—"

Charlotte emitted a little squeal of delight. "Oh my! I must fly! I see Lady Roxton with Lady Foxley-Graham."

Sophia tightened her lips against a grin. Lady Roxton and Charlotte were rivals in the pursuit of gossip and Lady Foxley-Graham often had tantalizing morsels of information to offer.

"Please," Charlotte said turning to Sophia and Dr. Christopher, "excuse me." She grabbed a surprised Helena's hand. "Don't give up hope, my dear. I'll return shortly."

"Yes, ma'am—my lady."

"Lavinia!" Charlotte called out in her shrill voice as she waved and sashayed over to her friends.

Bereft of Charlotte's distracting ebullience, Sophia found herself suddenly self-conscious in the presence of the alarmingly magnetic Dr. Christopher. Tentatively she caught his eye, and he smiled familiarly, almost seductively, with a charisma that instantly filled the weighty emptiness, wrapping around her, willing her to step ever so slightly nearer to him. His breath seemed to quicken at their closeness, the heat of him penetrated her, fanning the fire already smoldering in her core. She shifted her weight in an attempt to create a touch of distance and flushed at the arousal heavy between her thighs.

"As I was saying, Mrs. Phillips, I offer services to calm the nerves such as water therapies, massage, even conversation."

"Conversation?" Her lungs tightened against the word with a dizzying constriction.

He offered an alluring expression of gentle assurance. "You would be amazed at how many women simply need someone to talk to."

Sophia laughed, perhaps a bit too loudly. "I think not, Dr. Christopher. It is often very difficult to find someone who will listen, especially when one's woes seem so mundane."

The doctor smiled again, his face beaming with a glow that lit up his exquisite eyes which she suddenly decided were a pale Egyptian blue, then wondered what it would be like to see those eyes the first thing in the morning. The smoldering heat within sparked and flared, threatening to consume her on the spot.

Sophia licked her lips and swallowed.

Helena shifted on her feet.

"Oh my," Sophia exhaled with mortification. "We're really here for my daughter. It's her first Season."

"My congratulations, Miss Phillips."

Helena batted her lashes shyly in response.

"And I must congratulate the young men who will have a chance to dance with so magnificent a young woman."

Helena colored demurely.

Charlotte approached the trio with a slight huff and puff. "My dear," she said to Sophia, "I have not forgotten my duty." She wrapped Helena's arm around hers. "I have some very nice gentlemen to introduce you to." She nodded politely to the doctor. "If you will please excuse us, Dr. Christopher."

"Of course, my lady."

Sophia caught the doctor's eye and offered a smile infused with subtle promise. He smiled back graciously. As Charlotte whisked her and Helena deeper into the fray, Sophia cast a last glance at Dr. Christopher, once again feeling a touch of envy as the exquisitely beautiful Lady Foxley-Graham—her dress the very same color blue as his mesmerizing eyes—approached him accompanied by the brown-haired object of Helena's desires.

"That woman!" Lavinia huffed.

Nicholas chuckled.

Lavinia sneered at her lover. "Don't laugh. One really has to know her if one is to survive in London Society. Charlotte knows absolutely everybody—"

"Including, it seems now, even me."

Lavinia ignored his sarcasm. "But she's so overbearing! I think she plays the distracted fashionable old lady a bit too much, really."

Nicholas sipped at his champagne as his gaze wandered to Charlotte and her companions. "Who's she with now?"

His voice held far too much interest, and Lavinia saw immediately why. With her striking copper-colored curls framing her angelic face, a perfect figure swathed tightly in pale purple silk, draped tulle accentuating her hips, and richly decorated silver brocade underskirts distracting attention from her décolletage, Helena Phillips was possibly the most eye-catching debutante at the Wrexham ball. Nicholas gawked at the beguiling girl with a faraway expression, one Lavinia rarely saw but immediately understood. He was head-over-heels smitten. More than that, he was fantasizing an erotic scenario at that very moment as evidenced by the slight bulge in his trousers.

Upon looking back at the Phillipses and Charlotte, Lavinia was surprised to see Dr. Julius Christopher with them, being very charming—as he always was—to the ladies in question. Despite his status as a baronet and having a clientele among the families in the big houses, grand social occasions were not his usual milieu.

"Vinny," came Nicholas' entreaty to break her thoughts. "Who's the girl in lavender?" Mere interest had turned into earnestness.

"Ah, there's a scandal there." Lavinia sipped her champagne. "That's Sophia Phillips and her daughter. Mrs. Phillips was formerly Lady Sophia Harwell—well, I suppose she could still use her title if she wanted—until she went and fell in love with an American. Some sort of industrialist. Builds machines and such. She was more than three months gone when they ran away together."

"Outrageous!" Nicholas hissed sardonically.

"Yes, dear, you may well mock, but that puts the daughter Helena far out of your league. In order to redeem her twig on the family tree, she must marry a man high in the ranks of society." Lavinia brought her glass to her lips. "Someone like your brother."

That got a rise out of him. "My brother wouldn't know what to do with her."

"He knows how to fuck a woman, Nicky darling. And he only needs to do it until he's made an heir."

"Funny how he hasn't figured that out yet."

"Well, dear, Jack being childless and dissipated puts you in direct line to be Earl of St. Albans, and," Lavinia gave him a sidelong glance, "available to the likes of Helena Phillips."

"I left that life behind, Vinny."

Lavinia was afraid of that answer. Perhaps Nicholas wasn't as interested in the lovely Helena as she had guessed. Or he might need some prodding. "Then you will have to admire from afar."

Nicholas harrumphed just as Charlotte dragged the girl away into the crowd to find a dance partner.

That left Julius standing alone, although his attractive composed elegance would draw a curious female fairly quickly. "To take your mind off her, I'll introduce you to a very dear friend of mine." Lavinia took his arm and walked to where Helena had stood mere seconds before.

As Lavinia had expected, Julius beamed at her warmly, lifting one eyebrow provocatively.

"Lady Foxley-Graham," he said, bending over her outstretched hand. "How absolutely wonderful to see you."

"Julius." She indicated her companion. "May I introduce a longtime friend, Dr. Nicholas Ramsay. Nicky, Dr. Julius Christopher."

The men shook hands and mumbled pleasantries.

"And what sort of doctor are you, Ramsay?"

"I haven't settled on a specialty, sir."

"Nicky's only just returned from having been abroad for several years." Lavinia cast a proud glance at her protégé. "He's been learning about medical practices in the Near East."

"Well, I initially read medicine at Cambridge, sir," Nicholas added, "and I was in Edinburgh for some additional studies this past winter."

"Rather cold that time of year, isn't it?" Julius shuddered. "And with whom did you study?"

"Dr. Henry MacFarland."

"Marvelous! I know Hank from years back. He suggested I go into family practice. I've been doing that for over twenty years."

"Well, then, I suppose you must enjoy it, sir."

"It has its benefits, yes."

Lavinia squelched a giggle as Julius gave her a warning glare over his glass.

"Are you working with anyone in particular? Perhaps I know him?" Julius queried most solicitously.

"Not yet, sir. I had hoped to find a situation in London."

"Well, if you are at all interested in family medicine, you are welcome to join me—"

Lavinia gasped in excitement. "Really? Oh Julius!"

"I've two consulting rooms and more clients than I can handle, really."

Nicholas was profoundly impressed. "I would be very honored, sir."

"Come by the office Tuesday for luncheon, Ramsay." Julius handed his card to Nicholas. "You can have a look around and tell me more about your adventures." He made a slight bow to Lavinia. "My lady. I hear the music starting and I know how much you like to dance."

"And how much you hate it," Lavinia said nostalgically.

"Hate is a strong word, my dear." His smile shot a familiar heat through her that still tingled as she watched him walk away.

"You've slept with him," grumbled Nicholas.

Lavinia was slightly taken aback by the remark. Nicholas never cared about such things. "It was a long time ago, Nicky." She took a swallow of champagne. Julius had a unique understanding of women's pleasure, which made him a very good lover. Seeing him again filled her with giddy memories. "I think I need a dance now, darling. Are you going to ask me?"

That put Nicholas in a better mood. "Yes, love," he murmured. "Lady Foxley-Graham, may I have this dance?" Nicholas offered his arm.

Lavinia grinned. "Afterward, I promise, we'll find you a wife."

Julius could not wait to extricate himself from his social obligations. The second he had laid eyes on Miss Helena Phillips his cock had jolted to full stand. He could barely maintain his composure around the girl, a maddening feeling so very much unlike him. However, the mother proved to be a good diversion, allowing him to show off his usual charming self in front of the object of his desires.

With her auburn hair, hazel-green eyes, creamy flesh, and just a hint of a rosy hue on her cheeks, Helena was certainly the most beautiful woman in the world. But even better, she had that distinction of perfection…

She was a virgin.

Just the thought of her innocence made him once again achingly hard.

And he could not stop thinking about her, or him and her together. And Lavinia's appearance did not make things easier. Her perfume, the sway of her hips, her ample bosom straining against the deeply cut neckline, just reminded him of coition, and then, of course, he could only think about the act…

With a virgin.

Julius dug his nails into his palms as he maneuvered his way through the throng of party guests to the coat-room. He'd get past this obsession. He always did. He'd move on to something more practical, something more obtainable, something less virginal.

He'd have to settle for a whore tonight. It was obvious Lavinia was sleeping with the young Ramsay—a fine choice he had to admit, a good-looking lad, dark hair, tall, slim build—just like he himself had been when he had bedded her.

Julius took his coat politely from the attending servant and hurried out to his usual brothel.

CHAPTER FOUR

At precisely three-ought-four in the afternoon on Monday, there was a knock on the front door to Dr. Christopher's office.

"Grace Danby. How punctual," Julius said cordially to the slightly befuddled girl.

"I walked from the King's Road. You want yer bob back?"

Julius let the disbelief linger only for a second. "No, my dear girl. You keep the money." Most likely she had walked all the way from the East End and still held on to every penny he had given her. Dirty and disheveled, her appearance spoke volumes about the poverty she lived in. She wore the same tired coat and hat as the last time he'd seen her, although she had on a different dress, certainly not new, a little worn, a little too big, a hand-me-down probably given to her by Dr. Waddington's housemaid. Julius hoped the poor waif had at least spent some of his money on food.

"Grace, come into my examination room."

She followed obediently.

Julius pulled the bell cord and, despite her debilities and deafness, the ever dependable housekeeper appeared directly. "Mrs. Jennings, draw up a bath for our guest. Here, if you please. Use the medicinal tub."

"And the douching device, sir?"

He paused for a moment. It was why the girl was there, wasn't it? A hypothesis that needed to be proved? "Yes."

Mrs. Jennings shuffled out.

"Grace, please take off your coat and have a seat. Let's discuss my plans for you."

The girl shed her tattered wool sacque and gently untied the frayed ribbons of her faded velvet bonnet, then sat primly in the leather office chair. Not properly pinned, her brown hair sagged to her shoulders.

Julius began to pace, organizing his thoughts. "I am a doctor, a scientist. I treat patients. But sometimes I have ideas about ailments and I wish to study these, to see if my hypothesis is correct."

"'ipe—what?" She stared up at him with wide eyes the color of dark amber, the color of a memory.

Julius smiled. "Hypothesis. It is like an idea about something. You have the idea, but you don't know if it is the correct way of looking at things, so you need to test it."

Grace watched in fascination as Mrs. Jennings returned with a kettle and began boiling water on the small stove while the tub filled with tepid water from the pipes.

"Have you ever seen running water in a house before, my dear?"

"No, sir," Grace said with wonder.

"Well, before you get into the bath, I will need you to answer a few questions."

"Yes, sir." Grace dutifully returned her attention to him.

"Are you a virgin?"

The girl was utterly taken aback. She blushed and looked around confusedly. She lifted her head and bit her lip. "No, sir."

"And when you were with a man, did you find the experience pleasurable?"

Her face flushed beet red. She glanced over at Mrs. Jennings, who was, as usual, unconcerned about the interview and far more concerned with the temperature of the bathwater.

"I reckon."

"So, you would say 'yes'?"

"Yes."

"Think back to when you were last with a man and it was pleasurable. Was it as nice as the experience with Dr. Waddington's machine?"

Grace looked bewildered, but then began to consider the question put to her. "I think the machine was nicer."

Julius grinned.

"Dr. Christopher, the bath is ready. I'll take my leave now." Mrs. Jennings padded slowly across the wooden floor and creaked out, closing the door behind her.

"Take off your clothes, Grace."

The girl gave him the most enchanting look of astonishment, then slowly began to disrobe. She knew he was watching, he did not pretend he was not. It seemed she liked the attention, and why wouldn't she? He was not an unattractive man, although perhaps twice her age. Somehow, she made the act of divesting herself of her shabby clothing in a medical office profoundly erotic.

And when she was utterly nude, she stood unabashed before him, a magnificent specimen of young womanhood in her physical prime.

"Step into the bath." His voice was unwittingly hoarse with desire. He stripped off his frock coat and rolled up his shirt sleeves, then drew up a chair alongside the tub, adjusting the fullness in his crotch before he sat down.

With the water gently lapping around her beautiful figure, caressing her breasts and startling her nipples to excitation, Grace looked as if she were in sensual heaven. "I never 'ad such a treat before." She sighed artlessly.

She did not, could not know how intensely she was affecting Julius with her alluring blend of inexperience and experience enhancing her youthful nudity. He ran his hand along her thigh under the water, softly stroking the pale skin back and forth. When she adjusted her hips, he knew she had succumbed to his touch.

He reached between her legs and found her plump with desire, sticky with arousal. He inserted a finger, then two, slowly pulling them in and out, feeling her muscles react. She gasped then exhaled a little mewl.

"Grace, when a man is inside you it is very pleasing, is it not?" His tone was as gentle as his ministrations.

"Yes," she breathed, gazing up at him with those bewitching yet innocent eyes.

"And can you spend like this? If I were to continue to do this, would you reach your sensual climax?"

Her head fell back to rest on the small pillow hooked to the edge of the tub. "Yes."

Julius moved his fingers to caress her stunningly erect clitoris. "And if I were to continue to stroke you here, would you also spend?"

"Yes, oh, yes," was the euphoric answer.

Julius withdrew his hand. "And would the two experiences be the same?"

The look of annoyance from Grace was fleeting before she suddenly remembered why she was there. "No, sir."

"No? Are you sure?"

"I'm sure."

"Can you explain it?"

"I don't think so."

"Well, is one better than the other?"

"They're...I dunno, they're just different. Like with a bloke, it's just nice 'aving 'im there, you know? 'is body an' such. Maybe 'e's warm an' 'e likes to mug a bit. But with meself, I can think about anyone I want."

"By yourself?" Julius was flummoxed. "You mean when you masturbate, er, frig yourself? So, men don't touch you there?" He placed a firm finger on her clitoris.

"No, sir. I touch meself there. I mean maybe a gent or two's found the spot. But they really don't know what to do with it."

"Do you touch yourself often?"

"Well, I don't rightly know—"

"Every day? Every week?" Julius tried not to sound to enthusiastic.

"Well, not when I'm 'aving me courses. An' not every day. But more 'n just once a week."

"And why do you frig yourself, Grace?"

She looked at him with curious confusion. "'Cause it's nice," she admitted softly.

"Not because you're feeling poorly or upset or frustrated?"

"Well, then I think I might want to 'ave meself a good cry instead. Or a drink o' gin, donchya think?"

Julius grunted his concurrence as he considered this information. The girl admitted that the stimulation of her clitoris was a purely sexual act—that statement alone went against current medical assumptions. She achieved sexual satisfaction with men, and also alone with herself, each experience, by her own admission, different from the other. He would need to determine if the girl ever suffered from anything resembling so-called hysteria, or if she was able to fend off such feelings of frustration. And did she need the company of men to maintain a level of satisfaction, or could she manage on her own?

His frustration mounted as disorganized thoughts bombarded him. He needed a bit more time to structure his study, develop his methodology. But at the moment, he had a very lovely young woman nude and aroused in a tub before him. Science would have to wait.

He dragged over the douching device already filled with warm water.

"Spread your legs, Grace. Put one over the edge of the tub. Yes, that's right."

She lay spread before him. He placed the nozzle of the douche in the tub and turned the machine on. Bubbles from the force of the jets formed in the water. Julius moved the nozzle to hover over Grace's clitoris.

She jerked with a yelp when the jet made contact with her sensitive nub.

"Shh, shh," he calmed, "let me. Just feel it." He once again positioned the jet near her clitoris.

She closed her eyes, taking in the sensual assault, rocking her hips, then pushing them closer to the intense flow of water, moaning at the heightened sensation. Her whole body writhed, splashing, her fingers gripping the edge of the tub.

Julius was rock hard. He squeezed his cock with his free hand.

Her moans turned to cries drowning out the humming of the machine. He moved the jet closer until the full force of it was directed at her clitoris.

Grace thrust her pelvis against the jet and let out a long wail. A moment later, she lay panting in the lapping water.

Julius turned off the device and removed his hand from the tub and the girl. His other hand released his tormented prick.

"And would you like such a bath whenever you wanted, Grace?"

"Yes sir," she said with a relaxed smile. "If you please, sir."

"Good." Julius swatted her thigh. "You stay here as long as you need. Relax, clean up. I'll have Mrs. Jennings bring you some tea." He left to go frig himself in the water closet.

"Very fine luncheon, Dr. Christopher," remarked a sated Nicholas as he leaned back in his chair. "What did you call it again?"

"Vegetarian," the doctor said with pride.

"Ah, yes. I have heard of that movement." Nicholas glanced over at the servant patiently waiting against the dark oak wainscoting of the dining room. Grace, as she was called, was rather pretty, young, and timid. Somehow not what he had expected Dr. Christopher to have as a maid. He had learned a lot about the doctor during lunch and found him rather particular and exacting. The type of man who would have a cantankerous former schoolmistress for a servant instead.

"A bit radical for some in our profession, Ramsay. I keep a small garden with some produce specific to our climate." He sipped his coffee in a manner as refined as the gilded decoration of his French porcelain demitasse. "I'm sure you have seen wonderful gardens in your travels?"

He had regaled Dr. Christopher with stories of his exotic journeys and the state of medicine in foreign lands. "Oh yes. A stunning variety of fruits in the Near East. Have you also been?"

"I have. I was a bit younger than you are now. I do agree that travel opens the mind to new possibilities, new methods of living, new ways of seeing the world. Really, every scientist should make an effort to see as much of the world as possible. The Grand Tour should not be just for artists."

Both men chuckled.

"And now we are finished," Dr. Christopher rose from the dining table, "I should like to take you to the examination rooms. I have done some rearranging on account of your possibly joining me."

"You make me feel like an honored guest rather than a colleague, sir."

As they passed the servant the doctor murmured, "Thank you, Grace," with a touch of affection. Nicholas glanced at the girl again and saw her blush. Clearly she was not just a servant. The revelation was a little surprising. Dr. Christopher also seemed the type to have an erudite and refined mistress. Someone like Lavinia.

They walked downstairs to the offices on the ground floor. One examination room was next to the stairs, but Dr. Christopher led them into the opposite room. "It's larger than the other, not by much," he explained. "This will be your office."

Nicholas looked around, marveling to himself at every turn. There was a padded table for patients, a dressing area behind a folding screen, a children's corner with toys and books, a magnificent carved oak desk, ample cabinets and counters. Every surface was polished and spotless, every object in its proper place.

"This is too much, Dr. Christopher, sir," Nicholas stammered.

"Nonsense, Ramsay." Dr. Christopher patted Nicholas on the back. "To be frank, if I may, if you've been taken under Lavinia's wing, then you must be a very studious, responsible, and loyal young man."

Nicholas shifted on his feet nervously. It was the first time Dr. Christopher had brought up their mutual friend.

"You needn't be embarrassed, my boy. I know you're sleeping with her."

The admission was more than a little shocking. "Did she tell you this?" If she had, Nicholas would have to have a talk with her about discretion.

"Good God, no! She's an impeccably discreet woman. However, you are just her type, and she would not be wasting time with such a handsome young man if she were not bedding him. I dare say you could not do better."

"Thank you, sir." Nicholas did not know how else to respond.

"And what are her intentions for you?"

Nicholas was under no illusions that he was the first protégé in Lavinia's life, but it was disconcerting that Dr. Christopher knew so much about his relationship with the lady.

"My career, sir, to get me established in London. And," he lowered his voice, "to find me a wife."

That brought a grin to Dr. Christopher's face. "Good! Very good." He seemed genuinely pleased. "You'll learn quite a bit about wives working here." He indicated a chair by the desk. "Have a seat."

Dr. Christopher paced slowly, his head down, stroking his goatee before he steepled his hands under his chin to collect his thoughts. "Most of your patients will be young mothers with ill children. The children may not be terribly ill, but these young women have absolutely no idea how to handle such things. They're practically children themselves, some of them. It's basic care, you'll know what to do in no time.

"Some women will come to you with ailments of their own. Some of these will be quite obvious—a disease, a boil, a cough. Again, you'll apply your basic knowledge, or use my research library upstairs. But treatment will be straightforward.

"Then there will be the women who come in for themselves, or their pubescent daughter, complaining of very vague symptoms. They will use words they've heard or read in magazines like 'malaise', 'melancholia', 'ennui', 'nervousness'. They won't be able to describe the problem in definite terms." He stopped pacing and faced his pupil. "This is the type of ailment I specialize in."

Nicholas was intrigued. "What do you mean? What is it, this ailment?"

"Doctors as far back as Celsus and Galen have called this affliction 'womb disease'. Today we commonly use the term 'hysteria'. The treatment has been the same for a thousand years. We use it today, in fact. Generally, it is manual stimulation of the genitalia until what is called 'the hysterical paroxysm' is reached. It is, of course, a completely ridiculous malady with an equally ridiculous treatment."

Nicholas recalled his perusal of the medical journals. He himself had thought the same thing. "I don't understand, Dr. Christopher," he started tentatively. "If you offer treatment for this illness, what are you treating? And how are you treating it?"

"Don't worry, my boy," the doctor consoled with a touch of amusement. "You have not stumbled upon a quack out to bilk Mayfair's finest of their jewels. The malady is not some abstruse ailment called hysteria. The malady, as a matter of fact, is lack of sexual culmination. The treatment is not for a strange man in an office to touch a woman in her most intimate of places, but for her own damn husband to do it." Dr. Christopher sucked in air purposefully, as if to calm himself. "In lieu of a husband or other intimate partner, the treatment is for a woman to learn self-stimulation."

Nicholas was not sure he had just heard what he thought he had just heard.

Dr. Christopher must have read the confusion on his face. "Yes, Ramsay, that would indeed be masturbation."

Nicholas flushed.

"The lower classes figure it out, of course. There is no code of morality amongst them. But no one ever teaches it to the daughters of the wealthy or the middle classes. Of course, boys of any class don't need to be taught. But girls are much more mysterious."

Nicholas was still a tad nonplussed. He cleared his throat. "Dr. Christopher, sir, are you teaching women how to masturbate?" It was strange being a man of science as Nicholas thought he was and not being able to speak about medical matters without a little discomfiture.

"I would like to, I haven't done so yet. It's rather complicated, really."

Nicholas waited for further explanation but there was none. "How so?"

"Well, the medical community is not convinced of my theory at all. They do not see the connection between women's sexual pleasure and women's complaints. Sexual pleasure, you see, can only be achieved with penetration, so one theory goes, or semen, according to another. A woman does not need sexual gratification, like we men do. She only experiences it as a by-product of intimacy with a man." Dr. Christopher looked Nicholas straight in the eye. "Even if Lavinia has been your only lover, which I am certain is not true, you must know that women can and do experience sexual pleasure in the absence of men."

Nicholas did know that, and not just from Lavinia. "Yes, of course." He did find it a bit odd that, until recently, he had never realized such a topic was discussed in the medical community.

Dr. Christopher resumed his pacing. "I need to proceed with experiments to prove my hypothesis, to bring forth data and evidence, write a paper, that sort of thing. It is not an idea open for discussion in the Royal scientific societies at the moment. A great many doctors make a damn good living from what is essentially giving sexual gratification to ignorant women. And, what is worse, there are devices being invented and sold for such purposes. Really, it is these inventors and the doctors who buy their products who are the quacks."

"So, what is your course of action?"

Dr. Christopher drew in a deep breath. "In order to achieve my goals, I intend to use the very tools my colleagues use in their quackery. I hope to answer the question whether what a woman experiences with those devices is different from what she experiences with penetration. I have a douching machine and a brand new electro-vibrator at my disposal. And now I have Grace."

"Good God, man!" Nicholas blurted, absolutely stunned. "That servant girl? You intend to—to experiment on her?"

"She has agreed." It was said coolly. "She will be compensated and will receive lodging and food for all her work here, whether as servant or subject."

Nicholas was aghast, but still somehow fascinated. "And the part about, uh, penetration?"

"You mean, do I intend to fornicate with her? It would be difficult to keep a clear head during such activity, I admit, to keep a professional scientific separation from the matter." Dr. Christopher looked queerly at Nicholas.

He felt a slow twisting in his gut. "Oh no, sir. I won't. Don't ask me to do that, sir."

Dr. Christopher guffawed. "I was testing you, Ramsay. Of course I would never allow such a thing in my office. I would be professionally censured. As would you."

Nicholas quietly sighed his relief. "So how do you intend to proceed?"

"I haven't quite figured that out yet, to be truthful. It would be far easier if she had a young man of her own. I will have to give the scheme some thought. However, I do have an alternative trajectory of experimentation."

Nicholas was utterly intrigued. The crowding in his crotch made him realize he was unwittingly becoming aroused by the frank discussion. "Oh?"

"One way to prove that women do not need penetration for sexual gratification is to find a woman who maintains a level of satisfaction with mere clitoral stimulation without devolving into feelings of frustration. Of course, my detractors would claim that somehow memories of male penetration were surfacing, perhaps in a dream state. So really to prove this vein of my hypothesis, I will need a virgin."

"Oh, God." Nicholas sank in his chair. "And where do you intend to find a virgin?" he inquired meekly.

"It is a horrible matter, really, but they can be bought at the better brothels. Again, it would be a situation of maintaining a young woman, having her live here with me, that sort of thing."

The whole conversation was partly disgusting, partly intriguing, partly arousing, partly exhilarating. But Nicholas remembered his place. "Dr. Christopher, you would like me to come join you so I can treat the more straightforward cases and leave the more curious for your own analysis and cure, is that right, sir?"

"Yes, Ramsay, that is correct. I think your qualifications, training, and manner make you well suited to take over the practical aspects of my practice."

"Very good, sir. I think I shall like to take a bit of time to think this over. Not that I have any other offers, but your practice is rather unconventional."

"Yes," agreed Dr. Christopher. "Take all the time you need."

What Nicholas needed at that moment wasn't time. It was Lavinia.

It was a quiet, late afternoon staying in for Lavinia, a rarity during the Season for one of London's most well-known and sought-after widows. But she needed time to rest, to relax, to catch up on the week's newspapers that the butler, Mr. Sims, had stacked neatly and perfectly on a low table by the sofa in the library. No one was expected, and Sims had been instructed to take calling cards. The lady was simply not "at home".

For several hours she read her papers, the most recent first, stretched lengthwise on the sofa, bolstered by wonderfully plump pillows, shamelessly un-corseted and stocking-free, unconcerned with the drape of her dress, probably exposing an ankle or calf. Such unladylike behavior would surely shock most of her acquaintances, she laughed to herself as she picked up the previous Thursday's *Morning Post* and turned to the section on the Imperial Parliament.

She raised her head at a commotion growing slowly beyond the library door. Sims was talking very sternly to an unwelcome and assiduous man on the front steps.

"Oh bother, what is it now?" she said aloud as if someone could hear her. She sat up.

The door to the library crashed open.

Nicholas stood there, holding his hat in his hand, his dark hair wild, his brown eyes black with desire. And when he tossed his hat on the library table, he exposed the expectant bulge in his pants.

All Lavinia could think was that she had not inserted her Dutch cap.

"Nicky? I didn't expect you until tonight," she gasped. "I thought you were with Julius this afternoon."

He said nothing as he came toward her, tearing off his jacket and loosening his tie.

Oh, God. What debauchery did Julius introduce you to?

Nicholas pulled her up to standing, took the *Post* still in her hand, folded it, and placed it neatly on the table. One hand cradled the back of her head, while the other arm snaked around her waist. Her insides fluttered as they always did when he took control.

She looked up beseechingly. "Nicky? Darling?"

His mouth crushed down on hers, their tongues tangling before he plundered her depths even further. She steadied herself against him, gripping his shoulders, her body weakening under his demanding desire.

He came up for air, panting as if exhausted. "I need you," he murmured. "But…but, I need to pleasure you first." He seemed uncharacteristically abashed, perhaps even a little ashamed.

"Yes, of course." What else was she to say to that?

He drew her to the sofa, laying her back against the pillows, then pushed up her skirts. His hand reached inside the split in her drawers tickling her delicate flesh. The earnestness on his face contrasted with the gentleness of his touch.

"You're wet," he said as if he hadn't expected her to be. He eased her legs open, licking his lips as if she were a treat before him, then bent over and began his ravishment.

He was a man possessed.

Lavinia closed her eyes to concentrate on the momentary well-aimed flicks of his frenzied tongue, his lack of focus confusing her senses. She moaned her appreciation, smoothing his hair in encouragement, soothing him until he slowed his pace. His fingers dallied deliciously in her folds to uncover her clitoris before he sucked the pearl into his mouth, the tip of his tongue frantically stroking the sensitive spot, his pointed attentiveness sending her into spasms of vexatious ecstasy. As her body writhed against him, he followed her every move, digging his nails painfully into her butt cheeks, not wanting to let her go.

She cried out his name, grabbing handfuls of his curls as she thrust her crotch against his mouth, his smug chuckle vibrating against her as he feasted. He was relentless, he was determined.

She felt the buildup, the coiling of energy deep in her belly, the tingling in her toes, the anticipation hovering in the air, waiting…

He sucked harder, his tongue tormenting and teasing until she—

"Oh, God! Nicky!"

Lavinia opened her eyes and tried to calm her shallow breaths. She had never spent so hard. He had never pleasured her with so much enthusiasm.

But he wasn't finished yet.

With one hand he pulled her from the couch, urged her across the room, and thrust her against the door, while his other hand worked the buttons of his fly to free his cock. He was rampant, the prepuce already cowled below the glistening purple head. He bunched up her skirts and impaled her with a satisfied groan.

His movements were slow and even at first. Her body, sated and weak, found new resolve with the changed erotic assault. She clenched his shaft, sending tingling thrills through her, then released him with a tilt of her hips demanding he repeat his invasion. His thrusts picked up with determination until he was slamming inside her, meeting every moan with a vigorous lunge, holding her tightly as her arms and legs limply clung to his taut form.

His breathing grew ragged, his rhythm changing to a syncopated beat. He was going to spend.

She wasn't prepared.

She unwrapped her limbs and squirmed against him, her struggles eliciting startled protests. He let her go, pulling out, dejected annoyance clouding his face. She dropped to her knees and swallowed his wet, engorged cock.

Nicholas let out a curse as his hands slapped against the door for support. In mere seconds, her skillful mouth brought him to orgasm, his warm ejaculate spurting down her throat.

The sounds of his heavy breathing filled the silence of afterglow.

"Vinny," he panted hoarsely. "Did I pleasure you?"

Lavinia swallowed, still slumped on the floor. "Yes." *Why is he asking this?*

"Both times?"

"Yes." *Something's wrong.*

"And, was it…was it the same?"

She understood. "No, Nicky. It's different. The feelings are different. One is not better than the other. They are just different."

"Then you still need me?"

"God, yes, Nicky." She reached up and grabbed his hand. "I still need you."

CHAPTER FIVE

Sophia had explained to Lady Banbury that she wasn't quite sure anything was really wrong, but Lady Banbury had noticed her friend was subdued. "In a funk," she had said. "Nervous." Then she had enthusiastically recommended the services of Dr. Julius Christopher, and handed her his card, insisting she would not take no for an answer.

So now Sophia sat in Dr. Christopher's cozy waiting room, and if she hadn't been exactly nervous before, her hands were trembling—with anxiety or anticipation, she wasn't quite sure— now. She did not like going to the doctor's much, even when Helena was ill as a child, and she especially hated waiting. At least there was a selection of women's magazines and a sliver of sun shining through the window.

Her stomach tightened. It wasn't being at the doctor's office that was inciting her nerves, it was being at *this* doctor's office. After her brief conversation with Dr. Julius Christopher at the Wrexham ball, she had imagined him doing things to her only one's husband should be allowed to do. At first, she had felt alarm, but once realizing no one would ever know, she calmed.

Or would no one ever know? The thought made her a bit lightheaded. The man was a doctor, a man of scientific knowledge and perspicacity, a man whose job it was to uncover a patient's problems with a brief examination, perhaps a test, and, in Dr. Christopher's case apparently, with simple conversation.

A cold sweat broke upon her brow and Sophia fished her handkerchief out of her handbag. He would know, right? He would have to know. He'd be able to see her thoughts, sense her needs, then elicit essential information with pointed questions. Of course he'd know.

Sophia drew in a long breath, then exhaled her worries. That Julius Christopher would know why she was there was a comfort indeed.

"Really, my dear, it is nothing," Lady Banbury said to Helena. "I just felt a sudden need for air."

They exited through the French doors to the side terrace of Viscount Roxton's home, the setting for the day's entertainment, a musicale of voice and piano given by the just-presented twin daughters of Lord and Lady Roxton. Lady Banbury had patiently waited for a break in the performance to request Helena escort her outside. Helena was just glad to be out of earshot of the wretched noise. It appeared several of the guests had the same idea.

"I can call for your carriage to take us home, Lady Banbury."

"No, no, dear. I just need to spend some time in the out-of-doors. I need a little rejuvenation from the sun and breeze. We can go inside again once the refreshments are served."

Helena breathed in the fresh scents of spring, closing her eyes briefly to listen to the late afternoon twitters of dulcet birds, desperate to erase the memory of the past hour. She would have been mortified had it been her talents up for assessment in such a bald manner.

"Perhaps if I had a chair whilst I took in the soothing air, my dear."

Helena looked around, and spied an unoccupied ornate iron chair not far away in the shade. She went to retrieve it and found it much heavier than its filigree would suggest.

"Might I be of assistance?"

She looked up to find herself face-to-face with the handsomest man in the world. *Him.* The man from the Wrexham ball, the man Lady Banbury had said was not of high enough rank for her, the man who had unknowingly already broken her heart. Sun glinted off the waves of his thick mahogany-brown hair—unfashionable in its natural state and slightly tousled from the gentle breeze—and filled his brown eyes with golden glittery specs. Brown. They *were* brown. Rich brown. Like hot chocolate on a winter's morning, soothing, comforting, warming her very insides, the deliciousness spreading all over, rousing the tender flesh bound tightly under her stiff corset, settling and coiling voluptuously below her belly—

She had to stop looking at him.

"Yes, please." Her breath hitched in her lungs, but found relief when she turned her attention to the chair. "It's for Lady Banbury, sir," she managed.

"Lady Banbury?" He looked over at the older woman, shook his head with a wry smirk, settled his hat atop his glorious hair, and handily picked up the wrought iron chair.

"My lady," he said as he placed the requested seat before the countess.

"Oh! Thank you ever so much, Doctor… Doctor…"

Doctor?

"Ramsay." He lifted his hat and bowed.

"Yes, yes. Pardon me, please. I am feeling a bit overcome by the closeness of the music room." She sat down with a wheezing puff.

"Is there anything I can do to make you more comfortable, Lady Banbury?"

Oh! How very gracious and kind! Helena's heart skipped a beat.

Lady Banbury waved her hand and shook her head with just a touch of dramatic flair. "Thank you, Doctor, no. I'll be fine, presently."

The breathtakingly handsome Dr. Ramsay nodded and forced a smile with his lusciously full mouth, then stood beside Helena.

Despite the warmth of his closeness, Helena froze. They hadn't been properly introduced. Should she say something? But he should be the first to speak, right? She shifted on her feet, struggling to quell the turmoil within, and even with a refreshing breeze, forgot to breathe. She swallowed the dryness in her mouth, a sound that apparently was loud enough for Lady Banbury to hear.

"Oh my dear, I am much remiss in my duties as chaperon." The countess had whipped out her fan and was using it with vigor. "Dr. Ramsay, may I introduce you to Miss Helena Phillips?" She waggled her fan in their direction. "And likewise. Oh this heat."

Helena curtsied to the handsomest man in the world.

"Dr. Nicholas Ramsay, at your service." His baritone voice was enchanting, melodic. She could listen to it all day as she drank in his eyes and thought of those lips—

"Dr. Ramsay," began Lady Banbury, "whatever are you doing here? I didn't know men of science appreciated music."

"Oh but we do, Lady Banbury. So, to be truthful, I hardly know what I am doing here."

Helena let out a sharp laugh then stifled herself immediately. Dr. Ramsay flashed her a grin.

Lady Banbury seemed unaware of any merriment around her. "Are you here alone, Doctor?"

"I arrived with Lady Foxley-Graham."

"Of course, of course. Lavinia is a great lover of music, is she not?"

"She is. So much so, she left not too long after the event began."

The audacity of the man was unbelievable. And most appealing. It was simply unreasonable that Helena should be denied a lifetime of melodious witty intelligence with enchanting chocolate eyes.

But Lady Banbury seemed immune to his clever ripostes. And his charm. "Helena, dear, sit out of the sun over there while I rest my bones."

"Yes, my lady."

Dr. Ramsay politely offered his arm for the short walk to the shade. Helena's pulse raced at the mere idea of touching him, and when she slipped her arm through his, the rush of excitement stirred up such a dizzying frenzy, she feared she would faint right onto the flagstones suddenly rippling dangerously beneath her. She wobbled and clutched his arm, then, utterly embarrassed, released and went limp. Gentleman that he clearly was, he made no comment, but held himself perfectly steady as they strolled to the edge of the raised terrace. Inwardly, she sighed. Really all she wanted to do was lean her head against his shoulder and feel the rhythm of his gait.

"Lady Banbury appears to be resting her eyes as well as her bones," he said quietly. "Would you like a spot of sun instead of the shade, Miss Phillips?"

How very wicked! "Yes that would be lovely, Dr. Ramsay." Her heart fluttered as she took the opportunity to study him, the simple act of moving two chairs into the dappled sunlight becoming a display of strength and sensuality. He motioned gallantly for her to take a seat, then sat at her side and looked out at the view of the garden.

It was a beautiful day. Pink and white blossoms rustled on the Roxtons' apple and pear trees shading a sea of bluebells and bugles dotted with yellow cowslip. A bucolic scene utterly at odds with the event just witnessed. "Those poor Roxton girls," Helena sighed aloud.

"Yes, well, I suppose that is what a young woman has to do these days to secure an advantageous marriage."

His candid apprehension of the situation was disarming. "I suppose so. I should count myself lucky."

"That you don't have to grotesquely flaunt your talents to an audience of fashionable, unattached men?" His tone was teasing, but his estimation of her predicament astute.

"Well, not so obviously, at least," she sighed. She glanced around furtively finding the other guests scattered far beyond earshot. "Really, the singing and playing were quite dreadful," she confided. "And no one will admit to that! All the men I've met today are far too polite. It makes them seem insincere. I could not marry a man who is not honest, a man who pretends to be impressed by such things."

"And what sort of man could you marry?" he asked, raising a brow in anticipation.

Her cheeks turned hot. "Someone who is intelligent and kind." *You.* She bit her lower lip to hide a smile. "And thoughtful. Someone who likes to read. And to travel. And pleasant to look at, I should think." A nervous giggle escaped unwittingly.

"Yes, that would be nice."

"What would?"

"A wife who likes to travel."

"Oh! Have you traveled much?" she blurted before apprehending he probably meant a pleasant-looking wife.

He chuckled as he casually crossed his legs. "I've recently returned from a journey to the Near East."

"Oh! How romantic!"

His smile was devastating. "I traveled around Persia and Egypt."

This is too perfect.

"And I spent quite a bit of time in Turkey, Syria, and Palestine."

"Turkey!" she burbled. She leaned in a little. "Is it true the sultan wants young English girls for his harem?" she asked in a hushed tone.

Dr. Ramsay's forehead crinkled in surprise. "Where on earth did you hear that?" he asked, a twinkle in his chocolate eyes.

"A book—" Helena broke off, mortified. Heat rushed to her face as she sucked in her lower lip.

"What book?" he goaded, pursing his mouth in a vain attempt to restrain his amusement.

It had been a rather salacious tome in her parents' private library. She could never divulge such a thing.

He leaned toward her, so close she could feel his breath. "Be assured it is not true, Miss Phillips," he murmured, finally breaking forth with a knowing grin. "And I think you better not admit to your future husband that you've read such stories."

The glimmer in his eyes made plain he was teasing her again. Helena bit her lower lip and looked away, quashing her giddiness at knowing he too had indulged in such a story.

"And have you done much traveling yourself?" He changed the subject like a gentleman should, despite still being clearly diverted by the previous exchange.

"I've been to France and Switzerland. And America."

"America!" he exclaimed enthusiastically. "I've always wanted to go to America. What's it like?" He regarded her with a mixture of awe and reverence.

"My father is American, from New York state, so I've only really been there. The countryside is quite lovely. We've a home in New York City too. The city is big and busy and full of foreigners. Everyone is, well, familiar. Like they've known you all your life. So very friendly." She cringed inside. It was unlike her to ramble so.

"The Turks are like that too." He grinned again. "Friendly, I mean."

A rush of heat told her she flushed crimson. Still, she couldn't help smiling. His mirth, even at her expense, was infectious.

He politely turned his attention to the view of the garden and she took the opportunity to study his profile. Lady Banbury had deemed him unsuitable, but he was by far the most interesting, personable man she had met all Season. And, oh, so very handsome. He had to be something other than a doctor.

She surreptitiously looked at his hands, slender and masculine, one set on top of the other resting on his knee. Devoid of rings, meaning he was unattached, but also meaning he was lacking in a family heritage.

So he *was* just a doctor.

She mollified her disappointment by perusing his very handsome face once again. His nose was sharp, pointed, but balanced by a somewhat angular jaw and chin, so it did not appear to be a big nose. And besides, it was in proper proportion to his luscious mouth, twisted, as it seemed to be more often than not, in a smirk that revealed an active, interesting brain at odds with the frivolity of the afternoon's events.

He turned his chocolate eyes to her, catching her in the act of gazing at him. "So, Miss Phillips," he began softly, "what would you rather be doing than listening to the plaintive warbling of unmarried young women?"

Talking to you, looking at you, being at your side. "Reading."

"Something more edifying than *The Lustful Turk*, I hope?"

Helena giggled. And then she laughed aloud. Which appeared to wake up Lady Banbury.

"Helena, my dear," she called. "I see the party breaking up inside. Perhaps it is time for us to join them for refreshments."

"Yes, Lady Banbury." Helena stood to go help her chaperon out of her chair.

Dr. Ramsay stood too. For a brief moment, they were posed face-to-face, his comforting eyes and luscious lips mere inches away. Her heart thumped, pulsing heat to flush her cheeks.

Helena bit her lip and curtsied to Dr. Ramsay. He grinned wonderfully and bowed back.

* * * * *

"Mrs. Phillips, my apologies. My associate is out this afternoon and I am handling all our cases today."

Julius was, of course, rather surprised to see the lady, although he tried not to show it. He also tried very much not to gawk at her. She was stunningly beautiful, with rich auburn hair darkened by age, and full lashes framing mossy green eyes. Seeing her unaccompanied by her daughter made her own attractiveness rather apparent.

"Thank you, Dr. Christopher." She sat in the chair indicated. "To be truthful, I really don't know why I am here."

"Oh?" He took the opportunity to study her lovely features.

"You see, Charlotte, Lady Banbury I mean, suggested I talk to you. Specifically you."

"And for what reason?" Julius knew why. Lady Banbury was one of his most ardent devotees and she recommended him to all of her friends. She had, in short, made him a wealthy man. And now Sophia Phillips was to be his first experiment in his new way of thinking—teaching his patients how to heal themselves.

"I have been feeling, well, not myself of late. I usually love the Season, the parties, the people, the company—the gossip even. I'm meant to be an example for my daughter this year, to show her off, introduce her to the finest company. To get her married, really. But I feel uninspired, perhaps apathetic."

"If I may, Mrs. Phillips, I understand your husband is absent this Season. Is this the first time he has been absent at this time of year?"

She screwed up her face, trying to remember. Julius could not help thinking how endearing she looked at that moment. Beauty deep in thought. It was very appealing. He drew up a chair to sit and hide his arousal.

"I suppose you're right about that. He's always tried to be in England at this time. It is the best time of year to be here, really. He says California can wait for January."

Julius smiled—and when he did, the lady smiled back at him, an expression he swore was tinged with invitation.

"Mrs. Phillips, please do not think me impertinent, but I must ask." He leaned over, his elbows on his knees, further masking his growing erection. "Are you and your husband intimate when he is present?"

"Intimate?" She looked genuinely confused at the question. "We share all our secrets. How do you mean?"

"I mean in the marriage bed. Do you spend time together in bed, your bodies joined intimately?"

Mrs. Phillips' blush only heightened her perfect features. "Yes, Dr. Christopher. We have a very close relationship in that regard."

"Very good, very good." For the first time in a very long time, Julius found himself feeling a bit self-conscious. He drew in a breath and reminded himself he was a doctor treating a patient, no matter how exquisite she was, no matter how strong his desire. "I would imagine that you are finding yourself slightly bereft of your husband's presence and affections. You miss him and your relationship with him, especially during this most important time in your daughter's life. What I find helps in this type of situation is stimulation of the senses, re-enlivening them, if you will. I can provide this treatment myself, but what I would prefer to do is to provide you with the tools to help yourself. When you are feeling disquieted, this technique will invigorate you."

"Oh yes, please. Lady Banbury had mentioned you knew special methods to help women."

"Yes, well…" He really needed to stop hemming and hawing. "I use what is called pelvic massage. It is traditionally a treatment for hysteria but I find that it helps for other psychic maladies as well."

"Pelvic massage? Where? On the hips?"

"No, madam." Julius inhaled, his breath shuddering in his lungs. "Between the legs. At the apex of the thighs." He indicated on his own person attempting to simultaneously cover the insistent bulge.

Mrs. Phillips blushed crimson. "Dr. Christopher, do you mean where my husband and I touch my body for my pleasure?"

Julius could not believe what he had just heard. "Your husband touches you there? May I ask more details about where?" He sensed he needed to dampen his enthusiasm from the astonished look on her face. "Please do not be insulted. I only inquire as I have never heard any woman state this."

She shifted in her chair uncomfortably and could not look Julius in the eye. "He places his hand here," she indicated between her thighs, "and rubs a sensitive spot until I have…" she hesitated, glancing up at him for the briefest of seconds, "spent and am ready for him to take his own satisfaction."

Good God! "And, please, I find this a most unusual activity for husbands, I must ask, how did he come to know this?"

Mrs. Phillips glanced up again, perhaps emboldened by the doctor's admission of surprise. "He confessed to me that his father arranged for him to visit a woman—a courtesan—for his first time, when he was becoming a man. She taught him." Mrs. Phillips chuckled. "She taught him a great deal. I will say, Doctor, I am aware that my marriage is somehow different."

"And your husband taught this to you as well?"

"Yes."

"So you pleasure yourself, Mrs. Phillips?" Julius tried to steady his breathing.

She seemed a tad breathless herself. "Yes, Dr. Christopher."

It was the right thing and the wrong thing to say. He could not get the image of the lady stroking herself to orgasm out of his mind.

"Mrs. Phillips, my treatment for a woman complaining of your symptoms would be to release pent up frustrations with manual stimulation. Are you pleasuring yourself in this manner?"

"Yes, Doctor."

"With what frequency?"

"Every other day, sometimes every day."

Julius swallowed hard hoping against hope that it would somehow relieve the tension building in his trousers. He tried to remind himself, to no avail, that he was a professional. "Really, that is quite impressive," he choked. "I'm not sure what more I can do for you. I am so sorry, Mrs. Phillips."

She offered her hand upon taking her leave, her fingers cold and trembling even through her gloves, sending shock waves of desire pulsing through him. When she looked at him, her eyes held a touch of despair, a touch of regret, and a touch of pleading.

After Mrs. Phillips left, Julius sank into his chair, cradling his head in his hands. The woman missed her husband, the husband who could give her the one thing she could not give herself. Were his theories utterly devoid of merit? Was it true women could only feel ultimate release with male penetration?

Sophia Phillips had just presented to him some most interesting challenges. Women were indeed the more mysterious of the sexes.

When he had gone out on the terrace during the Roxtons' musicale, Nicholas could not believe the screeching noises he had just fled from were meant to be mating calls to all the available men in the audience. It was a shame Viscount and Lady Roxton had not thought to display other more obvious talents of their two daughters.

But when he had finally been introduced to the lovely Miss Helena Phillips, it all seemed rather bearable.

He remained on the terrace after she had left, leaning against the railing, turning his hat in his hand, looking out at the garden, thinking of her. How absolutely lovely she was, with her form-fitting dress of orange and olive that set off her hair and eyes perfectly. How wonderfully agreeable she was, their instant rapport indicative of a meeting of minds. How positively interesting she was, being more fascinated than appalled by an erotic novel.

How absolutely unobtainable she was given his recent choice to give up his titled heritage and try to succeed on his own. It was the first time he felt a pang of regret for his decision. But would Helena Phillips be worth the shameful groveling and possible violence he would be subjected to by his brother and father? And, even if he did debase himself before Jack and the earl, would they accept him back into the fold?

Besides he wouldn't really be the direct heir to his father, anyway, and Miss Phillips was meant to marry someone with a definite claim on a title. Someone, Lavinia had said, like his brother.

Nicholas sighed. He would have to simply content himself with dreaming of gazing into her mossy eyes, running his fingers through her brilliant coppery hair, wrapping his hands around her tightly cinched waist, nibbling on a delicate earlobe. He closed his eyes and lifted his face to the warm sun, breathing in her delicate fragrance lingering in his memory.

"Dr. Ramsay, sir. You're still here."

Her mellifluous voice drifted from behind him. He turned around perhaps a bit too quickly, hoping the action did not seem overly anxious.

"Yes. My employer generously gave me the afternoon off. I had thought I would enjoy the sunshine and view a bit longer before I returned to my office."

"So you are a working man." She seemed slightly disappointed.

"Yes, I am in the professions," he acknowledged apologetically. "A bit odd for a man like me to be at such an event. But I find myself in similar circumstances as yourself. Apparently, I'm here to find a wife."

"And, have you found one yet?" she teased.

He grinned at her. "I haven't seen enough talent flaunted in my direction."

She giggled and colored an alluring shade of pink, then let him gaze into her green-brown eyes probably a bit too long for propriety's sake. Feeling a touch of discomfiture, Nicholas glanced around the terrace. Except for a few furtive couples, they were quite alone.

"Miss Phillips, aren't you supposed to be chaperoned? Whatever would Lady Banbury think of you speaking to a strange man?"

"But you aren't strange. We've been introduced."

"But we are alone," he reminded her.

She glanced down and bit her lip. "Yes, I suppose we are. Well, not really. I mean, Lady Banbury is only over there." She pointed across the terrace.

There he saw Lady Banbury lying, probably asleep, on a chaise longue. He chuckled. "Why don't I escort you nearer your chaperon?" He held out his arm.

She slipped her hand around his elbow. As she had earlier that afternoon, she gripped him as if needing stability, sparking a pang of desire in his core. A moment later, she loosened her hold, the warmth of her touch and her closeness sustaining the excitement within him.

"And really, Dr. Ramsay, it's all right. You're just a doctor and I'm supposed to marry a duke or something."

Just a doctor. The words hurt even though he knew they weren't intended to. "What about an earl?"

"I think I can marry one of those too. Aren't they all old?"

"Earls?"

"Men with titles."

"I suspect your parents want you to marry an heir to a title. They're not always old." He leaned in just a bit. "Some are even handsome."

She glanced up at him, then quickly looked away, her cheeks rosy.

Her artless modesty was beguiling—and thrilling. The excitement deep down flared, warming him all over, a heat intensified with the afternoon sun. Never had such innocence aroused him, her arm in his, their perfect ambling rhythm, her subtly seductive scent—

"What sort of doctor are you?" she said at last, changing the subject.

"Family doctor. At least, I'm in training to be one."

"Like for children?"

"Yes, mothers, children, that sort of thing."

"Did you have to study a long time to do that?"

"Well, I have been studying a long time, but I've only just secured practical work in a medical office."

"Why did you want to become a doctor?" she asked with sincere interest.

He thought a moment. "I wanted to help people, to heal them." A memory of his mother flashed in his mind, distracting him for a moment before the delicate weight of Miss Phillips' hand on his arm brought him back to his rather enchanting present. "And I like science, I suppose."

"I like science, too," she said with giddy energy.

Nicholas stopped and turned to her, seeing for himself the enthusiasm in her eyes. "You do?" It was simply too much to ask.

"Oh yes. I've just read *On the Origin of Species*," she said proudly, then quickly lowered her voice. "Although Mama says I'm not to tell anyone that."

"You read Charles Darwin?" He had to dampen his incredulity so as not to appear impolite. He resumed their stroll as if he met debutantes who read scientific treatises every day.

"Oh yes! I found it ever so fascinating." She bit her lip, a charming little quirk that seemed to indicate girlish mischievousness. "Those are the sorts of books I usually read, Dr. Ramsay."

Nicholas laughed. "And what compelled you to read Mr. Darwin?"

"Papa bought a very fine copy for his library, and he recommended it. He knows I'm interested in the natural world, and we were discussing why some of the plants he sees on his travels are so different from what we have here." Her eyes twinkled at him. "I even know the Latin names."

"You know Latin?" This was too good to be true.

"No, not really. Just for plant names and such. I just studied by myself a little. Nothing formal in school."

Good God. She was inspired enough to learn Latin on her own? Nicholas broke out in a grin.

She giggled, at what he did not know, but it was a lovely sound, a sound that was music to his ears. She giggled again, then blushed and bit her lower lip. A very plump and enticing lower lip.

"What's so funny?" he asked.

"Speaking of Mr. Darwin," she said quietly, "I think we've witnessed a bit of natural selection today."

"Because the Roxton twins have only demonstrated they are quite unfit for the marriage mart?"

That made her giggle more, sending a thrilling quiver from her body to his. He wished she would clutch at him more tightly again, and lean into him. But alas, she kept her proper place.

His heart clenched when he realized they had almost reached their destination of Lady Banbury's lounging form, the landmark indicating a probable end to their conversation.

He could have sworn he felt her slow their pace at the sight of the good lady as well.

"Whom did you say you arrived with today?" Miss Phillips blurted.

"A very dear friend of mine."

"Oh?" Her eyes widened. "She's your lover isn't she?"

Every nerve in Nicholas' body fired at the sound of her voice saying that word—lover. What could he say? The lovely Miss Phillips had indicated she preferred honesty in men. "Yes," he admitted softly.

She stared at him, not in shock as he had imagined, but instead with awe and fascination. "She's the woman you were with the night of the Wrexham ball."

How could she have possibly known that? Of course he had noticed her across the ballroom floor…

"She's beautiful, isn't she?"

"Very," he uttered too quickly. He thought he was getting back at her for the snub of his professional status, but suddenly felt rather loathsome for it.

"Is she married?" she asked clandestinely.

Concern for his reputation, perhaps? Nicholas chuckled. "She's widowed."

"Then it's allowed, isn't it?"

Ah, a young woman's curiosity! So very charming. "Us being lovers, you mean? I think it would be allowed if she were married and her husband didn't care much."

"But would you do such a thing?" she probed.

An unusual query that he really had never given much thought to. "No, Miss Phillips, I think I would not. I prefer an affair to have an air of exclusivity."

She seemed to sigh at that, and slowed her pace to a crawl. "Do you love her?"

It was an innocent question, yet tinged with a sense of urgency. As if Miss Phillips cared about what he felt. His heart jumped. He could only hope as much.

"I like and admire and respect her a great deal. But I am not in love with her. My heart is free."

It was the first time he had confessed that to anyone. She looked up at him, her face glowing with the excitement of possibility, her luscious lips curling into a delicate smile. For a second he wished the world away so he could have the lovely Miss Helena Phillips all to himself.

"Helena! Where are you, my girl?" came Lady Banbury's barking cry beyond them.

"I must go," Miss Phillips said with a hint of regret.

"Until next time," Nicholas responded gently.

She livened at that, perhaps imagining there was to be a next time, and turned to attend her chaperon with what Nicholas perceived as a skip in her step.

CHAPTER SIX

Sophia knew why she was standing on the doorstep of Dr. Christopher's office at one in the morning, she just couldn't believe she had worked up the courage to do such a scandalous and wanton act.

The pretty servant girl who let her in flashed her a censorious expression as she led her into the wide hall between the two offices. It was as if the girl knew why she had come.

Abashed, Sophia suddenly questioned both her motives and actions.

Yet when Dr. Julius Christopher stood before her wrapped in his dressing gown, his hair disheveled but raked into place by his fingers, his lids still heavy from sleep, she knew why she had come. His unaffected sensuality devastated her senses.

"Mrs. Phillips, are you unwell? What is the matter?" He led her into his office and motioned for her to sit.

But she could not sit. She felt both trepidation and exhilaration. She looked nervously around the room. It was a different office from the one she had been in during the day, filled with odd machinery.

"Do you use these devices on women, Doctor?"

"Mrs. Phillips, I hardly think you came to my office to discuss my equipment."

"No," she said bashfully. She would simply have to say what she needed to say plainly. She looked at him. Lighted by the soft glow of an oil lamp, he was devilishly handsome. The thought that he had just come from his bed was terrifically erotic.

"Doctor, I came to you suffering from a malaise I know all too well. I also know how to take care of myself when I fall into these slumps of mine. You see, I frequently have this problem when my husband goes abroad, and I have always been able to handle my affliction. That is, until now."

He stiffened slightly, his breathing quickened.

She inhaled deeply. "When I was here last, you said you weren't sure what you could do for me. But now, Doctor, I think I know."

Dr. Christopher was thoroughly awake now. "Go on." He glanced briefly at one of the machines before returning his attention to her.

"When I pleasure myself with my hand to release my frustrations, I often think of my husband. Lately, though, I've been thinking of you."

His lips parted in surprise.

"I cannot get you out of my mind, Dr. Christopher. And I realize you have the power to fully relieve me of my frustrations."

His now-labored respiration resonated in the quiet dark office. "Mrs. Phillips," he remarked softly, "you are a married woman."

"And if I were not, would you be willing?"

He looked away briefly and drew in a long breath. "I would be more than willing," he said hoarsely.

Her heart leapt. "Please, Doctor, let me explain. My husband and I have an agreement, a somewhat modern arrangement. We are, the two of us, very passionate people. We both have our needs.

He's gone so much during the year that I've given him leave to visit a handful of his regular women. However, in all our years of marriage, I've rarely bothered to take the opportunity myself." She looked Julius directly in the eye. "But now I'm plagued by thoughts of you."

He stood still, frozen in place, but tautly pulled, ready to spring. "Sophia," he said hoarsely, "I also am plagued by thoughts of you."

She stepped forward until she was inches from him. Julius did not move. She untied his robe and slid it open to find him nude on top, his torso unexpectedly honed like an athlete's, the wondrously masculine contours covered in fine black hair flecked with gray. She took his hands in hers, glancing down briefly to see the shadow of his erection discernible beneath his trousers.

She leaned in and kissed him tentatively.

He swiftly enveloped her in his arms, clutching her to him fiercely, his insistent mouth covering hers, feasting on her desires like a starving man. She wrapped her arms around his body under the robe, the heated flesh and finely sculpted musculature flexing in need under her hands, a need so powerful it bordered on desperation.

"Julius," she said as he trailed kisses down her neck, "I've put a pessary in."

He stopped and stared at her in incredulous joy.

"I'd like you to spend inside me. I want you to have your full pleasure too."

He lost no time. "Come, let us go upstairs."

His fingers had trembled as he had unhooked her corset. His hands had felt clammy when he had rolled down her stockings. But now that she lay naked beside him in his bed, Julius felt only wonder and euphoria. His confidence had returned.

It had been a long time since he had been with a proper woman. Too long, really. And what a treat Sophia Phillips was. She was so utterly responsive, every inch of her flesh sensitive to his touch, every lick and nip eliciting an urgent cry for more. When he had massaged her clitoris, he had watched her orgiastic release with glee, reminding himself that it was the right reason for the act.

And then he had entered her throbbing, wet channel, relief coloring both their faces, groans of satisfaction escaping from both their throats. She had matched his every movement with her own, urging him onward to his release, as if she needed his culmination more than he did. Yet with every clench, she proved she was in great need herself, her need an insatiable craving that bordered on an obsessive wantonness.

"Faster," she had begged. "Harder."

And he had obliged, slamming into her like a younger man would, her body gripping him as though she did not want to let him go.

And then he came, his release accompanied by a howl of contentment, filling her with more than just his emission, but his desire, his satisfaction.

When they were both spent, he held her, not wanting to let her go, only for a second remembering she belonged to another man.

She stirred beside him, then stretched, pressing her belly against his abdomen. "Can you not sleep? It must be two or three in the morning. Surely you have patients tomorrow?"

He kissed her hair. "I do," he acknowledged.

The thought of his patients, of his work, spurred an idea. "Sophia, darling, I would like to show you a new device I have just purchased. A machine. I think you would be most impressed. It will produce a pleasurable feeling like no other you have ever experienced."

She propped herself up on her elbows. "Really?" she said with intense interest, her fingers dallying in the hair on his chest.

"Yes." He grinned. "Come, I'll lend you a dressing gown. Let's go downstairs to my office."

CHAPTER SEVEN

Lavinia threaded her way through the crowd in Lord and Lady Shotwick's ballroom as quickly as she could. Luckily for her, Nicholas was exactly where she had left him, standing next to a fan palm, holding a glass of champagne nicked from the refreshment room, and looking quite dull indeed.

"Nicky, dear," she chimed excitedly. "I've filled out your dance card for you." She waved it in front of him.

"My dance card?" He grabbed it and began reading the names as he gulped his drink.

"Don't worry, darling," she assured him, whisking the empty glass from his hand and hiding it in the palm. "They are each one of them hand-picked by me. Delightful girls. All over the ripe old age of twenty. All very pretty."

Nicholas looked overwhelmed. "Thank you, Lavinia. I think."

"The dancing is about to start, dear, so I best get you introduced to your first partner, Miss Prudence Waltham. She likes butterflies, so you'll have ever so much to talk about."

"Christ," he muttered. "I don't think I remember how to dance a quadrille."

Lavinia looked at the card. "Why that's not for ages yet. Come now, be a good boy."

They almost crashed into Lady Banbury leading Helena Phillips toward the dance floor.

"Charlotte! I had been wondering where you might be tonight."

"Running around like a shepherd's dog trying to get Helena a chance to dance with England's finest." The countess did seem a bit out of breath. "Mrs. Phillips put me in charge of her daughter, you see."

Lavinia glanced behind Charlotte to see Sophia Phillips talking very gaily with Julius Christopher. But more surprising was that the usually reserved doctor was drinking in the woman's every word, gazing at her like a man smitten. "Yes, I see." She then turned to smile at Charlotte's companion.

"So this is Miss Helena Phillips." Lavinia nodded to the girl who was flushed from running about or possibly from the sudden attention. She was dressed in a most eye-catching gown of reddish-purple silk with an enticingly low square-cut neckline presenting her bosom above the form-hugging bodice. She was absolutely ravishing. Certainly every man in the room had noticed—and probably desired—her already.

"Why, my dear Lavinia, I hadn't realized you two hadn't met! Helena, this is my good friend Lady Foxley-Graham."

As Helena curtsied, Lavinia noticed she flashed a glance at Nicholas, then blushed more deeply.

"I know your mother from years past, Miss Phillips. Why have we not enjoyed your presence before?"

"I've been away at school in France, my lady." Helena gazed up at Lavinia with admiration in her hazel-green eyes.

Now it was Lavinia's turn to blush at the unexpected attention. "Yes, of course. I had forgotten," she said gently to her new admirer.

Helena glanced at Nicholas again. "Dr. Ramsay," she said with a curtsy.

"Miss Phillips," Nicholas murmured reverently, obviously trying desperately not to stare.

"Oh how discourteous of me!" Lavinia exclaimed. "But you two already know each other?"

"We met at the Roxton musicale, Lady Foxley-Graham," Helena remarked sweetly.

"After you had left," explained Nicholas.

"Ah, yes," Lavinia remembered. It was a most unfortunate event.

"And what a success it was! One of the Roxton twins is already engaged," divulged Lady Banbury.

"Looks like Mr. Darwin was wrong," Nicholas mumbled.

Helena giggled, then raised her hand to her mouth in mortification.

They're already sharing private jokes? Lavinia was surprised that a friendship had blossomed from only one encounter. But Nicholas had found the girl quite beautiful the other night. From the look on Helena's face, it appeared she was more than just a trifle enamored of him as well. Her expression bordered on yearning, then swiftly changed to crestfallen when the orchestra struck up.

"Oh the music has just started. Nicholas, Miss Waltham awaits. And I'm sure Miss Phillips is eager to dance with her own partner."

"Yes, yes, of course." Nicholas gave a gentlemanly bow to the countess and her charge before they dived into the crush of the ballroom.

Lavinia pulled her lover close. "Nicky, if you continue with your life the way it is, you cannot have her," she cautioned under her breath. "You must stop thinking of Miss Phillips. Look, she's paired with Lord Acton of Northbridge. He's heir to the Dukedom of Cleveland. I am sorry, love. Concentrate on the charms of each of your partners. You'll find somebody. Trust me."

Nicholas sighed morosely. "Take me to Miss Waltham, then."

As they joined in the fray, Lavinia saw the most astonishing sight. Dr. Julius Christopher was dancing with Mrs. Phillips and looking as if he actually enjoyed it.

It turned out Nicholas did remember how to dance the quadrille. And if he made a misstep, Miss Penelope Hardcastle very generously covered his blunders.

Miss Hardcastle was really quite lovely, as Lavinia had said she would be. His partners at the Shotwick ball were all of them quite lovely. The problem was that he simply could not see spending a lifetime with any one of them. And he certainly did not want a middle-class marriage of convenience, where a wife was no more than a housekeeper, a man the breadwinner. Nicholas wanted a modern marriage, based on love, one where he and his wife could converse intelligently when he returned home from the office, then spend the rest of the evening in energetic pursuits in the bedroom.

It was well after midnight when he found himself in the garden of the Shotwick mansion, walking aimlessly, avoiding clandestine couples. The fresh air was a soothing respite to the stifling staleness of the ballroom. He took off his gloves, shoved them into his pocket and flexed his fingers in the cool night, inhaling deeply, realizing at that moment the real reason he was alone in the garden. All he could think about was Helena Phillips. He had watched her on the dance floor whenever he could, trying not to be too obvious in front of his partners. She even caught his eye every once in a while. He knew he wasn't supposed to encourage himself in that way, but ever since the Roxton musicale he could think of nothing else. Even when he made love to Lavinia, he sometimes imagined it was Helena in his arms.

A couple absorbed in conversation came toward him along the path. He quickly ducked behind the thick trunk of a gnarled tree.

"Ow!" hissed a female voice.

Nicholas turned around in the dark. "Who's there?"

"Dr. Ramsay?"

He would know her voice anywhere. A tingling heat ripped through his body and ended at his crotch. "Miss Phillips?"

"You stepped on my toe."

"Oh dear. Are you all right? Did I injure you?" His eyes adjusted in the dark to see her smiling demurely at him.

"No," she assured him with a soft laugh.

"It seems I've been stepping on a lot of toes this evening."

She giggled. "Did you like any of them?"

"Who?"

"Your dance partners, silly."

"They're all very nice and pretty. I don't think I want to marry any of them, though."

"But how do you know after only one dance?"

Nicholas drew in a breath. He knew, he just did. "I suppose I didn't feel anything. Like a spark, or a magnetic pull. I really don't know how to explain it. There was just no…no chemistry." *Like with you.*

"You make love sound so scientific, Doctor," she remarked with another giggle.

"Shh! Miss Phillips, we really oughtn't be alone in the garden like this."

"No," she agreed with amusement. "We really oughtn't."

"What are you doing here, anyway?"

"I could ask the same of you, Dr. Ramsay." She sighed. "It was so stifling in the crush of the ballroom. I'm supposed to be in the ladies' retiring room at the moment. But then I saw one or two of the ladies going out into the garden, and the lure of the starlit night was simply too much. I suppose they're escaping to the arms of their lovers with stars in their eyes." She sighed melodiously. "I have to content myself with the consolations of this old elm and the twinkle in the night sky."

Nicholas cursed the elm for offering comfort to Helena Phillips before he did. "I would have to agree, Miss Phillips, that being out amongst the stars and the trees is far more enjoyable than the disappointments of the dance floor." It seemed particularly dark, as if Lord Shotwick, or more likely Lady Shotwick, had purposefully left sections of the garden unlit. "Is stargazing another one of your pursuits?"

"Come," she said invitingly as she moved deeper into the recesses of the ancient tree. Nicholas was compelled to follow.

"Look up. You can see the constellation Virgo between those branches." She pointed. "That's Spica—the brightest star."

Miss Helena Phillips surprised him at every turn. "How wonderful," he murmured.

"There are various stories about who Virgo represents. My favorite is Demeter. She is the goddess of grain, of agriculture. She holds Spica—"

"Ah, yes, Latin. An ear of grain."

"Yes! She holds an ear of grain in her hand against her thigh, and another is held upward." Helena drew the goddess with her finger against the sky. "Do you know the story?"

He did, but Nicholas just wanted to listen to her melodious voice. "I'd love to hear it," he said as he leaned against the trunk of the elm.

She smiled. "Demeter had a beautiful daughter, Persephone, a girl pure of heart and soul who was her pride and joy. One day, Persephone was innocently picking flowers in a meadow when the ground suddenly opened and out of the fissure came Hades, the god of the underworld, riding fiercely in his black chariot. Hades coveted the beautiful Persephone and wanted to make her his bride. He grabbed her viciously and whisked her away to his kingdom in the center of the earth."

Helena's countenance grew earnest, her voice carrying a touch of intensity. She loved telling stories, it was clear. Probably because she loved reading them. Nicholas sank back farther against the thick trunk, contented, his heart swelling with the shared joy of her words.

"Besieged with grief, Demeter went looking for her daughter, but could not find her anywhere. She wandered the earth for four months, fasting, tearing her hair, pleading with the gods and man to help find her daughter. Her grief was so terrible the earth grieved with her. There was no sunshine, no warmth; only rain and snow and ice. The fields remained barren, and mankind began to die because of her mourning."

She painted the story with her hands, expressed the emotions in her intonation, her passion and utter engrossment affecting. Nicholas' heart thumped a little harder in his chest.

"Finally, Helios, the god of the sun, revealed to Demeter the horrific fate of her daughter. Hades refused to give up the beauteous girl, now no longer an innocent, having been subjected to his vile desires—"

Unable to tamp down his own improper desires, Nicholas' cock stirred.

"Until Zeus intervened. But Persephone had eaten four pomegranate seeds whilst a wretch in the bleak underworld, and as a consequence, Zeus required four months of the year she should endure with Hades as his queen. The rest of the year she would be on the earth, the center of her mother's loving attention." Helena bit her lip shyly. "And that's the story of the seasons. Four months of cold and winter, eight of warm spring, summer, and autumn." She smiled at him.

"Thank you." He smiled back. "You are a very engaging storyteller."

She blushed, or Nicholas imagined she blushed in the gray of the night. A moment of silence passed, and he realized they were quite alone. In the dark. A little spark of lust rose insistently inside him.

"And what about you?" he asked, trying to distract himself. "Did you like any of your partners?"

"Well, the best dancer was Lord Aldersley, the son of the Duke of Underwood. But all he talked about were his sheep."

"Animal husbandry is quite scientific, you know. You may grow to like being a duchess sheep farmer."

Helen giggled. "You make it sound so interesting. Unfortunately, Lord Aldersley made it sound awfully boring."

"Well, at least you like him."

"I liked his dancing. That's different."

"Yes, of course. I understand completely." Nicholas had liked Miss Hardcastle's dancing, too, but not her vacuousness. "One of these days, though, you'll meet someone you'll like for more than just his dancing. And, I suppose, you could learn about sheep," Nicholas offered.

Helena laughed softly. "I suppose. Mama learned about machines because of Papa."

"Machines?" Unwittingly, an image of Dr. Christopher's device flashed in his brain.

"Papa designs machines that make metal fittings for railroad cars and undercarriages. When Mama first met him, she knew naught of that. She just knew she loved Papa. So she was inspired to learn and now she consults with him on his business. She was the one who told Papa he should make his machines pleasing to the eye even if only laborers were to use them."

"They sound well-suited to each other." *Like us.*

"They are, very. And I simply do not feel the same way about Lord Aldersley. I like sheep, but he certainly does not inspire me to want to learn more about them than I already know."

Nicholas knew precisely what she meant. "Love as inspiration. Spouse as muse." *You.*

"Yes!" Helena looked up at him in the dark. "Isn't that like the chemistry you mentioned?"

"Yes, yes it is," he agreed. "And I was not inspired to marry and have children with any of my dance partners."

She grinned at that. "You don't need to get married to have children, Doctor."

"Miss Phillips!"

She giggled. "Mama and Papa weren't married when they had me."

Ah, yes, the scandal. Damn their impetuous hearts. "Yes, but they eventually got married to raise you, did they not?"

She giggled again, gently, melodically, not cruelly. "You want a woman who will inspire you to make children."

His cock stirred uncomfortably. "You are incorrigible," he said with a chuckle. "But yes, I want a family. And a wife who will be my companion and friend, someone with whom I can discuss my work."

She shifted on her feet and emitted a noise akin to a sigh. "Do you have family now?" she asked quietly.

"Only my brother and my father. We're not close." That was a subject Nicholas was most definitely not willing to discuss. "You? Do you have brothers and sisters?" he deflected. He already knew the answer.

"No. I am a solitary child. I know no other life, but I think it must be better to have more than one."

Nicholas empathized, "As long as the brood gets on with each other."

"But wouldn't they if their parents got on? Is it such a naive notion to think that if a man and a woman love each other their children would be happy and convivial?"

It was something Nicholas simply had no knowledge of. "Perhaps that would be the case. I suppose you'll discover the answer when you fall in love."

Helena shifted her weight from one foot to the other and back again. "What's it like?"

"What's what like?"

"Falling in love."

A spine-tingling shiver shot through him. How the devil was he supposed to answer that? *It's like what I'm feeling right now for you?* Well, at least he imagined that's what falling in love felt like. "It's a sensation of just wanting to be with someone, no matter how mundane the situation. I think magazines and novels will tell you it's all flowers and carriage rides, but really it's feeling comfortable and elated all at once. I think you'll know when you've fallen in love."

"And how will I know if he loves me back?"

That was something Nicholas could not answer. He hoped Helena felt something for him, thought she might, but short of outright asking, he really didn't know. "He might tell you."

"Then what do I do if he does love me?" she said timidly.

"What do you mean?"

"I mean, what if he wants to kiss me? I've never been kissed before. I wouldn't know what to do."

The shiver stirred inside, swirling around his heart. "Never? You've never kissed a man?" Why on earth no one had ever tried was beyond his comprehension.

"Never."

She stepped closer to the elm, to the crook of a large low branch. Nicholas joined her, moving until he could see her face illuminated by the tiniest sliver of pale moonlight. A stubborn root raised above the earth meant he had to be very close to her to get the view. Very close. The warmth of her flesh, her delicate perfume enlivened his senses.

"Is it nice?" she asked eagerly.

Nicholas felt his burgeoning arousal grow more insistent. "Is what nice?" he said, stalling.

"When you kiss Lady Foxley-Graham." She shifted again, ever so slightly, but enough that her hand touched his. Her bare, ungloved hand.

Every nerve in Nicholas' body came alive at the contact. "It is very nice," he choked out.

Her fingers, delicate and soft, threaded through his. "Will you…will you tell me what it's like?" Her eyes widened at the prospect of merely listening to him tell her about kissing.

Nicholas swallowed hard. "When two people kiss you don't just feel it on the lips."

"No?" she asked ingenuously.

"No. You feel it…other places." As if on cue, his cock twitched to full stand.

"Like where?"

His body ached from self-restraint until he could bear it no longer. He bent his head and brushed his lips against hers, his heart thrilling at how wonderfully soft and warm she was.

Helena flinched a little in surprise, a reaction that only encouraged him, his determination to explore emboldening her. Nicholas pecked gently at her upper lip, then the lower, then repeated the motion more languidly. She placed her hands tentatively on his shoulders, holding herself steady before sliding her hands around his neck drawing herself more closely to him. An eager pupil, she mimicked his tasting of her by eagerly tasting him back, her sighs of desire natural, instinctive. When he tantalized her with his tongue, she opened her mouth for him, letting him plumb her depths, letting him take his pleasure with a rumbling growl, mewling her yearning approval. She was an absolute natural at the game.

He pulled back, panting, incredulous. "That was your first time?"

"Yes." She was breathless. "I felt it."

"Felt what?"

"Felt the kiss in…in other places."

Damn and blast! It was outright seduction. "Helena—Miss Phillips, we mustn't do that ever again—"

"No," she sighed.

"We can't. Two people in our positions—"

"No." It came out as a little moan.

"You're supposed to marry a duke."

"Or an earl."

She couldn't possibly realize what those words meant to him. He had to remind himself he was never going to be an earl, never going to have the lovely Helena Phillips as his own.

But right now she was his. He couldn't stand it any longer. He had to have her again.

He reached for her, crushing his lips to hers in desperation. This time she knew what to do and confidence gave her leave to delve into her own cravings to touch and feel. Her hands wandered across his waist, gliding along his chest, wrapping around his neck as he leaned her against the crook of the old elm. He pressed his hips against her, and she responded with a tilt of her own, rubbing along his painfully needful erection. Their bodies undulated naturally, their mouths delighted in mutual cadence, she met every one of his actions with an equally enthusiastic reaction.

It would be this perfect when he made love to her.

When, not if…

He was a fool for harboring such fantasies.

Still, she was in his arms at that moment…

His hands spanned her back, her spine flexing and yielding to his hold, arching to give him access to more of her. He trailed kisses down her neck, along her shoulder, down to her heart thumping and pounding like his own. Her perfume, heady with arousal, filled his senses. Her breaths were ragged, each exhale intoned with a plaintive moan, her virgin body yearning for some unknown fulfillment.

It was wrong to lead her astray. He pulled back, still entwined in their dangerous embrace. "Helena, darling, we can't do this."

"I know." She gasped for air. "But I want to."

"I very much want to as well." He rested his forehead on hers, feeling the heat radiate from her flushed face. "But we mustn't."

She steadied her breath. "Nicholas, is it like that every time?" Her smile, her eyes, her face glowed with contented wonder.

"When you're with someone you love, yes, it is."

She emitted a yearning hum.

He shouldn't have said that, damn it, he shouldn't have. He shouldn't lead her to believe he was in love with her, even when he knew damn well that he was futilely fighting the feeling every damn day. Against his body's wishes, Nicholas released her. "Helena, darling, you must return inside at once." He studied her in the moonlight. "You may need to fix your hair. And put on your gloves."

"Yes, Nicholas." She had regained some of her composure.

"I'll follow in a few minutes. It…it shouldn't appear…obvious." He watched her go and heaved a sigh, not of regret but of relief. For one brief moment in time, she had been his. It was the best he could possibly hope for.

Helena did not want to return to the ballroom. She was already dancing on air.

He had called her "darling".

He had gazed at her adoringly.

He had *kissed* her.

The handsomest man in the world had kissed her and made her feel wonderful. The warmth of his lips had penetrated her very soul, as well as other very intimate parts of her body. Her breasts still tingled, and below, where she touched herself sometimes, she felt sticky and swollen, starved of a satisfaction she did not yet know, but now had an inkling of.

Until that moment, the moment when his arms enveloped her, holding her steady as he assaulted her with pleasure, Helena had only imagined such an act. She realized her imagination had been inadequate, lacking in specifics, not knowing what details to fill in. She certainly had not imagined the heavenly sensory experience that touched every aspect of her being. The touch of his fingers, strong yet gentle; the sound of his voice, sonorous and seductive; the look in his eyes, pleading yet determined; the scent of his flesh, heated with desire.

The taste of his mouth…

He tasted soft and comforting. It was the only way she could describe it. She traced a naked finger over her still-sensitive lips trying to relive his touch, his taste.

When you're with someone you love…

Helena pondered the words over and over. Did he love her? How could he? They barely knew each other. And yet, there was something electric, exciting, so utterly perfect every time they met. She became herself around him. She did not need to pretend to be something she was not, did not need to be dishonest for propriety's sake. She had been thinking of him since the first time she saw him, then more so after their first conversation, fantasizing he was with her when she pleasured herself, and constantly wondering when she might see him next.

Was that chemistry? Was it inspiration?

Was that love?

She really wasn't sure. Her mother always pined for her father when he was abroad, and they most certainly were in love. And when he returned, her father always kissed her mother in very much the same manner Nicholas had just kissed her.

She touched her finger to her lips again, then traced them with her tongue. They felt tender, almost bruised. Would everyone at the Shotwick ball know what she had just done? Could they tell just by looking at her?

As she pulled her gloves from her reticule, she realized how much she did not want to return to the ballroom. It was filled with dull, uninspiring men, men who did not thrill her, who did not attract her, who could never send her mind and body reeling, spinning, like Dr. Nicholas Ramsay could.

As she tugged her gloves on, she decided she did not care very much what anyone thought, even if they could tell she had just had the most incredible experience of her life.

She smiled. She still felt Nicholas' kiss in a million different places, some of them very far from her lips.

CHAPTER EIGHT

"Doctor, sir, who is that woman?" Grace asked from behind the modesty screen as she took off her dress.

"Which woman, Grace?" asked Dr. Christopher absently.

"The one what comes over and sleeps here." She tugged at the hooks on her corset.

"She is a very dear friend of mine. Her name is Mrs. Phillips."

Dear friend? "Is she in love with you?"

"Never you mind that, girl! Are you ready yet?" The doctor seemed annoyed.

Grace stepped out from behind the screen.

"On the table."

Grace got on the examination table and placed her feet in the stirrup-like holders. Propped up on her elbows, she watched Dr. Christopher make his preparations.

She liked watching the doctor when he was busy, when his handsome features were unclouded by insincere expressions of concern or interest. When Dr. Christopher concentrated on something scientific, his eyes became soft and dreamy, he would suck in his lower lip, wetting it, and he would even talk very quietly to himself, his seductive baritone growling indistinguishable syllables.

"Right," he concluded to no one. "Now, Grace, my girl—"

Grace loved it when he embellished her name with little terms of endearment.

"You understand what I need you to do, correct?"

"I'm to think about the feelings I feel, then describe them to you."

"Very good." He took off his jacket and laid it neatly over a chair. "Then we'll compare what you've felt with the vibration device with what you feel with penetration."

That was a word Grace was not sure she knew. "Doctor, sir? What do you mean? Penet—"

"Penetration. Inside you. When a man places his member inside you." He unbuttoned his waistcoat. "You said you were not a virgin."

"No, sir. I mean yes, sir, I haven't been a virgin for a few years. I like men." She was babbling, but his presence was quite distracting, especially when she was half dressed and he seemed to be taking off his clothes.

"Good. Then we will compare the pleasure you feel with the two events." He carefully laid his waistcoat over his jacket.

"Sir, will there be a man involved or a machine?"

He chuckled. Grace liked it very much when he chuckled. "It will be a man, my girl. It will be me." He sat on the chair and proceeded to remove his shoes.

Grace could hardly believe her ears. "You, sir?"

"Yes, me. I will be the one penetrating you."

Her breath quickened at the prospect. She and Dr. Christopher were going to engage in intimate relations? It was all she had imagined since he had first pleasured her in the bathtub. Where would they do it? Her bed? No, her bed was far too small for two people. Would she be invited into his bedroom? Would they make love on his four-poster? Since being his housemaid, she had been in his bedroom many times, making up the bed, changing the sheets, folding his laundry, placing it in his chest of drawers. Dr. Christopher didn't keep a valet, and Mrs. Jennings kept to the cooking these days, so it was Grace who did everything for him. Whatever he needed and whenever he wanted.

And she relished every minute of it. She would do so much more for him. Now perhaps he was finally asking her to do precisely that. Much, much more.

"Lie back, my girl," he said coolly as he lifted her petticoats.

Grace did as commanded. She had taken off her drawers like he had asked and now lay before him splayed open, all of her desires exposed for him to see.

"Good, girl. You're already wet." His warm fingers stroked her, spreading her sticky moisture. "Last time you had said you thought of someone while I stimulated you with the electro-mechanical device. Do you remember?"

"Yes, sir." It had, of course, been him she had thought about.

"Good. Let's see what you think about this time."

Still propped on her elbows, Grace watched, riveted, as Dr. Christopher unbuttoned his fly and pulled off his braces. He slipped his trousers off, then folded them and placed them on top of the pile of his clothes. Surprisingly the normally very particular doctor was not wearing drawers, tantalizing Grace with a view of his bare, muscular, masculine thighs. His magnificent member jutted forth, tenting his shirt. Grace wet her lips in anticipation.

He lifted the hem of his shirt. Grace sucked in air at the sight. Dr. Christopher was more than well-endowed. He was huge. And beautiful, the length and breadth of the smooth pink shaft in perfect proportion to the swollen glans.

He pulled the fabric of his shirt taut at his waist and tied one end in a knot. He touched her briefly again.

And then he entered her.

Grace gasped at the invasion, thick and delicious, suffusing her mind and body with a satisfaction she had craved. She looked up at him, wanting to know if he felt what she did. But the expression on Dr. Christopher's face was thoughtful, perhaps clinical, his mind absorbed in an analysis of what the rest of him was doing.

It was not at all like what she had imagined their union would be.

She closed her eyes, casting herself in a different scenario, one where Dr. Christopher was the solicitous lover Julius, leading her by the hand into his room. There he would undress her, draping each one of her garments delicately on his slipper chair. Enveloped in a sudden chill, she would shiver, and he would utter comforting consolations as he led her to the bed, tucking her under the goose-down comforter. She would watch him, wide-eyed with need, while he took off his own clothes.

Grace could now envision a complete picture of him utterly nude. Oh! What a sight he would be to behold! She had seen him working in his office at night in his shirt, his collar off, the placket unbuttoned, his sleeves rolled up. He had glorious hair covering his arms and chest. Grace would tangle her fingers in the silky strands as he hovered above her stretched out in the proper position of love.

He would cup her breasts one at a time, then languidly draw his hand across her belly to find she was ready for him, wet for him. And he would enter her, his magnificent cock stretching her, filling her, eliciting a rapturous cry from her throat. He would wait a moment until her ecstatic throes dissipated, then begin his erotic motions.

Grace would answer his movements with encouragements of her own, willing him to go faster as she rocked her hips in rhythm to his thrusts, letting him know her body craved him, needed him. His groans would remind her that he needed her just as much.

Her ravenous wail of ecstasy would spur him on to his crisis. With a deep jerking thrust he would spill every drop of his seed deep inside her satisfied cunt.

Grace would breathe a sigh of relief as Julius rolled over and wrapped his arms around her, kissing her in afterglow.

A waft of cool air nipped between her legs. Her eyes flew open. The office.

"Very good, my girl!" Dr. Christopher exclaimed, already half dressed. "Very good! Your orgasm was quite stupendous." He pulled out a small black journal from his desk. "Now, you must tell me everything you felt."

Grace stared at him blankly. He was everything yet nothing like the man of her fantasies. "I thought of someone," she said.

He raised his eyebrows in interest. "Oh? Tell me."

"It was the same man. A bloke I fancy. I thought about the two of us together."

"And what about a comparison of the two acts? Is one better than the other?"

"No…I don't think so." *Especially when it's with you.*

"Hmm." Dr. Christopher wrote in his notebook. "Could you live the rest of your life without one act or the other?"

"Do I get the bloke I fancy?"

He looked up at her in surprise. "I suppose. Is that important?"

"Then as long as I get the bloke I fancy, I don't think it matters much to me which act I would live the rest of my life with."

Dr. Christopher's surprise turned to befuddlement. He scribbled some notes. "Indeed this is most curious. Grace, my dear, women are fascinating creatures, are they not?"

She smiled. *Not as fascinating as you.*

* * * * *

"Nicky," Lavinia began with trepidation. "I received a letter from your father this morning."

Nicholas remained silent. He did not look up from his newspaper, but his fingers gripped the pages of the *Evening Standard* a little more tightly.

She adjusted her skirt over her legs stretched along the sofa in the library. "He says your brother is really awfully in debt, and he himself is not much better. He asks for money, of course."

Nicholas crushed the paper just a little bit more. "I don't give a damn about my father or my brother. They can both go to hell and rot for all I care."

"Yes, dear. I thought as much. I just don't like keeping secrets from you and thought you should know."

He looked over the paper at that, put it down, and reached for her. "Sometimes I wish I could just marry you." He pulled her into his arms and kissed her smiling lips.

Lavinia giggled as his attentions turned to her cheeks and neck. At the crook of her shoulder, he gave her a little bite. "Nicky!"

He pulled back to his side of the sofa, laughing.

"I received some other news this morning when Charlotte stopped by. The Roxton twin who got engaged, remember? It's to Lord Davenham."

"Good God! He's old enough to be her father."

"Well, that's not always such a bad thing. I married a man old enough to be my father and look where I am now."

"Sharing a bed with a man young enough to be your son."

Lavinia swatted her lover's leg.

"What else does Lady Banbury say?" Nicholas noticed his demitasse was empty and refilled it from the teapot.

Lavinia grinned devilishly at him. "Sophia Phillips is sharing Julius' bed."

"Yes, well, I know that. Puts him in a much better mood. I think the housemaid is a bit jealous though."

"And she says Helena Phillips has been acting queerly the last few days. Since the Shotwick ball, as a matter of fact."

"Oh!" Nicholas appeared genuinely concerned. "How so? Is she ill?"

"Nothing to pin down, Doctor, darling. She's morose one minute, then on a cloud the next. She's forgetful and distracted which is not like her at all. She even requested that her corset be tightened."

Nicholas blushed at that and resumed his perusal of the afternoon paper.

"Well, if you ask me, I think she fell in love with one of her dance partners." Lavinia looked over at Nicholas to see his reaction, but he had turned his attention to his teacup. "I think it might be the Marquess of Aldersley—you know, the heir to the Duke of Underwood? He's very handsome, and a good conversationalist."

"He's a bit of a bore, if you ask me."

"Perhaps it was one of the other dozen young men she danced with. Or all of them. Girls her age simply cannot make up their minds, really."

Nicholas crumpled the *Standard* in a huff. "Christ, Vinny. Stop it."

"Stop what, Nicky?" She glared at him, an inkling of the truth nagging at her. She wanted to hear him say it.

"I kissed her."

Lavinia stared at him in shock. "You did what?"

"I kissed her," he said succinctly, staring back.

She got up from the couch. "Nicky, how could you!" She began to pace.

"Vinny, how could I not? It was glorious, it was magical, and I would do it all over again."

"The poor girl. You're leading her on with romantic notions—"

"Good God, you're not jealous are you?"

"Darling, no!" Lavinia stopped. "No, I have no right," she said quietly. "But Nicky, to rile up a young girl's senses when you cannot follow through, it's…well, it's seduction."

Nicholas leaned his head on the back of the couch. "And what if I'm in love with her?"

Lavinia sat beside him. "You can't have her as Dr. Nicholas Ramsay."

"I know." He stared broodingly at the ceiling.

She nuzzled against his chest. "Please, darling, just leave her intact for her husband."

He kissed her forehead. "Yes, Vinny. I will."

Helena knew Dr. Ramsay worked at the medical office on Chelsea Manor Street, but the maidservant who led her in said Dr. Ramsay was with a patient, and that she was expected by Dr. Christopher anyway.

Mama had escorted her only to the front door. She seemed a bit embarrassed upon leaving but had said for Helena to be a good girl and to listen carefully to what Dr. Christopher would tell her.

For his part, Dr. Christopher was rather animated when greeting her. "Come in, come in, my dear. Have a seat. Thank you, Grace. You may go," he said politely to the servant.

Helena sat down. Dr. Christopher drew up a seat alongside her.

"Now, Miss Phillips, your mother says you have been complaining of fatiguing vexations. Is that correct?"

She really didn't know if that was a medical term or not. "Yes, I suppose so."

He put his hand on her thigh just above her knee, an action that was oddly intimate and not very clinical. "Tell me, in your own words, what you have been feeling," he said solicitously.

"So many emotions," Helena sighed. "I'm miserable one moment, but then something happens and I'm quite happy, elated even. Sometimes I'm cross. I think I've snapped at Mama once or twice. I don't know. I feel frustrated about something but I don't know what." The warmth of the doctor's hand seemed to have an unexpected calming effect.

"Might those frustrations have to do with your activities this Season?" His deep voice was lulling.

"Well, yes. The parties, the preparations, what to wear, how to act, whom I'm allowed to talk to, whom I'm allowed to dance with. It's all very unsettling, really."

"And what would you rather be doing?"

"Reading a book."

Dr. Christopher raised a brow. "Ah, well. Very different from social pursuits." He squeezed her leg a little. "Now, I understand you have been receiving attention from several young men."

Mama must have told him that. "Y-yes."

"It's all right my dear. I'm not here to gossip. I'm here to listen," he reassured.

"There seem to be so many of them. They call on me during the times I'm meant to be at home. They leave cards when I'm not home. Some want to take me for walks, others for rides in their fancy carriages. I've been given loads of flowers."

The doctor chuckled and patted her knee. "You are a very pretty young woman, Helena." His hand gently rubbed her thigh.

"Thank you, sir."

"You feel confusion by all the attention, do you not?"

"Yes!" She was surprised the doctor understood her. She looked up and studied him for the first time. He was really quite handsome for an older man. His eyes were the most beautiful color of blue she had ever seen. Like the summer sky.

"These tumultuous emotions of the heart are fairly usual in young women such as yourself."

"They are?"

"Yes, medical men call what you are feeling 'hysteria'. There are treatments for it. That's why your mother sent you to me."

"I'm suffering from hysteria?" Helena was astonished. "But I don't feel ill."

"No." Dr. Christopher stood up to pace slowly. "But the chaos of emotions, from the desperate melancholy to the ecstatic excitability, create a sort of illness of the mind." He faced her. "I have a method of resolving all of these feelings to make your mind well again. My treatment involves the body."

He must have seen the curiosity on her face. He touched the top of her head. "Your mind is connected to certain places in your body via a system of nerves. When certain nerves are aroused they send a message to the brain. Pain is one of those mechanisms. But so is pleasure." He folded his hands together as if emphasizing his point. "You are here to learn the method of pleasure."

Something about his voice, his expression—a touch of genuine enthusiasm, maybe—was very exciting. "What do I do?" she asked.

"I must ask you to take off your skirt, shoes, and drawers. And your hat, coat, and gloves, of course. There is a screen behind which you may do so." He pointed to a corner of the room.

He continued to talk as Helena took off the required garments. "I have my own three-step method to excite the nerves. The first is a manual massage, which I will teach you to use whenever you feel the need. The second is mechanical massage, which is needed at periodic intervals to give more stimulation to the nerves. The third step," he paused and Helena could hear him pacing again, "is penetrative massage. This keeps the muscles surrounding the nerves vigorous."

Helena stepped out from behind the screen. Dr. Christopher suddenly appeared enlivened, a state that only increased his attractiveness. Helena understood her mother's fascination with him.

He indicated a padded table, one end partly raised with a little pillow hung on the top edge. "Please lie down."

She did. "Am I to put my feet here?" she said indicating the metal stirrup-like brackets.

"Yes. Please."

He lifted her petticoats and cool air fanned between her legs, eliciting a new awareness of her body. He moved a chair and sat before her, looking attentively at the hair covering her privates, holding a jar of oil in his hands.

"I'm going to touch you here," he said indicating the hair. He dipped his fingers in the oil then lightly probed her.

Helena flinched, her knees reflexively smashed together.

"Relax, my dear. It is a new feeling, but you will come to like it very much. I'll help you."

He parted her knees, stroking them with a soothing gesture. He pulled up two leather straps on either side of the table then wrapped and buckled them around each thigh, making sure they secured her comfortably. With her legs wide, she could watch as he spread her open. His fingers were gentle, practiced, as he smoothed the oil on one particular spot, the spot she had discovered herself not too long ago.

Helena cried out involuntarily. She flushed in embarrassment.

"Yes, that must be it." He glanced up at her, an intensity in his blue eyes. He reached for a nearby hand mirror, then held it between her legs. "Watch while I touch you there."

Helena watched Dr. Christopher's finger as it stroked and glided across the very sensitive nub previously hidden under folds of pink flesh. She was fascinated by the sight, never having actually looked at herself since she only ever did the act at night in her bed under her sheets. She glanced back at the doctor's face to see him gazing at her intimate area with admiration. Her own body was mired in a mass of confusing sensations and emotions. The familiar thrill was mixed with a bit of unease.

"Now, Miss Phillips," he said taking the mirror away, "I want you to use your own fingers to do what I am doing to you. Choose either hand, whichever feels most comfortable."

Helena reached down with her right hand. Dr. Christopher helped guide her fingers to the spot. She flinched again when she found the smooth nub.

"Just keep rubbing there, my dear. You'll soon master the technique."

She hesitated. The act had always been private and daring in its secretiveness. Now that she was to do it in front of someone, it suddenly seemed so improper.

"It's really all right. It's what you came here to learn."

Helena touched herself slowly, her finger exploring the silky, oily area, causing a riot of thoughts and feelings to erupt inside her.

Dr. Christopher remained between her legs, now exploring the area just below. He gently pulled her open, then licked his lips. "I see you are a virgin."

"Yes, sir."

"Good, good. Now keep stroking, faster if you like." He got up. "I'll be right here with you." He walked to the other side of the office, disappearing from her view.

Despite the invigorating pleasures coursing through her, the confusion in Helena's mind lingered. She tried to concentrate on the movements of her finger, tried to focus on the physical, but her brain was distracted by the unusual circumstances. She drew in a breath and closed her eyes, willing herself to call up memories, very pleasant memories, one recent memory in particular.

She was in the garden again with Dr. Ramsay—Nicholas— kissing him, his arms wrapped around her, his hands clutching, massaging, kneading her back, her buttocks, her breasts. As their bodies undulated in a sensual rhythm, their breathing staggered unsteadily in unison. Nicholas' mouth feasted on hers at the same time his quiet moans surrounded her, echoing behind her, the sounds sparking a tingling warmth, hearing his breaths come faster and faster, lifting her higher and higher until he emitted a clipped grunt, shaking her from her fantasy, leaving her empty, unfulfilled. Her touch no longer satisfied.

"I don't know if I'm doing this right," she cried out in frustration.

Dr. Christopher was at her side immediately. "Let me," he said excitedly. "Close your eyes. Just feel."

Helena settled against the padded table and closed her eyes. Nicholas came back, enveloping her once again, rubbing himself between her legs, like he had done in the garden.

"Take pleasure from my caress, Helena, my sweet," she heard him say.

"Yes, oh, yes." She writhed in his arms, the confusion once again rearing its ugly head, but with his guidance she was able to grasp at a sensation of spiraling upward, until she was at the top, the top of what she did not know, but she knew she should hang on, clawing and clutching so she would not fall—

"Let go, my darling."

Yes, yes! She should let go and then she would shoot into the sky! Nicholas lifted her into the clouds, up, up, as she stretched her arms farther. Suddenly, like a firework she shot into the heavens, bright lights flaring before her eyes, the flares bursting into a million embers falling to earth—

She screamed.

"Shh, shh, Miss Phillips. It is all over now." Dr. Christopher's calm voice brought her back down to earth gently.

Helena drew in a deep breath.

"And did you find the experience soothing to your sensibilities?"

"Yes," she had to admit. She did not feel the queer frustrations anymore.

"Good. Now do you think you can do that on your own?"

"Oh yes." Of course he didn't know she already did. It was different this time, though. "Doctor, I thought of someone."

"Really?" Dr. Christopher seemed very interested in this.

"Yes."

"Was it one of the young men you've been spending time with?"

"Yes," she acknowledged.

"That's good, my dear." His lips were still at her ear, his voice sultry and low. "Think of that young man when you pleasure yourself in your room at night. And at your next appointment, I will show you a far more exquisite method for achieving this blissful state."

"Now, Mrs. Martin, you put that cream on your daughter's bottom if she has any more rashes."

"Yes, Dr. Ramsay. Thank you, Doctor."

Nicholas had never realized he knew so much more about babies than the women who bore them. He also never knew how much he liked babies. They were wonderfully delightful even when they were bawling their tiny lungs out.

He showed Mrs. Martin out of the office and to the front door. He let out a sigh when the door closed, realizing he finally had time for his long-awaited afternoon cup of tea. He headed back to his office to ring the bell for Mrs. Jennings.

That's when he saw Helena coming out of Dr. Christopher's office.

She blushed crimson.

"Miss Phillips," he managed to greet her amidst the pounding of his heart.

"Dr. Ramsay." Her voice seemed breathless, dreamy.

He took in her form, gorgeous—as it always was—in a claret and blue-gray walking suit, her face enticingly flushed, feeling his own body flush in her presence. "Are you well?"

"I'm fine now. My mother suggested I see Dr. Christopher for—" She broke off, abashed.

Nicholas' gut wrenched. He knew precisely what she had been sent to the doctor for. "Will I see you soon?" He tried desperately to keep the anger out of his voice.

"I do very much hope so, Dr. Ramsay." She nodded her goodbye and blushed anew.

The second she was out on the pavement, Nicholas stormed into Dr. Christopher's office.

"What the hell did you do to her?"

The doctor looked up from his paperwork. "I taught Miss Phillips how to masturbate," he said clinically.

Nicholas felt sick to his stomach. "You scoundrel, using an innocent girl for your perverted sexual deviance."

"It is most definitely not deviance, young man," he shot back. "Experimentation, perhaps, but not deviance."

"I've heard you and Grace in here and it is absolutely not the sounds of experimentation," he hissed. "You're fucking her, you cannot deny that."

"Grace and I are experimenting with the frequency and type of orgasm experienced by women during various sexual acts. I've charted it all. You may look at my notes." The doctor waved his hand casually in the direction of his bookshelf.

Nicholas clenched his fists to stop himself from throttling the conceited, cold-blooded villain. "I will not have you treat Miss Phillips in that corrupt manner," he growled.

"Would you rather one of my far older and less nimble colleagues manually stimulate the girl? It is why her mother sent her to me. I am an expert in the treatment of hysteria."

"Hysteria?!" he yelped incredulously. "Helena is not suffering from hysteria!"

Dr. Christopher narrowed his eyes. "'Helena'? You are overstepping your bounds. She is your better, you fool."

Nicholas wanted to scream at his colleague's cool arrogance. "You cannot continue this, you simply cannot. If you do, you do not deserve the title 'doctor'."

Yet even threats could not sway the man. He sat unmoved.

"Dr. Ramsay, I do appreciate your helping me in my practice. I would like it very much if you would keep to your work and let me continue with mine. You are, of course, free to find another position in another office, as you choose. However, I will continue to have Miss Helena Phillips as my patient no matter what you do."

"We'll see about that." Nicholas stomped out, rage tearing up his insides. He had to do something. He would do anything to save his beloved from such perversity.

CHAPTER NINE

"Oh, God, Vinny. Oh—"

Kneeling before him, Lavinia took Nicholas' cock deeper into her mouth until it touched the back of her throat. He was on the brink, ready to spend. He had been tense of late, and definitely needed the release. She squeezed his butt cheeks and pressed him into her, fluttering her throat around his glans.

"Christ! You're a bloody whore—"

It was rather amusing that he let loose with expletives whenever she did this to him. She loved sucking his cock—she loved everything they did together really, but this was the best she could do for him when she was having her courses.

His hands gripped the top of her head. "Yes, yes, yes—"

He was lost now, probably thinking about Helena. Lavinia didn't mind that he fantasized about Helena's lips wrapping around his prick, her tongue stroking his shaft. The likelihood of that ever occurring was slim, and if it did, that the girl would be as good as herself, even slimmer. All she cared about at that moment was making sure Nicholas was sated and relaxed.

She needed him in a good state of mind when she delivered the bad news she had for him.

"Arrgh!"

He jerked in climax. She held his hips steady, pressing her fingers into the taut muscles of his arse as she sucked the warm salty ejaculate and swallowed every drop.

Nicholas staggered backward and flopped onto the bed, flushed and breathless, utterly spent. He chuckled and pulled her up to lie alongside him under the covers. "You are magnificent, Vinny. You are not making it easy for me to want to marry someone else."

"Nonsense, Nicky. You know you would marry Helena Phillips in a heartbeat if you could."

He was silent. He wrapped his arm more tightly around her, the heat of his body warming her chilled flesh.

"Darling, I've said something wrong, haven't I?"

"No, love." He kissed her hair. "It's just that, well, I haven't told you, because of your past with Julius Christopher."

"Julius?" Lavinia propped herself up on her elbow. "What's he done?"

Nicholas sighed. "He has taught Helena how to frig herself. Apparently, it was Sophia Phillips' idea."

"Well, good for Helena then."

"You don't understand!" he blurted. He heaved a sign. "Dr. Christopher gets, well, 'aroused' is the only way to say it, when he touches women intimately. Other doctors take it in stride as part of their work. Most of them think it's not a sexual act anyway, and even if they do know the truth, they're able to separate the act of physical stimulation for therapeutic release from an intimate act of lovemaking. Not your Julius, though. He likes his work far too much."

Lavinia knew this. She'd known it for years. She had conveniently forgotten.

"Vinny, it makes me sick thinking of the beautiful, innocent Helena in his office and what he is doing to her."

"I suppose it doesn't help if I state the obvious, hmm?" She drummed her fingers on his chest. "That it was you who agitated the girl's passions to the point of nervousness?"

"And she's agitated mine but I'm allowed mistresses and masturbation because I'm a man?" he grumbled.

She ignored him. "Darling, if he has taught her how to pleasure herself, there will be no reason for her to continue visiting his office. Put it out of your mind. Or, at the very least, take a scientific view of the matter. Next time you see Helena, mark if she is changed."

Nicholas grunted.

Lavinia nuzzled against him as sweetly as she could.

He sighed. "Love, I'm sorry. I shouldn't have the grumps around you." He tilted her face up to his and kissed her mouth. "Hmm, do I really taste like that? It's positively wretched."

That made her laugh.

"Thank you, Vinny," he murmured. "You are the most wonderful lover a man could ever have."

A comforting warmth bathed her. It would be far more difficult for her to bring up the bad news now. She would have to strategize.

"Let's discuss your marriage prospects, shall we?"

Nicholas groaned.

"What about Emily Chambers? She's very pretty."

"Yes, I know."

"And intelligent."

"Mmm-hmm."

"And?"

"There's no chemistry with her, Vinny. I don't think she feels anything for me either. It was all rather awkward right after we danced."

"Well, there's Penelope Hardcastle. She's very friendly."

"A little too concerned with fashion and gossip for my tastes."

"But you've danced with her twice already at two different balls."

"She's a very good dancer."

"That's a good quality to have in a wife."

"You're a good dancer, darling. I wonder if it means Miss Hardcastle is as good as you are in bed?"

"Nicky!" Lavinia swatted the top of his head.

Nicholas laughed.

"It appears this conversation is going absolutely nowhere," she admitted with a bit of annoyance.

"Vinny, it's just that I really don't want any of them."

Lavinia sighed. "Darling, if you want Helena you have to change your mind about your father."

"I knew you were going to say that. And, it's probably too late anyway. And, they only want my money which is not unlimited I must say."

It was time. She could stall no longer. "Nicky," she started gravely. "There's something very important I have to tell you."

He sat up at that, leaning against the headboard. "Lavinia, what is it?"

"It's your father. And your brother. There's been an accident."

She heard his breath hitch in his throat. "What kind of accident?"

Lavinia gathered her courage. "Your brother was upset about some recent gambling debts. It seems that his creditors have not been too kind this time around." She inhaled deeply to steady the quiver in her voice. "He got very drunk. Very drunk. And belligerent." She met his eyes. "There was a gun—"

"Oh, God. Not again," he muttered.

The distress on his face constricted her heart. She turned away. "Jack shot your father in a blind rage. And then he turned the gun on himself." She looked up at him again. "Nicky, Jack is dead."

Nicholas stared blankly out the bedroom window into the fading afternoon light. "And my father?"

"He's alive. The letter I received was from your old butler Mason, who had talked to the doctor. The earl is very sick. The doctor removed the bullet, but it seems now there is an infection of the blood."

"Sepsis," Nicholas muttered darkly.

"Yes, that's it." Lavinia gazed up at him. "We both know what this means, Nicky. You need to see your father. Heal old wounds, so to speak."

"Christ, that is the last thing in the world I want to do," he said bleakly. "You know that, Vinny."

"Yes. But darling, you have a reason now."

Nicholas remained silent, his lips twisting and trembling in concert with the struggle going on in his heart.

She took his hand in hers. "It makes no difference what your motives may be. If you do it so you can win Helena's hand rather than make peace with your family, so be it."

"I always thought if this happened, I would disclaim the inheritance. Bertie is next in line after me and he's far more suited. He enjoys all the aristocratic pomp that I loathe."

"Yes, I suppose. I hadn't thought of that." Bertie was the eldest son of the earl's brother, George. The heroic Brigadier General George Atherley was elevated to the peerage posthumously as the First Viscount Ravensburgh for his valiant service to the queen during the Crimean War. At the tender age of five, Bertie had assumed his father's titles and bore them with the maturity and gravity of a young man many times his age. Nicky was right. Bertie would take to being the new earl quite readily.

"And all the debt...I don't think I could handle the responsibility." His voice was thin, conveying the beleaguering weight of the daunting tasks before him.

"Yes, you can," she reassured. "I can help."

"Does he even want to see me?" He looked at her beseechingly.

"Yes. Mason says he has called for you."

Nicholas rested his head against the headboard and stared up at the ceiling. "Christ!" he hissed. "I can never forgive him. What he did to Mother is abhorrent."

"You don't have to forgive him. But I think you should go see him."

Nicholas slid down to burrow under the covers. "I'll think about it."

"Nicky…" she hectored.

"Just when I was finally getting settled." He sighed. "I really like my work."

"You really like Helena."

"I do," he said with resignation. He hit his fist against the sheets. "Bloody hell! It will be like making peace with the devil himself."

"She's worth it. You know that."

He exhaled long and hard. "She most certainly is."

Julius watched the glow of the frosted-glass shade gently pulse as the flame danced inside the oil lamp. He really should be dancing too. He had just been vindicated. Grace had just proved his theory. Well, rather she had just disproved all of medical science.

Woman did not need man for sexual satisfaction.

It was contradictory to what he had come to know with his new lover. Sophia was a startling example of how a woman needed a man for fulfillment, at times to the point of desperation. Yet Grace demonstrated that a woman did not necessarily need a man.

Or even a dozen men.

The revelation made him elated and disappointed all at once.

Grace had gone to bed long ago, utterly satiated. His office was deserted, yet the stench of sex still permeated the cool air. The stench of men, working-class men.

The experiment had necessitated quite a bit of organization beforehand. No disturbance could be tolerated, so the timing had to be perfect. That meant it had to be done well after Mrs. Jennings had gone to bed. It also meant Julius had to inquire as to Ramsay's social habits, subtly of course, but still he had to endure awkward friendly chitchat about which nights the handsome young doctor was attending balls and such. Julius just hoped he had not raised any suspicions.

He needed time to set up the office precisely for this particular experiment. A row of chairs to line one wall, screened off from the rest of the office. The examination table was to be next to the door to allow quick exit, but shielded by another screen so anyone who entered would not see what was going on.

In the course of his experiments, Grace had proved to be quite a sexual dynamo, seemingly able to achieve orgasms without end during coitus, certainly never achieving a final climax. Yet, he could not know for sure as he himself spent far too quickly in the midst of her orgiastic frenzies. For proper scientific analysis he needed to discover the point at which her coital pleasure did indeed end. Her clitoral orgasms had finality, and an amazing display of wanton flailing it was, especially with the vibrating machine. But coitus, an act only undertaken with the male sex, did not seem to bring on an equally definitive satisfaction. Julius was determined to explore this tangent of inquiry, and for that, he needed more than one man. He settled on the nice round number of one dozen.

They were each one of them hand-picked by him, each about twenty-two years of age, each in wonderful physical condition, each of normal intelligence, each fairly good-looking. Simply put, Julius had gathered twelve men so similar as to act as one man, one man with a sexual stamina of heroic proportions.

He had asked the men to arrive at the office at staggered times. They were paid up front, then ordered to put on a blindfold before entering the office and forbidden to speak to each other. They were each given a number and forced to memorize it. Only one of the original dozen failed to show. After the remaining men were settled, Julius gave the command for them to begin frigging themselves, slowly, enough to bring on the required stiffness.

Grace lay on the examination table stripped from the waist down, her feet in the stirrups, the room dark with only enough light for Julius to make notes. The electro-mechanical vibration machine sat on the floor at the ready, just in case he felt he needed to use it. But he wanted to put that off for as long as possible. She would get her reward somehow. Grace was so very amenable, charmingly so, at times eliciting a little flutter of proud satisfaction in his heart.

He placed his hand between her legs to prepare her, studying her face as he did so. She had certain movements, certain expressions that betrayed when she was approaching a state of lubriciousness, and it was to observe these reactions—as a scientist, he told himself—that he watched her. She moaned and squirmed under his ministrations, then licked her lips and smiled up at him sweetly—almost innocently. He drew his fingers through her wetness, noting to himself that she was ready for his experiment, tamping down an annoying touch of protectiveness that welled within.

She would be fine. He had personally interviewed each of the men. She had nothing to worry about. And neither did he.

"Number one," Julius called out to the men waiting behind the screen. Once called, each man could take off his blindfold. The first one came stumbling nervously to the table, his cock fully engorged, its outline visible under his half-buttoned trousers.

"Come to the table. Drop your trousers and your drawers. Lift your shirt."

The young man did as commanded, his impressive cock jutting out eagerly at full stand.

Julius grabbed the man's prick and rubbed oil up and down the shaft until it was smooth and slick. Quite unexpectedly, the doctor felt his own cock stir.

"You may penetrate her now."

The young man looked at him with astonishment. "You really mean that, sir?"

"Yes. But be quiet. No more talking. Just copulate with the girl until you are finished."

Julius watched as the man's considerable cock entered Grace, feeling his own erection bedevil him at the sight. In a minute, the young man was up to speed, slamming inside her, his hands gripping her hips. Grace was already in ecstasy, mewling encouragements and blasphemies, as she did when Julius experimented with her.

The experience proved too much for the young man. He spent far more quickly than Julius would have wanted.

"Out. Take your clothes and exit through that door. Dress in the hall."

The young man staggered out.

"Number two!"

But he was taking too long. Grace should not be without some sort of stimulation or the experiment would not work. Julius turned on the vibrating machine and pressed the wand to her.

"Yes, yes, please, doctor," she moaned.

The second man came in, eyes wide in amazement.

"Trousers, drawers—off!" Julius hadn't counted on the decidedly unscientific attitude of the male subjects. He removed the vibrator. "Fuck her."

The young man did so with alacrity, and with a fair measure of skill. He worked in concert with Grace, moving in and out slowly or briskly depending on the girl's reaction. Julius knew she was reciprocating her lover's playfulness with her own physical dexterity. From her moans and wiggles, she was enjoying the act a great deal. And from the young man's earnest expression and surprised laughter, he was enjoying his part as well.

His vigorous endurance was a marvel to behold. Julius' pencil remained poised over his medical notebook as he watched the scene with astonishment and admiration.

After a spell, the young man picked up his pace.

"Yes, yes," Grace encouraged. "Spend in me. Go on. Oh yes, please."

Julius' cock was aching to be inside the girl. He gave it a quick squeeze and shifted on his feet.

The young man let out a long grunting howl as he arched his back. Unbelievably, he continued to plow into Grace as if he had not spent at all.

Grace was beside herself with pleasure.

"Number three!" Julius figured he better have the next man ready. He no longer cared if the men saw each other.

Number two pulled out finally, groaning his satisfaction.

"Out!" Julius commanded.

Number three was apparently intelligent enough to prepare himself as soon as he saw the incredible scene before him. He was embedded inside Grace instantly.

It was clearly the only way to continue with the experiment. Julius called out for the next man as soon as he could determine when the active man was going to spend. By man number five, Julius had deemed himself an expert in the variety of the course of male sexual response.

And by man number eight, Julius knew that Grace was an unconquerable subject as far as penetration by the male. She still writhed and wiggled, moaned and sighed. With the tenth man, she was still having orgasms.

After the eleventh man, there would be no more. Would she finally break with an even dozen?

His prick reminded him of his own desire. He could be the twelfth in the name of science.

Number eleven built himself to a frenzy slamming inside Grace, who only encouraged his efforts. A minute later, he gasped sharply, his body frozen as he emptied his seed in her.

"Out!" Julius growled impatiently.

Suddenly the room was quiet and still. Doctor and subject were alone. And Grace was still unsatisfied.

She looked up at him, pleadingly. "Julius, please. I want you."

Her urgency propelled him to undress without thinking. But then he looked down between her legs. The milky emissions of eleven men dripped out slowly, causing his stomach to churn briefly before his cock reminded him he was the last man. He could better them all. With him she would spend gloriously.

He entered her, her muscles embracing him in warm welcome. He pulled out slowly, savoring every sensation.

"Yes, that's right. Let me pleasure you." Her tenderness was excessively stimulating.

He hadn't realized until that moment how much he wanted her, how much he needed her. As he moved in and out, he forgot all about her desires, her reactions, her culmination. All that mattered was his own.

And Grace, the little devil that she was, was happy to give him whatever he wanted.

She gripped him with unflagging carnality, bringing herself once again to frenzied squeals of orgiastic delight, joyous sounds growing louder, louder than they had been with any of the other men, building to an ultimate peak. Julius was determined to get her there, determined to hang on as long as possible.

Luckily, a man possessed of maturity did not spend as quickly as youth.

But Julius had forgotten, in the midst of his own desire, that he had just watched the girl being pleasured for the last hour. His cock was ready even if his head—and his experiment—was not.

"Yes," she breathed. "I want you, Julius. I'm the only woman for you. Spend inside me. Make me yours."

He slammed into her, feeling her encouraging response, hearing her wails, then slammed into her once again. She pulsated around him, still not slaked, still strong, still squirming.

He wanted to feel more. He wanted to feel the end.

He knew he could only feel it if he pleasured the one spot that had nothing to do with the male.

He was defeated.

His cock did not give a whit about science. And, at that moment, neither did his head.

He grabbed for the vibrator and turned it on, pressing the wand against Grace. She screamed, thrusting her hips into the device, wanting more.

"Yes!"

She gripped him like she had never gripped him before, tightly, continuously, her clenching strength almost painful, threatening to stop his own climax before it happened.

And then she let out a roar.

He pressed the vibrator harder against her. Her body jerked, her cunt squeezed so tightly as to almost expel him. Julius spent instantly.

"Stop!" she shrieked.

He removed the machine. Grace lay on the table, exhausted, gulping air, trying desperately to catch her breath.

"Julius, that was wonderful." Her face glowed with joy and the flush of sex.

Julius' prick slipped out.

They were all wrong. All of them. The entire fucking Royal Academy of Science, the bloody Royal College of Surgeons, every man who claimed the title of doctor. Male penetration was not the end-all of female sexual satisfaction, instead it was secondary, a pleasant diversion. And contrary to his own colleagues' beliefs, women did indeed feel sexual pleasure in the absence of penetration.

Yet, if woman did not need man, would that mean Grace would not need Julius? A chill crept up his spine.

Julius. Grace had never used his Christian name until that evening, and hearing her say it sent an affecting pang through his heart. His name had rolled off her tongue cleanly, clearly, reflecting the effort she had put in to soften her accent to better help him with his patients. She had become useful, indispensable, and he had grown to rely on her. But it was more than that. Until she said his name he hadn't realized how fond of the girl he had become.

The flame in the oil lamp popped and sputtered, drawing him out of his reverie, reminding him why he was there, why he, a doctor, was in a medical office with a peculiar device. Grace, despite her youth, was overly experienced where it concerned men. She knew how to control her body, how, even, he chuckled to himself, to control men. She clearly loved the act of intercourse. But what if she had never had that experience? What if she had to rely only on herself?

What if she were a virgin?

Better still, what if he could garner a certain type of virgin, utterly untouched, a true innocent, not a feigning cockatrice from a brothel with a blood-soaked sponge up her cunt.

A woman of breeding, class, and intelligence.

Helena.

Julius stared at his notebook. There was only one way he could have unfettered access to Helena for several years. Luckily Sophia was exceedingly easy to persuade when the mood was right.

CHAPTER TEN

The office was dark and empty, but that only sent a thrill of expectation through Sophia. Julius had promised to use the vibration machine on her once again. Every time he had used it, she had reached climaxes beyond her imagination, each one better than the last.

"Tonight, my love, I have planned for something a little different."

Sophia loved Julius' erotic plans and schemes. They always left her breathless and satisfied.

"I'm ready, Julius."

She stood before him in the office utterly nude as he had requested. His attentions were freeing and decadent, his mesmerizing gaze wandering up and down her body while he sucked in his lower lip, biting it as his blue eyes narrowed lasciviously. She heard his breathing slow to an irregular rhythm.

"Sophia." It was said adoringly, hungrily.

She went to him and he took her in his arms to kiss her deeply, intensely, a man possessed. She knew his dark moods by now, his utter concentration on the matter at hand, his feigned distance, his bald desire. She felt his hardness through his trousers as he ground his hips against hers.

"We'll use the table, my love. But I want you to bend over and hold the footrests."

It was an odd request, to be sure, but she complied nonetheless. A night with Julius was certain to be a memory she would carry with her forever.

Sophia put her hands through the footrests extending from the table and held on. Julius placed his hand on her back, stroking encouragingly. She pushed her buttocks out playfully, shamelessly.

"Yes," he moaned. His hands caressed her, kneading the flesh of her cheeks, wandering to her inner thighs, massaging until she spread her legs enough for him to stroke her yearning labia. He spread her moisture over her clitoris, thoroughly wetting the sensitive nub. "You're so wet, Sophia. So excited."

She closed her eyes in anticipation, the sounds of his preparations more pronounced, the heat of him more powerful. He reached for something at her side, worked at an object behind her. He parted her butt cheeks then smeared an oily substance in the crevice. His finger dallied on her puckered hole, circling the ridge, breaching the unwilling orifice to lubricate it with a generous quantity of the viscous liquid.

Next he was undressing, and rather quickly. When the frenzied breaths behind her subsided, she turned around to see him rubbing the oil on his magnificent cock.

"Sophia, love, has your husband ever penetrated you in your arse?"

Oh, God, yes. Her heart beat faster. "Yes, Julius, he has." A tingle of anticipation pulsed up her spine.

He leaned over her, his slick cock sliding along her cleft. "But has he ever done so while you are being stimulated by a vibrating massage machine?" His breath was hot on her neck.

She swallowed her excitement, feigning a distance that had become her expected role in their sensual play. "No, Julius, he has not."

"Good." It was said with just a touch of smug self-satisfaction.

He flipped the switch. The whirring of the machine filled the room and her senses.

"Spread your legs, my love."

She did as instructed and he positioned the wand at her clitoris. It was set on low, but its pulsating vibration was enough to arouse her instantly.

She felt the head of his cock at her anus, insistent but gentle. He pushed in slowly.

Sophia flinched from the shock of pain, her muscles tightening against the invasion. She inhaled and concentrated on the pleasure of the vibrator.

He pushed in farther, stopping a moment to let her succumb, his hand resting on her lower back in reassurance, then proceeded with a jab as if it were her far more flexible cunt.

Sophia cried out unwittingly, then tried to steady her breath. It was a test of her ability to focus on her own pleasure. Julius had taught her skills of centering her thoughts and feelings on what she wanted, not what was actually happening to her, to move beyond the pain he subjected her to. She drew in a calming breath through pursed lips and relaxed her tensing muscles.

"Good, my love. That's right. Let me in."

He pushed forward, embedding himself fully, letting her accept him, then began moving in and out languidly, moaning softly, arriving at a gentle rhythm. Despite seeking his own pleasure he was able to concentrate on hers, holding the vibrator steady, taking the forbidden act to a point beyond ecstasy.

"It is wondrous, my love, is it not?" His voice did not betray the rapture she was certain he must be feeling.

"Yes, Julius." She could scarcely get the words out.

"Would you deny anyone this pleasure?" His steady baritone held a sinister edge.

"No. Of course not."

"Not even your own daughter?"

Sophia tensed at that. Julius paused.

"Ah, that is a delicate subject. Especially while I'm fucking you in a most unnatural way."

Confusion descended on Sophia. Why was he saying such things?

He took the vibrator away and turned it off, continuing his motions inside her. "Helena is a virgin."

It was not a question, but Sophia felt compelled to answer. "Yes."

"I've never had a virgin."

A chill spread over her.

Julius slowed his movement. "In order for Helena to garner a husband of sufficient status she must remain a virgin. Is that not so?" He picked up his pace, thrusting in and out of her more determinedly.

"Yes." She clenched her jaw against the pain now devoid of respite.

"I want her for myself, Sophia," he rumbled calmly. "You can either give her to me willingly or I will simply take her by force in the name of medical treatment. I call it penetrative massage."

Every muscle in her body tightened.

Julius groaned. Her body's reaction had seemingly provoked him to renewed vigor.

"Any aristocratic man worth his salt will require a virginity test given the family scandal." He pounded against her, uncaring. "Helena is a very beautiful girl. The daughter of a lustful woman. No man will believe her untouched."

Sophia fought back tears. She was the one who had set up her own daughter to see Julius for treatment of her erratic behavior. Couldn't she simply prevent Helena from returning to Julius for treatment?

He slowed his pace. "You know I can easily insinuate myself in her life, my love. I can easily convince her to come see me for further treatments. She knows the pleasure she feels under my care. She'll come."

He was right.

Julius thrust himself deep inside her and held his position. "A husband has rights over his wife that not even a father can deny." He clicked on the vibrator.

Every pore on her skin opened in anticipation. Like an opium eater to laudanum, she was addicted to his touch.

"Yes, Julius."

He held the vibrator away from her flesh. "You want your release, do you not, my love?"

God, oh, God, yes! "Yes, Julius."

"Tell me you give Helena to me willingly."

Her tears fell uncontrollably. "I give Helena to you willingly."

He moved the vibrating wand a bit closer. Pulsations rippled the air near her sex.

"You want me to use her body for my own pleasure."

"I want you to use her body for your own pleasure." Lust and fear, desperation and hate welled inside Sophia.

"Beg me."

An icy shudder ripped through her. Julius tauntingly moved the vibrator even closer.

"Please take my daughter, Julius," she choked out. "Please give me my pleasure." It took every last shred of effort to not sob her words.

He chortled darkly. "You won't regret it, Sophia."

He pressed the wand against her clitoris, then pounded against her relentlessly. She jerked in a mini-convulsion, squeezing him. His climax came quickly.

He held the wand steady, unrelenting, his cock still hard within her. She closed her eyes again, this time to block out the abomination she had just agreed to subject her daughter to. Julius was far too old for her, far too corrupt and perverted. Helena was chaste, naive, unaware such debauchery existed. But Sophia knew about such things. Sophia would do anything for Julius.

Including, it seemed, giving him her innocent daughter.

Sophia screamed her orgasm, her body gripping so violently she spewed out Julius' sated cock.

As she slumped over in despair she heard his gleeful laughter behind her.

Grace wasn't sure Dr. Christopher knew about the peephole under the stairs. He had to know, she convinced herself. There was an awful lot of bizarre equipment being stored there—probably medical devices he no longer needed—so he must occasionally go into the little room and fetch or leave something.

Besides, it wasn't so much a peephole, really, it was just that she used it as such. There had already been a tiny hole, probably because one of the wood and iron contraptions had hit the wall once when he moved it. But to be able to see—and hear—into Dr. Christopher's office the hole had to be made just a little bit bigger.

And what she had just seen through the hole had been astoundingly arousing. As she frigged herself she had reached back to touch her anus to see what an invasion there would feel like, especially an invasion by such a luscious cock as was the doctor's.

She stopped touching herself when she heard Dr. Christopher's ultimatum to the lovely Sophia Phillips.

It was one thing to share her Julius with a married woman whose husband would return eventually. It was quite another to share him with a beautiful young virgin who was to be his wife.

Grace remembered that Helena Phillips had inquired about Dr. Ramsay the day she had come in for her appointment. Perhaps the two were friends.

Perhaps Dr. Ramsay needed to be informed of Dr. Christopher's scheme.

CHAPTER ELEVEN

Thoughts of Helena and his rather eccentric employer occupied Nicholas to distraction, and thoughts of his father and why he possibly wanted to see him plagued him until his stomach turned. Did the earl want to make him his heir? It was the very first time in his life Nicholas actually wanted such a thing, and he wanted it because of *her*, to guard her and shield her from the likes of Dr. Christopher.

To love her with his entire being until the end of time.

Of course it was possible his father merely wanted to mock him, to let him know another more deserving heir had been chosen. Unfortunately, the earl was like that sometimes.

Such vexatious worries made the ball at Lord and Lady Quimby's rather tiring. But Lavinia had insisted he attend. "You need to keep yourself in the game, Nicky," she had said. "Who knows, you might find someone you like."

But it was the same as every other fashionable ball. Young ladies dressed in elaborate confections of ruffles, ruching, and lace, their necklines cut so low men young and old could get a glimpse of their wares, their pretty smiles flirtatious and beckoning, their waists nipped dangerously so partners could get an entire hand across the back, producing a sense of ownership and power.

After a while, it just got boring.

To be sure, he danced with some very lovely young ladies, taking the opportunity to surreptitiously glance at cleavage, feeling feminine bodies move under his command in the waltz. To be sure, he became aroused at all the attention. But it was his body's normal reaction. His cock would have got just as hard had he been at a brothel.

Then there was Helena. Unobtainable, beautiful Helena. While he was dancing with the light-footed Penelope Hardcastle, he saw Helena having the most awful go of it with William Peel— who was too young and rather gangly but must have been the heir to something otherwise why would Helena be dragged across the floor like a sack of flour in his arms? Nicholas swore he saw her look at him with a plea for help.

There was no garden at the Quimbys' Belgravia mansion— well, nothing to hide in at any rate. But the house was large, going several stories up. Which was where, it seemed, guests flocked to get a breath of fresh air.

Nicholas slipped through the throng of guests, out of the ballroom, and up to the third floor, passing several men and women going up and down the stairs. As if abiding by some unspoken rule, no one looked at or greeted any other. It created an air of licentiousness and possibility. Nicholas chuckled to himself. Whatever was he to find on the third floor?

It was purposely poorly lit, faces only shadows, colors faded into grays. He realized he was in a bedroom wing. Well, so be it. He could use a nice wingback chair in a gentleman's bedchamber after standing for hours on end.

Nicholas tried the handle on a door. Locked. Of course. He wondered what he would have done had the door not been locked and he had walked in on a fornicating couple. He was feeling so puckish he probably would have joined them. An unlocked door surely was a sign of welcome to such debauchery.

As Nicholas approached the next room, a young man dashed out. He moved along, assuming the fellow had already satisfied both himself and whoever remained behind.

He tried the next room. Open. He peeked in. It looked empty, but it was difficult to tell as it was almost completely dark with only a bit of moonlight glowing through the windows. The light revealed the coveted wingback. Nicholas entered, then closed and locked the door behind him. There certainly was no rule that a man could not be in one of the bedrooms all by himself, was there?

He glanced out the window at the night before settling in the chair, groaning as he felt his body relax into the stuffed cushions.

"Dr. Ramsay?"

He jolted up to standing at the sound of the familiar female voice.

"Miss Hardcastle?"

"Y-yes."

There was a tinge of shame in her response, as if she had been caught in a compromising position.

Oh, what a fool am I! He really should have asked aloud if the room was empty before entering. Now it seemed he would have to make absolutely sure he and Penelope Hardcastle left separately and at such an interval to avoid scandal.

"I didn't expect you," she said quietly. "I had thought you above this sort of thing."

Christ! "Miss Hardcastle, are you here for an assignation?" he asked incredulously.

She remained silent for a minute before answering. "Yes."

It was really beyond comprehension. Penelope Hardcastle fornicating with an unknown stranger in a dark room? And yet, the thought was surprisingly arousing.

"Miss Hardcastle, please understand, I had no idea there was something prearranged here. I came upstairs to sit in a comfortable chair and catch my breath. The garden here is really too small."

She giggled, then stepped forward into the shaft of moonlight. "Then I was right about you. I had hoped at one point, but you are so honorable and polite that I realized it was never to be."

Nicholas had never really studied her. Now with the soft light through half-open diaphanous curtains he saw how remarkably pretty she was. Her dress was cut provocatively and perfectly to suit her feminine attributes. A man would be a fool to not take the opportunity as presented. So his stiffening cock reminded him.

"Do you do this often?" he asked, then shook his head in dismay. "I'm sorry, I'm just somewhat surprised. Of course I assumed you were—"

"A virgin?"

"Miss Hardcastle, Penelope, this is most embarrassing, really. I do not know what to say."

She bit her lip and approached, reaching for his hands. Nicholas swallowed hard as she took off his gloves, slowly, one at a time, dropping them onto the arm of the chair.

She stood on tiptoe and brushed his lips with the most delicate of kisses.

It was his undoing. He pulled her to him and pressed his mouth to hers, devouring her, as she tore off his jacket and waistcoat.

"Nicholas, it means nothing, believe me," she whispered in his ear. "It's just a fantasy. I'm not interested in marrying you. We'll keep this our little secret."

Christ, but his cock was hard. "I haven't done such a thing as this in years, Penelope." His body reminded him of how exciting a furtive encounter could be.

She led him to the bed, bent over the edge, and lifted her skirts.

Between the tops of her stockings and the flounce at her waist she was naked.

"Where are your drawers?" he blurted.

She giggled. "Over there with my fan and gloves, silly."

He unbuttoned his fly and slipped off his braces to lower his trousers, only realizing then how excited he was. And, as he unbuttoned his drawers, how utterly rash. He was a doctor. He knew better.

"Penelope, should I pull out?"

"Oh yes, I think so, please. I wasn't able to put in a pessary."

She wriggled her glorious butt at him. In a second, he was embedded in her warm, wet cunt.

"Oh, God," he groaned.

Her muscles fluttered around him, gripping him tightly as he pulled out, releasing and flexing as he pushed in. She was most definitely not a virgin.

"Faster," she mewled.

He obliged. Her first orgasm was quickly followed by a second, then, astonishingly, a third.

Nicholas was stunned at how practiced the young lady was. He found her clit.

"Oh yes, please," she begged.

As he massaged the tender pearl her breaths became moans, growing louder and louder.

It would simply not do.

He grabbed his handkerchief and stuffed it in her mouth. She looked at him in surprise, her face quickly softening to lewd accession.

Nicholas slammed into her as his finger brought her to climax, her screams muffled by the handkerchief and the mattress. Her heated passage clenched so tightly he could barely pull out.

But pull out he must as she had made quick work of him. He wrenched her head up, grabbed the handkerchief, and spent into the hot, damp cloth with a satisfied groan.

Penelope stood up, adjusted her skirts, walked to where she had left her clothes, then dressed quickly and quietly.

Nicholas hastily jerked his trousers back on. He was speechless, but surely something should be said. "Penelope, that was fabulous."

She went to him and put a gloved finger to his lips before kissing him sweetly. "Thank you, Nicholas," she murmured.

And then she left.

Nicholas fumbled nervously searching the floor for the rest of his own discarded clothes. In his wildest dreams he would have never have thought such a thing would have transpired with such a polite young woman.

The sound of the door opening startled him. His heart jumped in his chest before crashing back down into his stomach. He was utterly spent, physically and emotionally. There was simply no way he could go through that again.

It was a woman, that much he knew from the rustling of silk and crinoline. She strode in purposefully as if she herself had been looking for an unlocked door and a wingback to settle down in. As she drew nearer he sensed her subtle perfume lingering in the air, a scent that his cock recognized before his brain.

Oh, God. No. It simply couldn't be.

As she strode toward the wingback Helena thought the empty bedroom was oddly humid, the windows peculiarly cast in a dissipating haze of steam. Then she felt a presence. A man's presence. She stopped short.

"Hello?" she called out meekly.

"Helena?"

It was him. Her heart leapt to her throat.

"Nicholas?" she croaked gleefully.

She watched as he ran to the door and locked it.

"Whatever are you doing?"

"Locking the door." He grabbed her hands. "Helena, you should not be in here."

"Because you're in here?" she asked plainly.

"Well, yes." He raked his hand through his hair nervously. "And what are you doing on the third floor anyway?" he scolded.

"I went to the ladies retiring room on the first floor and then I decided to explore," she began defensively. "There were so many people going up and down the stairs I thought there was nothing wrong with it. I was just looking for a little respite before I was expected back at the ballroom."

He shook his head. "I apologize. Of course your reasons are un-censurable. But darling, I don't want anyone to find you in such a compromising position." He exhaled, his expression twisted, trying to think what to say. "You see, the third floor is where guests go to have illicit love affairs."

"Oh." She should have been completely scandalized by such a notion, but she was far more enthralled that such things happened at formal occasions.

Nicholas led her to a window as if to consider how he could manage her escape, but seemed to realize how foolish that was.

In the pale moonlight, she gazed from his worried expression down to his untucked shirt bunching where his braces met his trousers. His half-dressed appearance suggested a recent adventure of sorts. "Then did you just have one?"

"One what?" he asked distractedly, reconsidering the window.

"An illicit love affair." She relished saying the words aloud. She could never talk like that in front of anyone but Nicholas.

He glanced down at his state of dishabille, then regarded her apologetically. "Helena, please believe me," he implored. "I came here as innocently as you did, to find some peace away from the crowds." He looked away, abashed. "But I found someone here, someone I knew, someone I liked." He brought her hands to his lips and kissed them as he gazed at her. "It was base and contemptible. I hope I have not lost esteem in your eyes."

"Was it wonderful?" she asked eagerly.

Nicholas was taken aback by her response. "I—I suppose it was, rather."

"Oh, how romantic!" She wandered over to the wingback and flopped down into it, his gloves falling from the arm to her lap. "I wish I could do something so wicked," she lamented, smoothing and straightening the kid leather. It simply was not fair that others could be so free.

He knelt at her side. "Helena, you should never have to do such a horrid thing! Your husband…" He faltered. "Trust me, your husband will worship you. You will find all the love and romance you'll ever need with him."

Your husband… Helena didn't even know who he was going to be. Tears welled in her eyes. How could she possibly love a man she did not even know? Meeting Nicholas in third floor bedrooms sounded like a much preferable life. The tears were insistent. She wiped her cheeks, staining her gloves.

Nicholas jumped up. "Darling, what is wrong?" He pulled her out of the chair and led her to the bed. "Sit with me. Talk to me. Tell me what is bothering you."

She sniffled as she sat on the mattress. "Do you have a handkerchief?"

"No," he responded brusquely. He slipped off his braces and offered the hem of his shirt. "Please, use this," he said gently.

She wiped her eyes and her nose, pulling the shirt up as she did so, revealing his torso little by little until she had completely forgotten about her tears and was simply staring at his stomach. She had never seen a man unclothed before and the sight was affecting her in an unexpectedly physical way. "May I touch you?" she asked quietly, unable to quell the awe in her voice.

"Yes," he said with a yearning quiver.

Nicholas lay back onto the mattress and Helena knelt next to him, gazing at his uncovered flesh as she nervously removed her gloves. She touched him tentatively, finding his skin marvelously soft and excitingly warm, then glided her fingers over the taut muscles of his abdomen, through the fine hair of his chest. He responded with moans and sighs, encouraging her, emboldening her, compelling her to bend down and kiss his bare flesh, his hot belly burning her wet lips. His throaty growl provoked her to lick, his exhaled blasphemy incited her to outline tiny circles around his trembling navel with her tongue before following the trail of downy hair to the waistband of his trousers.

Nicholas sucked in air at her intrusion. "Darling, no!" He sat up. "We mustn't."

For only a moment they stared at each other wide-eyed, puffing shallow, astonished breaths before Nicholas took her in a devastatingly needy kiss.

Helena gave in to his demands, letting his tongue tangle with her own, letting him twist her to lie back, letting him place his weight on top of her, letting him trap her against the mattress. Her hands explored his back, discovering the muscles masculine and exciting as they moved and reacted to her gripping fingers steadying herself against the assault of pleasure. His hips rocked against hers in a slow rhythm. She responded instinctively, pressing up and tilting down to his sensual cadence.

He lifted his head, gazing beseechingly. "Darling, your very presence drives me mad with desire." He stroked her cheek. "Then to be with you like this, to love you like this, to touch you like this, I am beyond my senses."

"Me too." She smiled and drew her fingers down his spine tracing every ridge, every valley of every vertebra until she reached his waistband. She slid her hands under the fine wool, hesitatingly, slowly. She hardly knew what she was doing, but it felt perfect.

She sensed a new energy surging through him at her touch. His lips pecked a string of kisses from her ear to her décolletage, his tongue darting under the fabric of her neckline. "My love, Helena, we oughtn't be doing any of this." Despite his speech, he did not stop.

She did not want him to stop. She wanted to ride the tumult of emotions from confusion to delirium. But his truth made her remember why she had to get away from the crowd in the ballroom in the first place. "No, we really oughtn't," she said, the words choking in her throat as fresh tears smarted in her eyes.

Nicholas abruptly pulled back. "Helena?" He slid to her side. "Oh, God, I've been a brute."

"Nicholas, no, please, it's nothing you did." She took the edge of his shirt again to wipe her eyes. "When I'm with you I feel nothing but…but joy. Absolute joy, unfettered freedom." She smiled up at him, his face racked with concern and delight. "I fear I will never experience such feelings with another. I know I could not." She drew in a bracing breath. "My mother has found a husband for me. I don't know who it is yet. She said he is a kind man but an older man."

Nicholas gaped, then fell back onto the mattress in defeat, gasping, stunned and disheartened as she. "I'm sure whoever your mother has chosen for you will be a suitable match," he said, staring up at the canopy.

Helena rested her hand on his belly shuddering as uneven breaths coursed through his torso. "Nicholas, I'm afraid. How can I love him if I don't know him?"

"Perhaps he is a good man. Perhaps love will grow." He didn't sound convinced.

"But I want to feel what I feel when you kiss me."

He wrapped his arms around her and pulled her close. "Perhaps he is an interesting man. A man of science."

"Can dukes and earls be men of science?" she lamented.

He chuckled. "Yes, I think so." He gave her a little squeeze. "Why do you not know who it is?"

"My mother said she has written to my father in California. I think I have to wait until he approves."

"Oh." He could not hide the disappointment in his voice, and yet there was a hint of something akin to hopefulness. "Do you have any idea who it might be?"

"I've thought it through. It has to be a duke. I've met a couple of those who were at least forty, I think." She gazed up at him. "Nicholas, I don't want to think about it right now. I want to be with you." She slid her hand across his stomach, stroking the silky strands that disappeared tantalizingly beneath his waistband.

"All right." He kissed her hair and grabbed her hand, holding it away from him as he tugged down his shirt. "But I don't think we should continue with what we were doing. I'm not sure I could restrain myself. And I would have the wrath of both your father and your future husband to deal with."

Helena giggled. "Tell me about the girl you were with."

"No! Absolutely not."

He didn't seem angry, so she pressed. "Do I know her?"

"I will not besmirch the name of a fine young woman." Despite his stalwart words, he was smiling.

"So you admit what you did was wrong?" she taunted mischievously.

"What? No! I mean, yes, it was very naughty, but if two people—" He broke off.

"Yes?" she said expectantly.

"You are incorrigible, you know that."

"I do." She smiled.

"How any man will put up with that, I don't know."

"You would."

"I would," he agreed. He pulled her close again. "Tell me about the stars, Helena. Tell me about the constellations."

He was changing the subject to make her feel better. She nuzzled into the crook of his arm. "When I was a child, Mama and Papa used to tell me bedtime stories about gods and goddesses. One night, Papa took me outside on the lawn of our house in New York. We lay there and he told me the same stories while we looked up at the stars. I spent that summer reading about the constellations and the myths during the day, and studying the sky at night, watching it change as the hours passed." She sighed. "I suppose the wife of a duke doesn't really need to know such things."

"You never know." He kissed her hair and threaded his fingers through hers. "I didn't think it would happen so soon," he said quietly, his voice betraying his disbelief. "I thought I'd have a bit more time."

"Time?"

He pressed his face against her. "Time to be with you."

It was a curious thing to say. Even all the time in the world would not have changed the fact that he was a doctor. Still, an old duke might not mind if she had her pleasures once she bore him an heir. "Nicholas, could we be lovers after I am married?"

She felt him tense briefly. "I would very much like that, Helena."

"We could make love in third floor bedrooms."

He smiled and looked down at her. "How positively wicked." He pulled her close and took her in a deep kiss.

She opened for him letting him consume her, her lungs tightening against the sobs threatening to break forth, knowing it was probably the last time they would be together. She tugged him on top of her to envelop him in her arms, gripping for dear life, letting his body crush hers, just needing to feel him more.

He broke away reluctantly, loosening her hold on him yet understanding the urgency, letting her run her hand inside his shirt. His muscles trembled under her frenzied fingers.

"Darling," he said softly, "I have to go away for a while on business. I mean, there's a family matter, an illness, and I must attend to it. I don't know when I will see you next, but I will see you. Even if you are already married, I will find you."

Helena nestled against him. "And then we can become lovers?"

"And then we can become lovers."

It was said with a hopeful note.

CHAPTER TWELVE

Nicholas had lost her. His beloved Helena, gone, to another man, a stranger who did not love her.

Still, Lavinia—dear sweet, practical, intelligent, beautiful Lavinia—had convinced him he had to see his father even without the hope of Helena. Once the Earl of St. Albans died, the press would discover Nicholas' relationship to him. It was best for Nicholas' future—and his marriage prospects—if he made an effort to reconcile with his family. Women adored honorable men, she had said.

Mason the steadfast butler showed no surprise when he opened the front door to the sprawling estate and saw the proverbial prodigal son returned.

"Good afternoon, Lord Saxondale."

The reference to the courtesy title was jarring. "Good afternoon, Mason," Nicholas said kindly. With Jack dead, the servants would just assume he was the new Viscount Saxondale. There was no point in admitting his reservations.

He was led in and his hat and coat dutifully taken. "I'm here to see my father, Mason."

"Yes, my lord. Right this way."

As they climbed the stairs, passing paintings of his ancestors, Nicholas saw how much the house had been left to deteriorate. Along the corridor of the second floor, where a maid would have usually cleaned, dust clung to woodwork and covered the tops of tables, less thick where objects had been removed, probably to be sold. The patent disregard for their once-esteemed heritage disgusted him.

"Where are you taking me, Mason? This is not at all where I remember my father's bedroom was."

"Yes, my lord. The bedroom wing was closed a few years ago. Much of the house is no longer used. It saves on the expense of coal and other things, my lord."

Yes, of course. Jack had acquired his nickname not just because it was a diminutive of his Christian name, Jonathan, but because of his gambling habit, developed, unfortunately, during his university days when he became known as Jack of Diamonds. Nicholas knew his brother had recently been excessively in debt, and now the magnitude of that debt stared him plainly in the face. Jack and his father seemingly had fired the entire staff—save for Mason and perhaps a cook—sold family heirlooms, and closed off most of the house. It was amazing how much devastation vice could bring upon a family in just a few years.

Mason stopped before a room Nicholas remembered as his mother's summer morning room. "We are here, my lord."

His heart thumped nervously. "Tell me, Mason. What state is he in? Can he speak?"

"Yes, my lord. Your father is bedridden, but he can speak. He will be delighted, I am sure, to see you. He has much to say."

"Thank you, Mason." Nicholas drew in a fortifying breath and went in.

The room was as he had remembered it when his mother was alive, except a narrow servant's cot had been placed before the fireplace, and, instead of the scent of lavender, the stink of death hung in the air. The Earl of St. Albans, a formidable man when in his prime, lay shriveled and pale under a dense goose-down comforter in the small bed.

"Nicky, is that you?"

Nicholas' heart dropped at the sound of the frail voice.

"Yes, Father, I am here."

"Good, good. I have been waiting."

Nicholas drew up a chair and sat at the bedside.

"The bullet went close to my heart, if you would like to see it, Doctor."

Nicholas was taken aback. The earl was trying to humor him.

"If I may, Father."

Nicholas drew the comforter down. His father's left shoulder was covered in a bandage—expertly done, he had to admit. He loosened and pulled back a corner. The stench of infection hit him first. The wound was beyond repair, discolored and decaying.

"I wish I could have been here to help, Father. I learned how to treat wounds in the mountains of Anatolia."

"The doctor did what he could when he could, Nicky."

"Yes." Nicholas tucked the bandage in place and sat back in his chair.

"Thank you for coming, son."

"It was Lavinia who convinced me."

"I know." The earl's breathing was labored. "Nicky, I know what you heard, but I did not kill her. I did not kill Louisa."

Tears welled in his eyes at the sound of his mother's name. Nicholas fought hard to calm himself, hearing Lavinia's voice in his head telling him he should listen to whatever his father had to say. "Go on."

"I admit I was cruel to her. I regret that. I was selfish, foolish, a criminal. I did not deserve such an angelic woman as she." He gasped for air.

"All I read was that you and Jack beat her to death."

"No! It was not like that." There was a heavy silence as the earl bolstered himself to tell the tale. "Jack had taken up with a young man named Percy."

"The Duke of Amesbury's son?"

"The very same."

"Why, he is just a child!"

"He was when you left us, yes. He was a handsome youth when Jack began his affair with him."

Nicholas really liked Percy, a delightful boy full of fantastical notions who amused him with stories of pirates and fairies.

"I really think at one point Jack loved Percy. I had even hoped the boy would be his savior from drink and debt. But it did not last long. Jack fell back in with his old friends and began drinking again. That's when he started abusing poor Percy."

Nicholas tamped down the anger boiling within.

"Your mother and I did not know for the longest time. We would see Percy injured, but he always had an excuse. We thought nothing of it. He had always been such an active boy."

The earl drew in a tremulous breath. Nicholas' stomach clenched at the sound.

"I'm not quite certain how it all happened. Your mother must have heard Jack and Percy arguing, must have realized Jack was beating the boy. She found him alone in Jack's bedroom, crying and bleeding, so she took him and hid him in her own room and cared for him there.

"Jack came home later that night, more drunk than he had been that afternoon. He looked for Percy everywhere, eventually finding him in Louisa's room. He flew into such a rage."

The earl stopped. He was crying. Nicholas' head ached from restraining his own tears.

"It was Jack who beat your mother, Nicky. He hit her as if she were a man equal to his strength. I heard her screams. The whole house did. We ran upstairs to her aid, but he had a gun and threatened to kill her. He was raving that Percy was his to do with as he pleased. I knew I had to do something. In my foolishness I leapt for the gun. In the melee, Jack pushed my Louisa down the stairs."

The earl made an effort to catch his breath again. "The servants went every which way, some to help your mother, some to tackle Jack. She died on the landing, Nicky. She broke her neck. In her last breath, she spoke your name."

Tears blinding his eyes, Nicholas took out his handkerchief. The "R" for "Ramsay" emblazoned on the corner sent him over the edge of grief. The earl weakly reached out his trembling fingers. Nicholas squeezed the frail hand.

"I went to Percy, guarding him, while the servants sequestered Jack. At that moment, in my sorrow I realized I was the one to blame. Jack learned such abhorrent behavior from me and the way I treated your mother."

Something did not make sense. Something was missing from the story. "Father, why did I read that you were involved?"

"I was involved, really. But it was for the boy's sake. A son of a duke in a pederastic relationship would not sit well with the ton. That he had been beaten by his lover would have been worse. I had to feed the press something. I told them it was an argument with your mother that ended in tragedy. Of course the gossips embellished the story with Jack's drunken involvement, that he had been seen with a gun, even daring to insinuate it was murder."

Nicholas tried to absorb all he had just heard. Three years ago, he had read newspapers, listened to gossip, and had burned every letter his father had sent to him via Lavinia. Had he actually read them he might have known the truth earlier. Still, it would not have saved his mother.

Mason knocked lightly before entering the room. "Master Nic—pardon, Lord Saxondale, I think it is time your father rested."

"Yes, of course."

"Nicky," came his father's weak voice. "Will you be staying?"

Nicholas hadn't bothered to think that far ahead. "Yes, Father, I'll stay."

"Good. We have some catching up to do."

Once outside, Mason led Nicholas down the hall. "I'll put you up here, my lord. I think it was once a parlor of sorts."

"Yes, it was." His mother used to entertain close friends there. "Tell me, Mason, why is my father not in his old bed? Surely he'd be more comfortable."

"I had no one to help me move the bed, my lord. And, to be frank, as your mother was killed in the bedroom wing, your father did not want to die there too. He hopes to feel her spirit in the morning room, where she spent so much of her time."

"Thank you, Mason."

"Marry Dr. Christopher!" Helena screamed in horror. "Why am I to marry Dr. Christopher? I thought I was to marry a duke!"

Mama's fingers fumbled at the buttons on the back of her walking dress. "Now, Helena—"

"He's not a member of the peerage, is he?"

"He's been made a baronet, darling."

"Oh but there are gobs of those, aren't there? Even Papa could be made one and he's American." Helena tugged at her bodice until it fit properly. Her lady's maid had the afternoon off, and clearly Mama was too anxious to be of much help.

"I should not have told you," Mama sighed. "Everything will be settled once your father returns." She pushed on Helena's shoulders making her sit at the dressing table.

"When will that be?" Helena flinched as her mother roughly brushed her hair.

"I've already written him in California—"

"Mama! It could be months!"

"Yes, well, it could very well be. But you needn't concern yourself with that." She inelegantly pinned Helena's hurried chignon.

"But in the meantime I could be meeting someone far more…appropriate."

Mama gaped at her in the dressing table mirror. "Dr. Christopher is a fine man, Helena."

"But he isn't a duke, Mama. And you always said I had to do better than what you did, I mean as far as station is concerned."

"I should strike you for your insolence."

"That wasn't meant as an affront to Papa," Helena said quietly. "I love Papa. You know that. But you have been telling me since I was fourteen that I needed to marry well. And why."

"Yes, of course." Mama appeared uneasy. "Well, sometimes things change."

Her mother's nervous fragility emboldened Helena to dare say aloud what she, and probably others, had been thinking all along. "Why should I marry him when it is you who is sharing his bed?"

Mama's eyes flashed in panic, her forehead twisted in worry. "Who told you that?"

"No one, Mama. But I know you leave after you think I've gone to sleep. And he is ever so attentive when we see him at parties, perhaps overly so."

"Dr. Christopher is spending his private time to treat me. With your father gone, I have no one to turn to."

It was more than that. There must be a certain physical intimacy between the doctor and Mama, otherwise, why wouldn't she just seek out the company of her daughter?

"Mama, if you need someone to talk to, I would love to be your friend. To comfort you, as you have always done for me."

"My sweet child." Mama pulled her from her chair and drew her into her arms. "It isn't that simple."

Which only confirmed her suspicions. "It's his pleasure machine, isn't it Mama?"

That elicited a sigh. "When your husband goes away for months at a time, you'll understand."

"But why would a London doctor ever need to leave me?" she blurted impertinently.

Mama let out a little grunt. "Yes, of course. Why would he?" She smiled and patted Helena's shoulders. "You'll be a lucky wife."

Helena had to say it, she knew she had to say it. It was her last appeal. "Mama, I don't love him. I mean, I like him, I suppose. He's polite and kind. But I certainly don't love him."

"You'll grow to love him. Trust me."

"I really don't think he loves me, either."

"He esteems you, dear. That is sufficient."

"But why can't I marry the man I love?" she lamented. "You married the man you loved."

Mama lifted Helena's chin to look her squarely in the eye. "Are you in love with someone, dear?"

Helena felt herself blush. She couldn't tell her mother about Nicholas. He wasn't a duke. He was only a doctor, just like Dr. Christopher. There was nothing to recommend him except that she was absolutely, positively, irrevocably in love with him. And she was certain he loved her back. "There are some men I feel a certain way with when I dance with them. I think it might be love. I certainly don't feel the same way around Dr. Christopher."

"Ah. I see." Mama smiled in understanding. "I think what you need is another visit or two to Dr. Christopher's office. He can set your heart at ease. You'll see."

Helena sighed as she followed her mother down to the parlor where they would wait for Lady Banbury's carriage to whisk them off to some tea or other. She didn't much care anymore. What was the point if she was already engaged?

She pouted, and played with her gloves, stretching them and picking at the buttons. Why was she the one who had to redeem her mother's name in the eyes of the Marquess and Marchioness of Richmond? She barely knew them and certainly did not care what they thought. Why didn't she get to marry for love, too?

Nicholas, oh, Nicholas...

She bit her lip to hide a smile. Thoughts of him inflamed her body, inspired her dreams, and provoked her brain to scheme.

What if she could do exactly what Mama had done? If she became pregnant with Nicholas' child, then she would have to marry him! Mama and Papa would insist upon it. The plot gave her hope. But seduction was hardly her forte, and every time she saw him it was by utter chance. Surely they would have to be left alone for quite a bit of time. But how to make that happen? She simply did not know how to begin.

Nicholas' time at the estate proved to be an exhausting, but very rewarding, few days.

The Viscount Ravensburgh—Bertie—came to pay his last respects to the earl. The dying man was happy to see his nephew, remarking in awe how much like his brother George Bertie had become. Before Bertie left, the cousins were able to spend a morning reminiscing. Nicholas intimated that he hoped the viscount would be chosen as the earl's heir.

"If the honor befalls me, Nicky, I will certainly accept my duty," he had said quietly. "But right now I am in love and I would like to immerse myself in that luscious feeling for a moment. I really don't want the headache of this estate. I'm sure you understand."

Of course, Nicholas had said, quashing a pang of envy for his cousin's love affair. But Bertie had been nothing but responsible and duty-driven from far too young an age. It was time he experienced the pleasures of life.

By chance, the boy Percy—who, it turned out, was no longer a boy but the very handsome and dashing Marquess of Norrington—had also decided to visit the earl on his deathbed. Percy had put the unfortunate relationship with Jack behind him, although he still felt tremendous guilt about the Countess of St. Albans' death. He was going abroad on a sort of Grand Tour to put some distance between himself and his old life.

"My father doesn't know, Nicky, about the affair with Jack. He hopes I'll find a pretty girl of some venerable European aristocratic bloodline and settle down. But I'm not entirely sure I want a girl, even a pretty one."

If only Percy could marry Helena. She and Nicholas could be lovers without her husband really caring.

In his final discussions with his father, the idea of Nicholas himself settling down had been brought up several times. His father seemed overly enthusiastic to pass on nuggets of wisdom to his one son who had any sense. And who was still alive.

"And your medical practice, how is that?"

"I am working with a rather eccentric doctor. But I think I will be able to go out on my own very soon."

"Good, good." His father's breathing had become torturous by the end. "You'll be able to support a wife and children?"

Nicholas had flushed at that. "Of course, Papa." He found it had become easy to agree and obey, to slip into old childhood ways now that it was the child caring for his parent.

"Lavinia writes that you are looking for a wife."

Nicholas had chuckled. "It is rather Lavinia who is looking for a wife for me."

His father's gaze was eerie. "And have you found one yet?"

"I thought I had, but it turned out she was promised to another. I'm still looking."

"You're a handsome young man, Nicky. I'm sure you have women falling head over heels for you every day."

Nicholas knew he had blushed at that. "It's more difficult than you might think, Papa."

"Well, you have a lifetime to find someone. When you find her, you'll know. You must cherish her, Nicky, as well as love and respect her."

"Yes, Papa." Nicholas had held back tears knowing full well his father was looking to him to rectify the mistakes of his past and redeem the family name.

"Will you bring her to live here?"

Nicholas had been utterly taken aback by that. He had then tried to convince his father that he was not interested in inheriting the title and that Bertram would be a far better candidate to replace him as earl.

His father had agreed quietly that Bertram had very admirable qualities and had not broached the subject again.

That night the Earl of St. Albans had died. Nicholas had been in the room, but had dozed off, the exhaustion of worry finally having caught up with him. He left the next morning, saddened and dazed, Mason assuring him that he could handle the matters of the estate with the solicitor.

On the train home to London, Nicholas had no idea what to expect when he got there. Would Helena already be married? It had only been a few days, so, of course not. She would probably be formally engaged, though. Maybe there would be a soirée in her honor. Perhaps it would turn out that she was fond of her fiancé. Maybe Nicholas himself would realize the lucky man was the better choice.

Then, for some reason, Nicholas found himself wondering if Penelope Hardcastle would be attending any of the same events as he in the coming days.

CHAPTER THIRTEEN

"Dr. Ramsay, sir, I take it you had a nice visit with your family?" Grace wanted to be as polite as possible. She needed the young doctor on her side.

"Thank you, Grace," he said uncharacteristically morosely. "Actually, my father died. But I am glad I was able to spend time with him at the end."

"Oh Doctor! My condolences, sir."

She busied herself about the office, tidying up children's toys and books, shuffling papers, putting pieces of equipment and furniture in their proper places. Dr. Ramsay's first day back had been a full one, with almost no break between patients.

Mrs. Jennings knocked on the door before entering with the tea tray.

"Thank you, Mrs. Jennings." Poor Dr. Ramsay seemed rather tired.

"Can I fix you a cup of tea, sir?" Grace asked as she shooed the old lady out.

"Yes, please. Thank you, Grace." He wolfed down a sandwich.

"Busy day, sir." Grace hardly knew how to begin. She suddenly felt a little nervous.

"Yes. I take it Dr. Christopher saw very few of my patients while I was gone?"

"He saw them what came in without an appointment. Urgent matters, you know. Otherwise, he's been busy with his research, sir."

"Hmmph." Dr. Ramsay gave her a dubious smirk. "And how has he been treating you? He's not taken gross advantage of you, has he?"

"I really don't know what you mean, sir. I like Dr. Christopher. A lot."

"Ah, I see." He eyed her with concern. "Then you don't mind being party to his little, uh, experiments?"

"Oh no, sir!" She warmed and knew she had blushed crimson at his insinuation. "And his experiments are really quite clever. Did you know, sir, that the electro-mechanical device can be used on a man?"

He started at that, his third sandwich poised before his mouth. "A man?"

"Yes, well, really it is a most delicate subject, but a man has an area inside that can benefit from such stimulation."

Now it was Dr. Ramsay's turn to blush. "And you witnessed this?"

"Yes, sir. We hired a nice-looking young man. I watched, then I held the wand while the doctor took notes."

"Good God," he muttered under his breath. "The things that man makes you do."

"If you must know, sir, I quite fancy the doctor. I'd do anything for him."

Dr. Ramsay clearly did not know what to say to that, at first. He took a sip of tea then cleared his throat. "Grace, I don't want to see you hurt. Dr. Christopher is far above your station. I fear he might not see you in the same way as you see him. It's best you do not get too emotionally attached."

"I do understand that, sir. But if I may be bold, sir, Dr. Christopher and I are very much alike. I would hate to see him with someone who would not appreciate his motivations and desires."

"Well, your heart will be safe for a while at least. I'm not sure he's really looking for someone at the moment. I know he's been involved with a woman recently, but that is a temporary arrangement."

It was said with genuine regard for her emotional well-being. Grace was deeply touched. It made what she had to tell him all the more difficult.

"But sir, if I may, there is someone the doctor wants to be with. I think it's horrible really. She's young and, well, rather innocent if you ask me. I don't think she quite understands what he's all about."

"Well, well, well. So the doctor has found love in the few days since I've been away. I certainly was not expecting that."

"I don't think it's proper love, Dr. Ramsay, sir. I think it's like part of his experiment."

"His experiment?" His brow crinkled.

"Yes. You see he needs a virgin."

"A virgin?" He paled as realization descended upon him.

"Yes sir. You see, he's got what he needs out of me for the experiment, but, well, I'm not a virgin." She flushed at her admission. "He was going to get a virgin, like, in another way, see, then he met this young woman. She's very beautiful. He told her mother that if she does not let her daughter get engaged to him, he is going to have relations with her so she's no longer fit for anyone else. He really wants to use the machine on her and take notes, and when he's done he'll have a proper honeymoon, if you know what I mean, sir."

"Good God." Poor Dr. Ramsay looked horrified. "Have you met her?"

"Yes. So have you."

"I have? Grace," he said with exasperated annoyance, "who is she?"

"Miss Helena Phillips, sir."

All color drained from the doctor's face until he looked as if he were going to be sick. "Are you sure?" His voice was ghostly.

"I am, sir. I know how upsetting this must be for you. So I need you to stop him. I need you to make sure my Julius does not marry that girl."

Nicholas was beside himself with rage and grief. When Grace had told him about Helena it was as if he had been hit over the head then revived in the middle of a bizarre nightmare. He had dashed out of the office straight to Lavinia's.

"Is this true?" Nicholas stormed right past her beleaguered butler into her study.

She was standing in the middle of the room, frozen, holding an open newspaper, her usually lovely dark amber eyes bloodshot from tears of disbelief.

"My God, Nicky. I don't know what's got into him." Lavinia held out the *Daily News* for him to see. It was the engagement notice for Miss Helena Phillips and Dr. Julius Christopher.

"Christ!" Nicholas slumped onto the couch. "She can't possibly want to be with that man."

"No, no, she can't. I don't understand how this happened." She crumpled the paper in disgust and threw it on the floor.

"I'll tell you how it happened!" Nicholas stood and began to pace frantically. "The mother! Somehow he's blackmailing her."

"Julius does not need money, Nicky."

"No, of course not." He paused briefly. "It's some sort of perverted sexual blackmail."

"Hmm, I suppose I could see that."

"Mrs. Phillips and her damn clouded judgment! If Helena doesn't need to marry a duke why can't she marry me?"

"I don't know. I simply do not understand." Lavinia stared vacantly at the *Daily News* on the carpet.

"Yes, well, I'll tell you why! It's his blasted experiments with women and their sexual desires. He told me once he was going to buy a virgin at a brothel. Now it looks as if he has his sights set on Helena. And he's blackmailed Mrs. Phillips into giving her to him."

"Oh dear." Lavinia plopped onto the couch.

"I heard this from Grace, his maid. She's in love with him, it seems, and wants to stop the marriage. She asked for my help."

Lavinia steepled her fingers pensively. "Well, Nicky, it seems to be in your best interest to help Grace, then."

"Yes, I had actually thought of that. But how? What could we possibly do?" Nicholas hesitated at a wicked thought. "There's always seduction."

"Nicky, don't you dare!" she hissed. "With Helena's family history, Mr. Phillips would take you to court. He would win too."

"Because I'm from a family of violent libertines?" he said snidely.

"Don't be daft." Lavinia glared at him. "Because current practice by our upstanding judges is to defend the moral fabric of our society. I might be dragged in for conspiracy even."

Nicholas offered his hand and pulled her into his arms. "Vinny, I would never, really," he assured her. "It would disgrace us both. I'm just so…so lost." Lost didn't begin to cover it. Anger, hatred, desperation, anxiety, need… With so many emotions it was difficult to put any of them into words.

Lavinia took his hands in hers. "I'll have to think about this, darling. And we must be careful. If anything goes wrong, Julius could sue for breach of promise."

Nicholas' stomach turned. "As if Helena has actually promised anything to that man. Besides, he can't. She's not twenty-one."

"The engagement could last for years, really."

Which meant years of so-called experimentation. "Not if I can stop it beforehand."

"Look darling, I'll talk to Charlotte. She must know how to contact Mr. Phillips. He cannot possibly accept such an arrangement. He'll think Julius is after her money."

"Which is the one thing he doesn't care about."

"Well, most men do. Mr. Phillips will just assume."

"I'm stopping this marriage, Vinny, by any means necessary."

Lavinia ran her fingers through his hair. "Go upstairs and take a bath. I'll call on Charlotte. She'll know it's important if I show up at this time of evening. And if you're still upset when I get back, I'll help you relax."

"No. I'm going home. I really need my own rooms to think."

"All right, darling." She kissed him tenderly, trying to soothe him.

Nicholas wrapped his arms around his lover and kissed her in return, only then realizing how much he needed release.

"Go," he said hoarsely. "Before I seduce you."

Charlotte had indeed been as upset as she and Nicholas were about the news.

"This will not do. I simply do not know what has got into Sophia!"

Lavinia knew precisely what—or who, rather—had got into Sophia.

"Can you contact Mr. Phillips, Charlotte?" she had asked.

"I've already sent word, my dear. They can't possibly marry without him present. My understanding is that he is in California, although I've telegrammed a few other haunts of his. It could be months before we hear from him."

"So that means we have some time to try to convince Julius that this is not the best of plans, wouldn't you agree?"

"Yes, Lavinia. I will leave that up to you. You were close once. He'll have to listen to you."

And that's how Lavinia found herself in Julius' parlor pacing on his Persian carpet while he watched her admiringly, comfortably ensconced on his couch.

"You've a lovely figure, Lavinia. That dress shows it off quite well."

His suggestive tone and pointed gaze were unnerving. "That's unlike you to comment on such frippery, Julius. Or are you trying to get in practice to please your young wife?"

He chuckled. "I wondered why I was being dignified by your presence. So you've heard." He calmly sipped his port.

She rounded on him. "Of course I've heard! It was in the bloody paper! Why the hell did you publish it so soon?"

"To take her off the market, so to speak. It is the height of the Season, you know."

"You are infuriating." His scrutiny of her body continued to fluster her. "Has her father been informed?"

"Not yet. Sophia has written him. He will know presently."

Lavinia hoped Charlotte's telegrams arrived before whatever missive Sophia thought to send. Mr. Phillips would know that the ton of England were not happy about his daughter's impending nuptials, no matter what balderdash Sophia decided to write.

"How can you, Julius!" Lavinia paced more rapidly. "She's an innocent."

"Yes, she is," he concurred lewdly. "So very innocent, beautifully innocent. In fact, I will not even kiss her until my violation of her has begun. I want to watch her experience everything at once." His wicked smile dripped with insinuation.

Lavinia pursed her lips, suddenly glad Nicholas had kissed the girl. At least Helena would have a memory of her first kiss being with someone she adored.

"Yet," Julius continued, twirling his glass and watching the ruby liquor cling and drip down the sides, "my only regret is that I must give up my affair with the mother. Such a wondrous response to my touch." He took a sip of port. "So wanton. So generous." He glared at her. "So much like you."

Lavinia crossed her arms and turned away in exasperated irritation. But Julius was standing behind her in an instant.

"You remember don't you, my love?" His arm snaked around her waist while his other hand found the buttons of her bodice. "Your inattentive, flaccid husband and my fervent potency?" His breath was hot on her neck.

She damned her inconstant desires as the heat rose in her body. "Julius, please," she pleaded meekly.

He rocked their bodies in unison. "You, too, were something of an innocent, were you not? He barely touched you, the fool."

Lavinia closed her eyes to more fully indulge in his touch, his closeness. "I couldn't wait to see you," she breathed. "I could never get enough of you." She craved him even now.

He drew her into his arms and kissed her tenderly, nostalgically. Twenty years ago, their affair had been intense, passionate. An imaginative lover, Julius had been a welcome respite from Lavinia's impotent husband. Against her better judgment, she had fallen in love with him. But when she discovered she was with child, his child, Julius had insisted the pregnancy be ended. The affair quickly cooled but with the distance of time, it proved too easy to resume their connection.

"We've always been good together." He drew his tongue up the pulse point in her neck. She did not realize he had opened the top of her dress until he began unhooking the front of her corset.

"Darling, don't…" Her protest was weak.

His hand found its way under her chemise, cupping a breast, his thumb and forefinger delicately pinching her awakening nipple.

His intense blue eyes held hers with a familiar intimacy. "You are so unique in your lustfulness, my dear. Does your lover know you can climax thusly?"

He bent down and took her breast in his mouth, his tongue rolling spirals over the sensitive peak, thrilling her as he used to. Lavinia closed her eyes and grasped his head as he attended her, trying to imagine Nicholas, realizing that no one else tortured her like Julius.

She moaned softly.

She should have known it would only encourage him.

With experienced precision, he nipped at her now-hardened peak. Her body convulsed in orgasm, collapsing in his waiting arms.

"Please," she begged. "You must stop."

"Whatever for, my darling?"

"Because I hate you now, you monster." Even she realized her plaintive pout was pathetic.

Julius let out a sharp laugh as he draped her pleasure-weakened body over his shoulder. She struggled, futilely, of course. He was stronger than his lean frame led one to believe. His strength had always surprised her, her willingness to let him subdue her had always frustrated her.

He took her downstairs to his office, ably unlocking the door with his free hand. Once inside he laid her gently on the examination table right in front of what she realized was his electro-mechanical vibrating device.

Lavinia studied the contraption with wonder. A small wooden peg was screwed at a ninety-degree angle to a brass baton, which looked to be the housing for a machine. It sat on a tray attached to a cart, a flexible cloth hose leading down to a motor on a lower shelf.

"Ah, you are admiring my latest acquisition? It turns on down here at the motor," explained Julius. "Electricity goes through the hose to the wand," he picked it up, "which contains a small engine and causes the end to vibrate." He pointed to a tray in the middle of the cart. "As you can see, there are various shapes which can be affixed to the end."

Lavinia glanced at the rubber attachments. One, to her utter astonishment, perfectly resembled a penis. She gasped.

Julius chuckled. But his mirth was short-lived.

With the nimbleness and dexterity of a wrestler, Julius flattened her against the table, strapping her arms at her sides. Despite her kicks he grabbed her legs, securing those in metal holders attached to the edge. He pushed up her skirts and tore open her drawers at the split in the crotch.

He leaned over her face, an eyebrow raised sinisterly. "Remember those games we used to play? As I recall you enjoyed being tied up."

"Oh, God, Julius, please, don't." Back then he would torment her with swats from a paddle and stings from a switch. What would he do to her now?

"I think it best you experience firsthand what the lovely Helena Phillips will feel. You'll come to accept she should not be denied such pleasures herself."

Lavinia sucked in air.

"Don't bother about screaming, my dear." His hand cupped her mons. "The deaf Mrs. Jennings is in her room on the upper floor. And Grace is probably watching at the keyhole. She likes to watch."

Lavinia tried desperately to not expose her inexorable excitation as his finger massaged her expertly.

"Good," he said smugly. "How lusciously wet. You arouse so quickly," he leaned in to brush his lips against her ear, "just like I remember."

She hated her body for giving in so readily to his touch.

Julius grabbed the wand and applied a small rubber tip, then bent down and flipped the control to the motor. The most fascinating whirring noise ensued.

Holding her gaze with his own, Julius brought the oscillating end of the vibrator down and gently pressed it against her clitoris.

Lavinia yelped in shock, almost fainting from the overpowering sensation.

It was like nothing she had ever experienced before, nothing like the insistent solitary finger of a lover. This was one thousand fingers stimulating her all at once, their ministrations filling her

entire body with ripples of aching desire, rolling into waves of lubriciousness, curling, peaking, hovering, retreating to begin all over again. Her mind reeled from the chaos, grasping at each instance of pleasure, reaching urgently as it dissipated only to be quickly replaced by another assault to her muddled senses.

"It helps to close your eyes, my dear. Think of happier times between us."

His smooth voice conjured up erotic memories—a masquerade, her husband's study, the beach at midnight—intensifying the sensations, helping her to focus. Sharp pleasures surged forth, this time she held on, gripping tighter, undulating with the sensual upswell, wrapping herself around each crest, sliding down with a moaning sigh, to be tossed once again in a sea of decadence. She did not want it to stop.

Yet an end was inevitable, and the dreaded harbinger of culmination reared its unwanted finality against the waves of endless pleasure. She struggled to tamp it down, to prolong the lulling voluptuousness, but her climax was stronger than her resolve. She gave in, her senses shattering as she screamed her carnal completion.

She lay on the table, panting, puffing, absolutely stunned by what had just happened. It had been the most extraordinary feeling, beyond anything she could have imagined. Helena would certainly succumb to any man who could deliver such a pleasure.

Julius chuckled.

Lavinia's eyes flew open. Her tormentor loomed above her.

"I'm not finished with you yet, my dear."

In one swift movement he loosened her bindings and pulled her down toward him at the end of the table, impaling her on his iron-hard cock.

She shrieked. She was too tender, too sensitive. "Julius, please, I—"

Her orgasm was unexpected. How could her body still not be satisfied?

Julius let out an arrogant groan of approval. "So delicious, so—"

Lavinia clenched around him, stifling a cry.

His piercing blue eyes bored into hers, mockingly, angrily. "Very good, darling. Let's have another shall we?"

Oh, but she hated him! There was a time when she loved their games, but now his cool condescension was as stultifying as his prick was arousing.

Her third orgasm left her utterly spent.

Sensing her submission, Julius concentrated on his own culmination. He thrust into her with a familiar rhythm, quickly building speed.

Lavinia could not help but climax again.

His fingers tightened cruelly on her thighs, his pace slowed imperceptibly, his breathing became labored. She knew the signs when he was about to spend.

"Julius, please, pull out. I'm not prepared."

"Pity," he growled. "You should always be prepared when you come see me, my dear. But don't worry. Your doctor-lover can take care of any consequences. You remember, Lavinia, like what I did."

He slammed into her one last time, holding his hips against hers, twitching inside as he emptied himself into her.

Abruptly, he pulled out.

"You won't change my mind, Lady Foxley-Graham," he said as he wiped his cock with a handkerchief. "No matter what the aristocracy thinks. Sophia already has shocked the ton with her marriage to an American businessman. No one will think twice about the daughter marrying a man of the professions. Poor girl was simply not raised properly, is what the gossips will say."

Lavinia tried to steady her ragged breaths and the beating of her angry heart.

"Go. Back to your lover. Do not meddle in my affairs again."

Lavinia dressed, then left, defeated. She hated Julius. But even more, she hated her body for still wanting him.

CHAPTER FOURTEEN

"Telegram for you, Mr. Phillips. It arrived this morning."

Joseph Phillips took the card from the concierge at the New York hotel. "Thank you, Jones." He glanced quickly at the dispatch. London. "So they found me, eh?"

The pert Mr. Jones smiled boyishly. "It's a big country sir, but I've learned in my work that if someone wants to find you, you'll get found."

Joseph chortled and took the missive to the lounge, finding a quiet corner with an opulently overstuffed chair. He sank into the cushions, feeling his muscles and bones relax in relief. His trip to New York had been unexpected. The anarchical violence of the Western states had proved too much even for a hardened businessman like himself. He abhorred that he had to carry a gun in order to build a railroad. It smacked of barbarity, not of progress.

So, whatever the news was in the telegram it was important enough that it had been delivered to a place where he was not meant to be, a place where he only might be if someone were looking everywhere for him.

He read the note. His heart fell briefly before it tightened with irritation.

The correspondent, the Countess of Banbury—Charlotte, as Joseph preferred—was absolutely correct. He should come home to England immediately. He would arrange passage on the next ship out and he'd be across the Atlantic in just over a week.

He crumpled the card. What the hell had Sophia been thinking to allow an engagement to a commoner? It was not what they had agreed on for Helena. And a man in the professions, no less. A doctor.

Joseph sighed, wondering just what this doctor looked like, imagining a suave seducer in a well-tailored suit. Marriage to a highly passionate woman had its distinct advantages, but every once in a while it had its definite drawbacks as well.

Nicholas had forced himself to congratulate Julius on his engagement when he saw him that morning in the office. What else could he do? His patients still needed him, and he still needed to maintain some sort of cordial working relationship with the villain until he found another situation. Lavinia had promised she would help him get out—had insisted on it, really.

She had arrived at the doorstep of his flat late the night before, disheveled and in tears. She confessed all that had happened when she went to see Julius, was deeply ashamed that she had let him degrade her, and desperately needed Nicholas to console her.

And while he had helped her with a vinegar douche, then held her wretched form in his arms throughout the night, Nicholas felt the sting of reality. He had willingly given up his claim to a title. Had he not done such a rash thing, possibly he could have pleaded

his case to her parents. But now all was lost. Helena could never, would never be his.

And then we can become lovers?

He consoled himself by imagining their trysts in third-floor bedrooms, his fantasies disregarding the certainty that Julius would never let his perfect bride out of his sights. His only hope was that Helena's father would disallow a marriage to the corrupt doctor. Most likely, though, by the time Mr. Phillips arrived on the scene Helena would have been violated, then, her innocence lost, discarded by the vile man. At that point Nicholas would step in and offer his hand.

It would be a dreadful way to start a marriage. But he would have saved his love from a lifetime of depravity.

Nicholas tried to go on with his workday as if nothing were wrong. His patients sensed his sullenness, some even attempted to cheer him up. He choked up when he saw beautiful, bouncing babies, his failed fantasy kicking him in the gut with the realization that such happiness would not be part of his future.

Mrs. Jennings had even noticed his mood and gave him an extra-large slice of pie with his afternoon tea. He had skipped his midday meal due to lack of interest in food, but was starving by four o'clock. Grace came to take his tray away.

"There's no more here to see you, Dr. Ramsay," she said spiritedly.

"Thank you, Grace. I think, then, I will go home."

"Very good." She stood a little too close to him as she took his cup and saucer from his desk. "I think you should know, Doctor," she began very quietly, "that she's coming here tonight."

Nicholas gasped in horror. "Helena?"

"Yes. He's sending around a carriage at nine. She's to have a 'private consultation', I think that's what Dr. Christopher said. I've been told to disappear as soon as I've shown her in."

"Oh, God." His heart sank. He sat frozen at his desk, not quite sure what to do. He didn't want to stay but he didn't want to leave, either. He wanted to be there for his love.

Grace bent down closer to his ear. "I think maybe you should make sure he sees you when you leave just now. I can let you back in through the service door when it gets dark out."

It sounded like Grace had a plan. "And then what?"

"You get to her first. Tell her to go back home. I know a cab driver what can take her. I'll have him waiting. You'll accompany her, of course."

She had certainly thought things through.

"Yes, that could work. But wouldn't it be easier if I just stop her from getting into the carriage in the first place?"

"Dr. Christopher's got a man watching her house. Probably because of you."

"Good God!" Nicholas growled. He raked his fingers through his hair. "So what if I do come here and stop her? How will we cover it up? The doctor will wonder where she is."

"We'll have her send a note around saying she felt ill in the cab or had second thoughts and she found her way home. You'll have to take her directly home and won't be able to get out of the cab yourself or you'll be seen."

It seemed Grace had worked out every last detail. "Oh. I see." Nicholas had to think the whole scheme through before he agreed to it. Dr. Christopher could be a bit of a brute when he was upset, and if things did not go his way—as Nicholas and Grace were planning—he would be very upset.

But then, again, Helena was to be violated. Nicholas simply had to save her no matter what.

"Yes," he finally agreed. "I'll come by around eight-thirty tonight. Be waiting for me at the service door because I don't want to have to knock. Any unusual noise will be suspect."

Grace took his hand and smiled. "Thank you, Dr. Ramsay."

Julius drew in a deep breath, savoring the night, feeling something wonderful, something electric in the air. He hadn't

frigged himself all day anticipating the evening's events. He sat back in his office chair and closed his eyes to better hear the sound of her approaching carriage, her footsteps in the hall, her tender voice call his name, smell the fragrance he had requested she wear. The anticipation made him remarkably hard.

He started at a noise coming from downstairs. He'd thrash Grace if she did anything to disrupt—or, God forbid, prevent—his escapade. Helena wasn't expected for about twenty minutes. He left the peace of his office to investigate the unwelcome disturbance.

He certainly didn't expect to see Dr. Nicholas Ramsay in the servant's hall.

"What the devil are you doing here, Ramsay?" he said with calm annoyance.

Ramsay's eyes betrayed the seething acrimony roiling inside. "I wanted something in my office," he said curtly. "I thought maybe the service door would be unlocked as I've forgotten my key."

"It will have to wait for tomorrow." Julius pointed to the back door. "Out. I'm busy and I cannot let you upstairs."

Ramsay did not move. The space between them lay thick with tension. Something else was going on. Something else indeed.

Ramsay narrowed his eyes. "If you must know, I left some medicine for Lavinia on my desk. I've got—"

"Well, get it at a chemist's. There's a man open all night up on King's Road, and, I don't need to remind you, you're a doctor." He had no time to put up with this nonsense.

But the young man hesitated, seemingly in no hurry to get badly needed medicine for his ill lover.

"Ramsay, I will not tell you again—out."

Ramsay pursed his lips and exhaled with an annoyed growl before turning to leave. Julius watched him close the door behind him and listened for his footsteps as he walked away.

Then he ran up the stairs to Ramsay's office, threw open the door, and looked around. Everything was in its proper place.

Everything. The damn room was even cleaner than it had ever been when he himself had occupied it. He glanced at the desk. Also clean, notebooks stacked neatly. There was no medicine.

He ran halfway down the stairs and spied Ramsay quietly returning through the back door.

Damn. He should have locked it.

Ramsay looked around before stepping onto the bottom tread.

You bloody fool. "You're not going anywhere, son."

The young doctor looked up in frozen surprise.

Julius lunged at him.

Ramsay's shock quickly jolted into fury when Julius knocked him down, sending them both tumbling onto the hard floor. Ramsay was quick to push his knee between Julius' thighs, clamping his other leg on top, squeezing, gaining leverage to try to twist Julius to the floor. It was a surprising move.

But Julius was on top and had the advantage.

He grabbed Ramsay's thigh and pulled up, leaning over him, pushing his near shoulder to the ground opposite. Ramsay struggled against the counter-twist, releasing his hold to gain leverage, giving Julius the opportunity to crush him to the ground facedown.

"You forget I also spent time in the Near East." He hadn't had to use such a dangerous maneuver for a long time, but his body still remembered the skills.

Then, in one final swift move, Julius grabbed Ramsay's right arm and twisted it deftly behind his back.

"Ow!"

Julius smiled to himself. Ramsay would know such a lock hold could do more than just immobilize him. "Keep your mouth shut and I won't fracture the bone," Julius sneered. "It would be rather troublesome to explain to your patients how their doctor had broken his arm."

That hit a nerve. The young man relented.

"Now get up."

And, like the intelligent young man he was, Ramsay complied.

Adding a pinch to his victim's hand, Julius steered him up the basement stairs and toward a low door behind the stairs to the upper floors. A door, from the look on his captive's face, he had never noticed. Julius opened it and pushed Ramsay through.

The room was dark save for the soft glow coming from the hall behind them and a brighter light coming through a small hole in the wall.

"What the hell is this place?" asked Ramsay in utter astonishment, his head bobbing back and forth, up and down, trying to take in his surroundings.

Julius tightened his grip and pushed him farther into the room. "You will do as I say or I cannot entirely guarantee her virtue."

That hit an even bigger nerve. "Yes, of course," he mumbled.

It had been a very long time since Julius had used the room for its intended purpose. From time to time, he checked the equipment to make sure it was in working order, just in case. It was not long after Grace had joined his staff that he had noticed the peephole in the wall. He had left it there, thinking no harm would come from a randy girl watching him bring the occasional female patient to climax. Now he realized how useful it could be.

"Left arm up," he commanded still holding on to the right.

Ramsay obeyed and watched in disbelief as Julius strapped his arm into a leather manacle hung by a chain from the ceiling.

"Other arm."

Ramsay was too stunned to do otherwise. With the looming threat to his precious Helena he simply complied and let Julius strap him into the other binding.

The foot bindings were just as easy.

"If you wish to watch the proceedings, you may." Julius pointed to the peephole as he narrowed his eyes at Ramsay.

The idea astonished the lad. His mouth fell open in shock.

That would simply not do.

Julius went to a small cupboard and took out a length of knotted leather. To be extra careful, he shoved his handkerchief in Ramsay's mouth before gagging him.

When he was finished, his attention was diverted by a noise upstairs.

"Ah, the carriage," he said with a taunting smirk. "And right on time."

The chill of anxiety crept up Nicholas' spine. Or perhaps it was astonishment. Or discomfort. His arms and shoulders were terribly uncomfortable. His neck and jaw too. The bindings were not altogether tight, it was just that he had never been in such a position in his life, even when he had been captured by Turkic tribesmen in the wilds of Asia.

Thoughts flooded his mind. Thoughts of Dr. Christopher having such a peculiar thing as a bondage room. Thoughts of how he might use it. Of course, Nicholas was not so innocent he did not know such things existed, he had just never seen, much less been in, such a place. Then there was Helena. Beautiful Helena coming to visit the man of her own free will. A man who had a bondage room. *Christ!* Nicholas struggled futilely against his bindings in frustration and growing anger.

She was there now, in the examination room, talking very politely to Dr. Christopher. All could be seen through the hole in the wall, and Nicholas watched every detail with immense interest and horror.

At the doctor's direction, she disappeared behind a screen for a spell, reappearing almost utterly devoid of clothing. She wore only her chemise and stockings, thin, delicate garments that clung to every sensuous curve. The fine linen gently draped around her perfect breasts, her nipples, hardened from the slight chill of the room, tented the fabric. She did not blush, but appeared to be somewhat comfortable, perhaps confident, in her state of undress.

She was innocence, beauty, and desire all at once, and Nicholas could not stop staring. His mouth watered, wetting the crumpled cloth silencing him, as his cock stirred flagrantly between his bound legs.

She lay down on the padded table and put her feet in the holders, spreading herself willingly before Dr. Christopher and unwittingly before him behind the peephole. Even the detestable doctor's wolfish expression could not stop Nicholas' irrepressible arousal. He was rock-hard.

Dr. Christopher bent down over his patient and said something very quietly in her ear. Helena smiled, a sort of naughty smile it seemed, and nodded. Dr. Christopher gave a little bow, then covered her eyes with a blindfold.

Nicholas cringed as the doctor reached out to touch Helena, then flinched when he pressed a finger to her most intimate of places. His stomach churned as Dr. Christopher massaged gently, taking far too much enjoyment in the act. Her view of her molester obscured, Helena writhed in response to his ministrations. Nicholas hoped against hope she imagined a fantasy lover, hoped she dreamed of him. Riveted, he could not wrench his eyes from the despicable sight. His prick was painfully hard.

Helena let out a little moan, a joyous sound, and Dr. Christopher flipped the switch on his vibrating machine. The soft whirring could be heard in the small chamber under the stairs. Nicholas and Helena tensed in anticipation.

"Good God, how the bloody hell did you get in here?"

Grace's hissing brought Nicholas back to his own predicament. She ran to the peephole and glimpsed at the scene on the other side, then looked down at the bulge between Nicholas' legs and smirked.

"Well, well, what have we here?" She cupped her hand over his balls and stroked her finger along the erection straining against his trousers.

Nicholas recoiled against the restraints, trying to shake her off. Grace pressed against him. "You just watch the show. I'll make sure you feel it too." She pushed his head closer to the peephole, then knelt down in front of his crotch.

Dr. Christopher positioned the vibrating wand over Helena's clitoris.

Grace unbuttoned Nicholas' fly and drawers and freed his rampant cock.

The wand touched Helena and she bucked up with a cry.

Grace took Nicholas' length into her warm, wet mouth.

As he stimulated Helena, Dr. Christopher uttered encouragements in her ear, his face unabashedly reflecting his arousal. But Nicholas was far too distracted to consider such dreadfulness. His prick was being attended to with the utmost skill by his medical assistant. She was amazingly good. And thorough. He relaxed in his bindings.

Helena writhed rhythmically, her moans measuring the erotic beat. Dr. Christopher's free hand hovered over her perfect body, outlining her shape, her curves, not touching but trembling against the urge to do exactly that.

As Grace's tongue tortured Nicholas' glans, as her fist clutched his shaft, Helena rocked her hips, thrusting up against the wand, undulating back down, scooping up again to press herself against the source of her pleasure. Her hands gripped the sides, pulling at the sheet covering the table. Her moans of ecstasy were music to Nicholas' ears.

Dr. Christopher took her hand and murmured to her, eliciting nods and questions in response. He guided her hand to the wand, holding it steady while she took hold and became used to its shape and vibration. She nodded and voiced her consent. Dr. Christopher withdrew his hand and smiled lasciviously as he watched Helena begin to stimulate herself with the instrument.

Nicholas stared, enthralled, as his love held the device against herself. Helena did not waver, but pressed the wand as if she knew exactly where she would feel the most pleasure. Her body responded with sensual squirms, she voiced her ecstasy with dulcet moans.

He knew precisely what she was experiencing. Grace held his hips steady as she took him to the back of her throat. Tears welled in his eyes as he fought back every groan.

Dr. Christopher positioned himself on a low stool between Helena's opened legs, studying her sex, fluttering and swollen in excitation, his face the semblance of dissolution. A sudden lurch revealed what he was doing.

Nicholas gasped. Dr. Christopher's enormous prick stuck out through his opened fly. He stroked it, watching Helena, still murmuring encouragements to her, his fist gliding along the shaft in a rhythm to match Helena's excited moans, growing louder, more frantic.

She thrust up her hips, holding the wand with stronger resolution, her breath heaving, almost at her peak.

Nicholas was on the edge. Grace sucked his prick resolutely, squeezing his balls gently in encouragement.

Helena screamed, her raised hips hovering motionless for just a second before crashing down onto the table with a howl of contentment.

Nicholas shot his seed into Grace's hungry, swallowing mouth.

Dr. Christopher continued to frig himself, more vigorously now, a touch of desperation beading on his brow. Helena stirred from her afterglow, moving the still-vibrating wand to her belly and reaching up to remove her blindfold.

"No!" Dr. Christopher's barking command resounded clearly in both rooms. Helena froze. The doctor masturbated himself in earnest. His free hand reached out tentatively, then glided along Helena's bare skin above her garter. His fingers stretched to stroke her satisfied labia.

The blood boiled in Nicholas' sated body. Anger replaced arousal.

But Dr. Christopher never touched his prize. His head fell back and his body arched for a second before jerking forward. He pumped his cock, shooting the milky ejaculate onto the floor between Helena's legs.

Grace buttoned up Nicholas' fly, kissed his cheek with a giggle, then left without a trace.

Dr. Christopher made himself decent before he shut off the vibrating machine and removed Helena's blindfold.

For the rest of the time she was there, nothing untoward happened. Helena got dressed, doctor and patient talked, she said her goodbyes without ever noticing anything amiss on the floor. Dr. Christopher showed her out, then returned to the examination room to clean up and put the equipment away.

It was ages before he freed an extremely stiff and stunned Nicholas from his bindings. Not a word passed between the colleagues, only the clink of metal filled the void. Once unbound, Nicholas fought against the urge to thrash the man, his baser instincts tempered by his abhorrence of solving problems with violence, and knowing Helena could still be put at risk.

Instead, he left through the service door and walked home in a daze.

CHAPTER FIFTEEN

Nicholas had to soldier on the next morning as if nothing irregular had happened in the medical office the night before. There were patients to see, mothers and children who had come to depend on his attentive and compassionate services.

The reminders were, however, palpably present. He had aches and bruises in places he had forgotten about. The formerly unnoticed door under the stairs mocked him in the daylight. He flushed at the first sign of Grace. She, however, took it all in stride, going about her business as if sucking the prick of her employer's colleague was an expected part of her work. She tidied up his office and set out the tea tray with her usual cheer. His stomach churned when Dr. Christopher grunted the requisite "good morning" with a scowl. After that, the villain disappeared for the rest of the day.

Nicholas, of course, had no idea what he would say to Helena—if he ever saw her again. She was engaged now, and attended fewer luncheons and soirées, having, he supposed, a wedding to plan for instead.

Lavinia insisted Nicholas stay in the game despite his morose mood. After an uninspired tumble in bed, they settled against the pillows. He asked her about the bondage room. She laughed with a toss of her head.

"He still has that, does he?" A memory glinted in her golden brown eyes as she threaded her fingers through the hair of his chest.

"It seemed ill-used of late."

"He's a scientist, Nicky, like you." She drew spirals on his stomach with a finger. "He liked to see how the mind and body reacted to certain, well, stimuli. He took a lewd enjoyment of it all, but that really wasn't my fancy."

Nicholas wasn't quite sure if it was his own fancy, either.

"Darling, there's a ball tonight—"

"Good God, another one?" It was growing difficult to continue to be pleasant amongst the ton.

"Yes. And, you are escorting me," she said, punctuating each word with a jab of her finger.

He sighed.

She smiled and cocked her head to look up at him. "I saw Penelope Hardcastle at the hat shop the other day. She expressly wondered if you would be there tonight."

"Ah, yes. Miss Hardcastle. I see now what you mean by girls on the shelf gaining confidence in their third seasons."

Lavinia's mouth opened in surprise. "You dog! You didn't!"

"It was she who seduced me, I'll have you know. At the Quimbys'. Third floor. Surely you know what goes on up there? I certainly did not."

Lavinia laughed, then cozied up to him. "Yes, well, just save some energy for me, darling."

* * * * *

Lavinia glanced about the entry hall as soon as she and Nicholas arrived at Lord and Lady Hawkhurst's home for their annual mid-Season ball. She knew most everybody and was ready with a blithe comment or sympathetic ear. But really she was looking out for her Nicholas, and if there were any young women of fine character he had not yet met and with whom he should absolutely dance.

She spied a certain young lady whose third or fourth season she was sure it was. "Nicky, have you met Margaret Withers yet?"

"No, darling. Is she very handsome?" he asked in an overly charming manner.

Lavinia looked Miss Withers over. The young lady stood out wearing a dress in the Aesthetic style with a Greco-Roman pallium crisscrossed over her bosom. "Oh, terribly so. I think she reads books in Greek or some such odd preoccupation."

"Well, that sounds ideal." His tone dripped sarcasm.

Lavinia shot her lover a snide look. "You read Greek."

"I do. And German, and Latin, and a smattering of Turkish, Arabic, and Persian. Are there any lovely young ladies here tonight who can entertain me thusly?"

Nicholas was being rather puckish and abominable that night, making Lavinia wish Julius had kept him chained up in his dungeon. Through her kid gloves, she dug her nails into his arm as he escorted her into the main ballroom. Nicholas held his head high as if to annoy her.

They both stopped their childish games when they saw Helena. She was gorgeous, dressed in a stunning turquoise blue with cobalt underskirts, her mother similarly attired in sea green and deep forest, pendants on either arm of a smiling Julius Christopher. Lavinia heard Nicholas suck in a fortifying breath.

"Steady, Nicky," she cautioned quietly.

But she smiled graciously as the trio came forward. "Julius, how lovely to see you." She nodded. "Mrs. Phillips. Miss Phillips, congratulations are in order, I hear."

Helena looked away with a blush, biting her lower lip. "Thank you, my lady," she said almost inaudibly.

The two men barely looked at each other as they muttered polite greetings.

"Lavinia, dear, I wonder if you would do me a favor," asked Julius abruptly.

Always wary where it concerned her old lover, Lavinia kept her cool and merely answered, "I will try my best."

"It seems Mrs. Phillips is feeling a little faint and I thought it a good idea she have a lie down. I would like to take her upstairs to the third floor. Some fresh air from the balcony and a rest would enliven her, wouldn't you agree, Ramsay?"

Nicholas stared at his employer. "A glass of cool water as well, I should think."

Julius nodded his response and returned his attention to Lavinia. "Would it trouble you much to take Helena under your charge while I attend to her mother?"

Lavinia seethed. "Not at all, Julius," she responded as if nothing were wrong. "I would love to spend some time with Miss Phillips. Wedding chatter, you know."

Sophia looked quite distressed but was nimbly whisked away by Julius before she could utter a word.

Lavinia's anger was mollified by the sight of Nicholas and Helena gazing at each other in awe. Just then, Penelope Hardcastle approached, her demure smile at odds with her gown. The lace edging on her square-cut neckline gave the illusion of modesty, when in fact quite a bit was on display.

"Lady Foxley-Graham, what a beautiful dress," she said as her eyes flickered toward Nicholas.

"Miss Hardcastle, thank you. My dressmaker is right near that hat shop. I should give you the address."

"Please." Her gaze did not waver from her target. The girl clearly had far more invigorating topics on her mind than dresses. "Dr. Ramsay," she greeted casually.

"Good evening, Miss Hardcastle. Very nice to see you." Like a boy trying to choose between a puppy and a pony, Nicholas seemed overwhelmed.

"It occurs to me that the two young ladies might not have been formally introduced," announced Lavinia. "Miss Helena Phillips, may I present Miss Penelope Hardcastle."

The two young ladies greeted each other as young ladies ought.

"Miss Phillips is engaged to be married, Miss Hardcastle," Lavinia taunted.

"Are you?"

It worked. Helena and Penelope began to chatter away as if they had known each other for years. Lavinia nudged a besotted Nicholas.

"You know what that cad is going to do to her upstairs, don't you?" she hissed.

"Lavinia, please don't remind me," he groaned under his breath.

"Well, I'll see how I can make it worth your while, darling."

"Dr. Ramsay," came Penelope's sweet voice. "May I inquire if you will be free for a dance later tonight?"

Lavinia could see the distress on poor Nicholas' face. "Perhaps later, Miss Hardcastle," she offered. "I fear he has been requested to look after Miss Phillips for the time being while her fiancé is otherwise occupied."

"Of course. I'm sure Miss Phillips needs a bit of protection from those men who do not yet know of her engaged status." Penelope shot Nicholas a sly, knowing smile as she took her leave.

Relieved of the distraction of Penelope, Nicholas and Helena once again gazed admiringly at each other, all the while trying desperately to not be too obvious.

"Nicholas, be a dear, the waltz will begin soon. Partner Helena, please?" She turned to the young lady in question. "I'm sure you won't mind a dance or two with Dr. Ramsay? I fear he's still getting his ballroom footing after having been away for some years."

Helena looked absolutely thrilled at the prospect. "Yes, Lady Foxley-Graham. I would love to dance with Dr. Ramsay."

Lavinia smiled graciously. "That would be most appreciated. But please, one moment, I would like to confer with my companion." She stood on tiptoe to whisper in his ear. "Take her outside during the dance, Nicky. No one will notice. There's the grotto in the back corner of the garden to the left."

Lavinia's heart was jubilant as she watched Nicholas and Helena, their faces glowing joyfully, walk arm in arm to the dance floor.

Dancing with Nicholas was a welcome respite from the horrid nightmare of her engagement to Dr. Christopher. And an amazing opportunity to put her plot into action. The Hawkhurst mansion had a third floor absolutely full of bedrooms.

As she clung to him, Helena looked out onto the crowd fringing the ballroom. So many couples still on the dance floor would mean the upstairs would be empty…

"I feel somewhat deprived of your full attention, Miss Phillips. Is there another man you've set your sights on?"

Mortified, Helena looked up at Nicholas, his eyes twinkling teasingly. "I was just admiring your companion, Dr. Ramsay. Lady Foxley-Graham is quite beautiful tonight."

Nicholas grinned at her. "I think she would be supremely flattered if you told her that."

"Me?" Helena envied the woman who was such a special friend to Nicholas. The woman who saw him naked, who was free to touch him, who enjoyed his attentions in bed—

"You are one of the most beautiful women to grace London this Season, Miss Phillips. Surely you know that?"

Helena blushed. "Thank you, Nicholas." It felt good to be waltzing in his arms, almost familiar, and yet so new. "You know, we've never danced together before."

He pressed his hand more firmly against her back. "I was wondering when you would realize that. Now that you are an engaged woman I suppose you may dance with whomever you choose." He leaned in a little. "We should dance together more often," he murmured.

Helena flushed at his flirtation. "We should. You're quite good."

"Thank you," he said, whirling her about handily.

She giggled and he did it again.

He pulled her more closely to him. "Are the turns making you dizzy, Miss Phillips?" he whispered conspiratorially in her ear. "So much so you must repair to the garden for a breath of fresh air?"

His insinuation made her giddy. "Dr. Ramsay, please, no more," she complained aloud. "It is a bit warm in here, and I'm afraid I need some air."

"Of course, Miss Phillips." He offered his arm and escorted her off the dance floor.

Once out on the flagstone terrace, they became like any other couple escaping under cover of moonlight, arm in arm, seeking a *tête-à-tête*. They quickly descended the stone staircase leading down into the garden.

The cool air was refreshing against Helena's heated skin. Her closeness to Nicholas set her ablaze, letting loose a flood of fantasies, fantasies still stoked by the fire of her last visit to Dr. Christopher's office. Blindfolded, she had imagined Nicholas as her lover, his sensual ministrations torturing her exquisitely. She bit her lip. Did Nicholas think of her when he touched himself? Oh, God. Just the thought of him touching himself…

He guided her to a dark corner of the garden where they were very much alone, then slowed his pace. He took off his gloves and laced his fingers through hers.

Grateful that her glove concealed her sticky palm, she squeezed his hand and turned to him.

He put a finger to her lips. "Not here. Come."

The moonlight and the dim glow of lanterns revealed his destination—an exedra, a large semicircular vault encrusted with shells, pebbles, and bits of glass looming majestically before a pool with a softly splashing fountain. The famed Hawkhurst grotto. Lots of shadowy corners and far from the crowds. Helena bit her lip again. Better than the third floor.

Nicholas led her to a low bench running along the curve of the vault and chose the darkest spot for them to sit. He took both her hands. "I hoped I would see you tonight. I never envisioned being with you like this ever again."

"Like what?"

"Alone."

Helena's heart skipped a beat. For a moment he looked as if he were going to kiss her. Instead, he wrapped her in an arm and pulled her back against him.

"How have you been, love?" He gave her shoulder a comforting squeeze.

She sighed. "Nicholas, I don't know why my mother chose Dr. Christopher," she said quietly. "He's not at all what my parents had wanted for me."

"Surely she gave you some explanation?"

"Not a reasonable one. I think she's fallen in love with him. Or his machine."

His breath hitched at the mention of the device. "I fear your mother is being deceived in some manner."

"I think something is amiss, as well. It is she who spends so much time with Dr. Christopher."

He bent down to her. "You don't call your fiancé by his Christian name?" he asked in surprise.

"I don't feel comfortable calling him 'Julius'. It feels strange."

"And yet, you no longer call me 'Dr. Ramsay'." He nuzzled his nose against her neck.

"That's because you kissed me," she said shyly.

"He hasn't kissed you yet?" Nicholas was incredulous.

"He says I should remain completely chaste until my wedding night."

"Oh, God." It was said with a measure of disgust. "Be cautious around him. Never be left alone with him. No doubt he has some debauchery planned."

The thought chilled her. "Well, we still have to wait for Papa's consent. I hope he—I know he won't approve of such a match. Dr. Christopher's only a baronet. If I'm allowed to marry a doctor, why can't it be you?"

He chuckled. "Well, first of all, I'm not even a baronet."

"Can't you be made one?"

"I suppose. But I am descended from earls. I think that's a bit better."

"Earls?" Helena jolted back to face him. "Are you in line to be an earl?" *Please let it be true!*

He chuckled. "Probably at some point. It's my cousin who's the earl."

"Oh." It was really too remote to satisfy her parents.

"And," he squeezed her again, "I haven't asked you."

She looked up at him smiling down at her, obliged to the night for hiding her flush of abashment. He tenderly touched her heated cheek with the tip of a finger, tracing tiny circles along her jaw to her chin. She desperately wanted to kiss him. Could a girl do such a brazen thing?

She reached up to press her palm behind his head, then drew him down toward her.

A giggling couple scurried along the path on the far side of the fountain.

Nicholas pulled back. "Darling, there's a far more private place."

He stood and gallantly offered a hand, then guided her behind the grotto's vault to a set of stone stairs leading down into the earth.

She held on to him as they descended into the pitch blackness together, their eyes adjusting slowly to a view of a magnificent underground chamber. Beams of moonlight and lamplight shone through small holes in the ground above, creating a starlit canopy over the subterranean space.

He led her to a stone bench carved with ancient motifs. There they sat and looked up at the false stars, the sound of the fountain above echoing faintly around them. She leaned into his welcoming embrace.

It was dark and quiet. And they were truly alone. Perfect for lovers.

Helena snuggled deeper, reveling in the comfort of his body surrounding hers, the rhythm of their breaths and the tempo of their hearts merging in unison. He bent and kissed her neck, then nuzzled his nose against her shoulder. "I love being with you like this. Just the two of us in the dark." He chuckled, his breath hot against her. "It always seems to happen when we meet."

"It does, doesn't it?" she agreed with a giggle and a realization. Each time had been a step forward, each time she had seen more of him, touched more of him, kissed more of him. But this time, she didn't want a furtive fumble with a quick return to the ballroom. This time she wanted all of him and wanted to give him all of herself, a desire that verged on desperation, inciting her, emboldening her. "Nicholas," she said, turning to him, "I think of you often…how we were together at the Quimbys', when I touched you, your response to me."

He threaded his fingers through hers. "I feel the same. I can't get you out of my head. I think of you frequently. Far too frequently," he confessed. "Even when I make love to Lavinia, sometimes I imagine you."

Helena swallowed her excitement at his admission, but it welled up, refusing to be tamped down inside her. "My body hungers for you. In my bed at night, when I pleasure myself, my thoughts are filled with images of you, and I find myself no longer alone."

He pulled her more closely to him as he inhaled deeply, the fine linen of his shirt warm, his shirt studs cool against her bare shoulders. His slow exhale jittered with emotion. "Helena," he murmured morosely. "I have to know. His machine, would it be enough to keep you from me?"

How does he know? She turned to face him. "Did he tell you?"

He took another deep breath. "I saw it. I was supposed to have rescued you, but everything went awry. He locked me in a closet next to the examination room. There was a sort of peephole…"

"You watched me?" The very idea was astonishingly arousing.

"You're not completely appalled?" His forehead crinkled in disbelief.

Perhaps a girl could be brazen after all. She pecked his luscious lips agape and slightly smiling at her enthusiasm for his voyeurism.

The peck turned to passion as he held her head steady and melded his mouth to hers. He pulled back, panting. "Where have you been all my life?" he murmured with a chuckle. "Darling, I saw you in ecstasy. I cannot express what that did to me, still does to me." His gaze flickered as he caressed her face. "Would I be enough for you?"

"Yes," she answered quickly. "Yes, oh, yes." She traced his lips with a finger still imprisoned in a glove. "All the pleasure I felt with the machine cannot compare to the pleasure I feel when I am in your arms." She licked her lips. "Nicholas, I want to give myself to you."

"Oh, God." His head fell into his hand.

She placed a palm against his chest. "Nicholas?"

He lifted his head and looked into her eyes. His tears glistened in the pale light. "I burn for you, Helena. I cannot tell you how much I burn for you."

His mouth descended on hers, their lips and tongues merging and twining urgently, frantically, perfectly. Somehow, after only two encounters, she knew what he wanted, what he needed, and how to give it to him. And he understood her desires before she even knew them herself. Their quick familiarity reassured her that when he made love to her it would not be shocking and disagreeable as she had been told at school, but liberating and sublime, the stuff of poetry.

He clutched her closely, humming his satisfaction against her mouth. She threaded her fingers through his hair to hold his head steady as she dared to break free and kiss his cheeks, rough and masculine under her delicate lips.

His mouth trailed down her neck, sizzling against her tingling skin, his lips searing her shoulder, not stopping, his fingers working the buttons at her back. She sighed when he kissed the tender flesh of her bosom, shuddered as his tongue flicked under the neckline of her dress. Her bodice loosened and slipped from her shoulders, exposing the layers of fine undergarments. His hands slid along her waist to gently cup her breasts, pushing them above her corset, pulling aside the cambric corset cover, the linen chemise, exposing her naked flesh to the night's chill.

She gasped when his thumbs teased the tender peaks, and discovered a new thrill when he drew an excited nipple into his mouth, a thrill that shot all the way to the most intimate of places between her legs, now hot and moist like the tongue tormenting her.

She now knew what her body craved when she pleasured herself.

Him. Inside her.

She arched her back inviting further invasion. "Nicholas, my love, I want you. Now. Please."

He suddenly stopped, his labored breathing burning her décolletage. "Oh, God, Helena, darling," he whispered against her. "We both know we should not be doing this."

"Do you want to do this?" His lips and tongue met her heaving chest with every inhale.

"God, yes. This and so much more." He lifted his face, his expression like a guilty, needy boy.

She placed her hand on his thigh. His muscles tightened and tensed at her touch. He stared at her apprehensively. She slid her hand along the fine wool until she found the heated hardness between his legs. Nicholas sucked in air as she glided her thumb up and down the wondrous length.

"Is—is this what you want to do to me?" she asked brazenly.

"Yes."

She grasped the shaft thick with lust. "Will it make me faint?"

"Faint?" he queried unsteadily.

"Like in the books." Each stroke of her palm elicited a sigh of masculine need. "I mean, will it hurt?"

"No. It feels wonderful." His voice was rough and hoarse.

He shifted, moving one leg until he was straddling the bench. Helena kept her hand on his crotch, exploring with utter fascination. She looked up at him, questioningly. He nodded.

With a boldness she had never imagined, Helena took off her gloves, unbuttoned his trousers and drawers and pulled up his shirt. His erection jutted forth, its smooth tip inviting touch. She hardly knew what to do, and fingered him tentatively.

Nicholas gasped with a grunt. "Oh, God."

"Do you like this?" she said stroking him up and down. He was as hard as stone, but warm and vibrant.

"Yes." His voice trembled.

A small drop of liquid emerged at the tip. Captivated, Helena bent down and tasted the musky dew.

"Christ!" Nicholas hissed from between clenched teeth.

Helena licked and kissed his heated shaft, encouraged by his responses to give him more pleasure, drawing him deeper into her mouth. Nicholas twitched against her with a clipped groan.

"Darling, darling," he said placing his fingers under her chin. "We should not, we must not, do any of this." He lifted her head off him.

Helena saw the expression of utter abandon on his face and kissed his lips. "But I want to give myself to you."

He held her head steady between his hands. "You cannot, you simply cannot, Helena. He'll know if you are not a virgin."

Nicholas' words ripped her back to her horrible reality. "I don't care," she said resolutely, shaking his hands away. "I do not want to be married to that man. I do not love him. I love you. Why can't I marry you?"

"We've been through that—"

"But what if I have to marry you?"

Nicholas studied her. "What do you mean?"

"I mean, what if I were with child. Your child. What if we had physical intimacies and I carried your child?"

He exhaled his astonishment. "You mean right now?"

"Yes. Now."

He wrapped his arms around her. "It doesn't quite work that way, darling. I mean it does, but it might not happen on the first try."

"You mean we'll have to keep doing it?" She certainly would not mind that.

"Yes—I mean no!" He sighed. "Helena, once a woman is engaged, there are certain expectations about her conduct. Any deviation might mean legal action."

Helena's jaw dropped. "Dr. Christopher could take you to court?"

"If the engagement is deemed legitimate, yes. Your father could too. For seduction."

That was not how it happened with her parents. "But if I am with child, then they'll have to let me marry you."

"Not necessarily. You might be sent away and your child—our child—taken from you."

"Taken from me?" Was that why Uncle Arthur had kept Mama sequestered at his house during her confinement? Why Papa had stayed in England the entire nine months? Protecting mother and child from legal action by the Marquess of Richmond? "Truly?"

"It is unfortunately so."

"But what about my uncle Arthur? And Lady Foxley-Graham? What about your cousin the earl? Surely they'll help us?" She knew she was grasping at uncertainties.

"Darling, we can't count on any of that." Nicholas raked his fingers through his hair. "I don't know much about what happened when your mother and father had you. I take it your uncle Arthur had a hand in protecting your family. Still, the gossip mill says your grandparents were not happy about your parents getting married, nor about you. They disowned the lot of you."

"Yes, that's true," she admitted glumly. "But Uncle Arthur will be the next Marquess of Richmond and he doesn't care about titles and lineages. He'll let me marry you."

Nicholas took her hands in his. "Helena, I no longer have any close family. My father and brother just died in an accident. My mother died a few years ago. To have my own children, to love and play with them, to watch them grow and have families of their own, this is so very important to me. It is a dream of mine. I do not want to take such a risk."

"That's why you went away, isn't it? Your brother and father." She could not fathom such a great loss all at once. "And now you have no one."

"Well, there's my cousin the earl." He smiled at her concern and brushed away a stray lock from her face. "I would love to give you children, Helena. I would love to be married to you and raise them together. One day, I hope to be your husband. But there is simply too much uncertainty in your proposition."

His words moved her. "Yes, I understand." She watched as he tucked in his shirt and buttoned his flies, adjusting himself in his trousers, then met his eyes in the dark.

"Don't look like that." He cupped her cheek, then took her hands in his. "Have hope. There may yet be a chance for us."

His voice held conviction, enough to mollify her, enough to fuel her fantasies once again, fantasies of him and her... "Nicholas, I want to give you something of myself."

He quickly pressed his lips to hers. "You have given me something." He pecked her face as he tugged her clothes back into place. "You gave me your first kiss, your first touch. That is all I can accept from you for the moment." He positioned her until she lay back against him, his arms encircling her. "We have to be content with what we've had with each other, love, and dream about what we hope will come." He kissed her neck. "Now, you tell me something, a story, anything. Just talk to me. I want to listen. I want to simply be with you, share this moment with you."

Helena leaned into him, letting his heat and strength comfort her. He was right, of course. Until this mess was settled, she would have to content herself with a kiss, a dance, and a little daring exploration. She sighed morosely, realizing what she shared with Nicholas in a few furtive meetings would be more than what she would share in a lifetime with Dr. Julius Christopher.

CHAPTER SIXTEEN

Nicholas found himself retreating to Lavinia's house after work more often than not. It wasn't the sex so much as the refuge from the bizarre situation at his office.

"Darling, there's a note from your valet on my desk," Lavinia said, pointing to the missive. "Apparently, Mason is waiting for you at your flat."

"Mason?" Nicholas queried distractedly.

"Your family butler."

"I know who Mason is! What the devil is he doing here in London?"

"Well, perhaps you should go home and find out."

Certain that whatever news Mason had would not be good, Nicholas persuaded Lavinia to go with him for support.

The three gathered in his study, Mason looking quite official with a dossier under his arm. He opened the contents onto the bureau as Nicholas and Lavinia sat in matched wingbacks.

"Lord Saxondale—"

Lavinia giggled.

Mason lifted a scathing brow in her direction. "Sir, your father's will has been read. There are some matters of importance I must go over with you before you see the solicitor yourself."

"So he left you something after all, Nicky dear." Lavinia was cheerful.

"Indeed, Lady Foxley-Graham, the earl did leave something to his lordship."

Nicholas, however, was not at all curious. It was probably a few heirlooms, valueless trinkets left over from his father's and brother's creditors. "All right, Mason, let's have it. What do I get?"

"You 'get', sir, to be the Earl of St. Albans."

Lavinia gasped.

"W-what?" Nicholas was not quite sure he heard correctly. "Mason, what did you just say?"

"Your father has made you his heir."

Nicholas shook his head. "What about Bertie?"

"The Viscount Ravensburgh, it seems, did not reflect the qualities your father would like to see in the future Earl of St. Albans. You, apparently, do."

"Really, Nicky, you should be flattered," remarked Lavinia.

"Flattered? I'm stunned! Absolutely stunned!" Nicholas stood up and began pacing. "Flabbergasted, alarmed, bewildered. Me? I'm not suited for such a life! I've purposely kept a distance from all of that nonsense." He stopped, standing stock still with his hands on the top of his head. "Good God!"

"I know this comes as a shock, given your history with your father and brother, sir."

"Well, yes, Mason, quite a shock." He let out an exasperated groan.

"What is it, Nicky?"

"That also means I inherit the family debt." Nicholas turned to his butler. "Doesn't it?"

"Yes, my lord," Mason agreed. "However, once the creditors were secretly informed of the choice of you as earl, they pulled back. They are quite prepared to negotiate with you given your principled reputation, it seems."

Nicholas sighed. "I'll have to learn about running the estate now, I suppose."

Mason cleared his throat. "Well, my lord, if I may, owing to the dearth of silver to polish and guests to satisfy, I spent my days these last few years learning about estate management in general and the running of the St. Albans estate in particular."

Lavinia sat up in attention.

"Oh?" Nicholas raised his brows.

"There is a lot of profit to be made, my lord. With the proper management, of course."

"Of course." Nicholas shook his head in awe. Mason, it seemed, had been planning for this precise moment for years. "And what if I disclaim the title? What then?"

"Well, you would also forfeit the right of your son to inherit—"

Lavinia raised an inquisitive eyebrow at Nicholas.

"But given that you are childless as far as we know, this is not an issue. Your cousin, 'Bertie' as you call him, the Viscount Ravensburgh, is successor after you."

"Good. Then he is second," Nicholas mused.

"Yes. He would have to be called back from Italy or wherever he happens to be traveling with the Marquess of Norrington."

Lavinia gasped with glee.

"Bertram's with Percy?" Nicholas chuckled. "Well that's a damn sight better than Jack."

"Yes, my lord." Mason looked him squarely in the eye, his expression stern. "You should know, my lord, your father expressly stated that he did not want you to disclaim the title." He removed an envelope from his jacket pocket and handed it to Nicholas. "He knew you might consider it so he left a personal entreaty. He wanted you to be the one to restore honor to the title."

On the front of the envelope was scrawled *Nicky* in his father's handwriting, recognizable despite the shaky script. It was probably the last note he ever wrote.

Lavinia beamed. "Darling, I think you should just accept it."

Nicholas turned to her, hastily wiping the tears threatening to run down his cheeks. "And give up my profession? Vinny, I've just spent seven years forgetting about that old life and forging a new one. I know you'd rather see me as a peer, but I must admit I truly like being a doctor."

She tilted her chin with a challenging look. "But darling, think of Helena."

He shook his head. "Isn't it hopeless?"

"No, darling. Mr. Phillips still needs to consent to the marriage. There is a possibility that he will not. Not only has Julius been sleeping with his wife, he's quite a bit older than Mr. Phillips. Some men don't take kindly to those sorts of things."

Nicholas resumed his pacing. "And if the marriage goes through, I'm stuck with being Earl of St. Albans. Alone. God, what a bore."

"I'll be there for you, Nicky. I can help you over some of the hurdles."

"As can I, my lord," said Mason with a faint touch of hopefulness.

"Besides, can't you be the country doctor of your little village or some such? And," Lavinia winked at him, "I'm certain Penelope Hardcastle will make a fine countess, don't you think, love?"

Well, at the very least she'd be fashionable. And lively in bed.

Joseph Phillips paced a path in the carpet as he waved his hands in the air. "What the hell were you thinking, Sophie? Who the devil is this man?"

He had stormed into the morning room of his London townhouse the second he arrived without even a "good day" to his wife. Conveniently, Helena had been diverting herself in the library.

Perched nervously on the edge of the sofa, Sophia began to sob.

He hated to see his wife cry. "Sophie, honey, look, I need to know what is going on here." He knelt before her. "I received a telegram from Charlotte Banbury that seemed rather urgent. You were the one who expressly said that Helena should marry a highborn nobleman, and here you are giving her away to a doctor. I know you, sweet. What is really going on? Who is this Dr. Julius Christopher?"

"He's…he's," she stammered. "Oh Joseph!" She threw her arms around him.

Joseph knew at that moment his wife was sleeping with the man. While he did not care so much about that—they had a very modern arrangement—he was more concerned with the fact that Sophie was going to allow the same man to sleep with their daughter. Of all Sophie's affairs, this was rather irregular.

"What has this Dr. Christopher done to you, love?" He sat down next to her on the couch.

Sophia wiped her eyes. "He has a machine," she sniffled.

That was an intriguing bit of news. "A machine?"

"An erotic machine. It forces one to experience pleasure."

Joseph started at that. "Really?" If this was true then no wonder his wife had succumbed to the doctor.

"It's a new medical device. Doctors are using it now for hysteria treatments."

"Hysteria!" Joseph was nonplussed. If there was one thing his wife did not suffer from, it was hysteria. An obsessive need for physical stimulation, perhaps, but that only calmed her. She was never really of a nervous disposition.

"Well, yes," Sophia admitted sheepishly. "But as I have learned from Julius—"

Joseph eyed his wife disapprovingly.

"I mean from Dr. Christopher, when doctors treat hysteria they are really only bringing women to sexual climax, to orgasm. And as not all women achieve this type of release as easily as, well, I do, it can be quite a tedious undertaking, sometimes taking an hour."

"Good God! An hour?" Joseph said in amazement. "I feel very sorry for the poor husband whose wife takes an hour."

"Well, I dare say, and this is Julius' theory, that these doctors simply do not know how to massage women properly."

Joseph grunted. "Then I feel very sorry for those doctors' wives."

"And so this vibrating machine has been invented to, shall we say, speed up the process. Really, dear, as a modern man of business you should be impressed. These doctors are using machines to increase the numbers of patients they can see in a day, thereby increasing their income."

Joseph stood and resumed his pacing. "Yes, well, I can see how this would be useful for a doctor treating a patient with hysteria, but Sophie, love, that is hardly your condition."

"No, Joseph," she said in hushed embarrassment.

"So what the hell was he doing to you? Making false claims about your health so he can cure you of some ailment you do not suffer from so he could get your money? Does he know who you're married to? Is that it?"

"No, darling. Julius is an honest man. He refused to treat me after I told him I knew how to assuage my own urges. But I couldn't satisfy myself completely. For that I needed a man."

"You seduced him." Joseph knew all too well how his wife could behave.

"Yes, I suppose I did. Then we began using the machine not as a medical tool, but as an amusement."

"And then you became dependent on what it could do for you, wanting more?"

Sophia stood and walked to the window in frustration. "I'm sorry, Joseph, I got caught up." She hung her head. "I did grow to need it. Julius knew."

"So how does Helena fit into all of this?"

She turned and faced her husband. "Your daughter really was suffering from hysteria, you really must believe me, darling. She's been nothing but nerves since the beginning of the Season."

"For God's sake, Sophie, she was thrown to the wolves with this damn marriage business!" A meek glance from his wife mollified him. "So, she went to see Dr. Christopher and his machine?"

"First he taught her how to placate her own desires—"

"Oh, God, I don't think I want to hear this, Sophie," he growled.

"Well, I don't think I could have taught her," she said defensively. "It was all very medical, really. And, yes, he did use the machine."

"So then what? He fell in love with her? Surely this man must see countless women and have his pick."

"Joseph, as her father you really have no idea how absolutely stunning Helena is to men."

"As I am in love with her ravishing mother, I know precisely how beautiful our daughter is."

Sophia blushed. "Yes, well, Julius fell in love with her. He made me agree to the engagement under duress."

"And you call him an honest man?"

"Darling, please don't raise your voice."

"This is my house and I will raise my voice all I want," he bellowed. He pounded his fists against his thighs in utter astonishment at his wife's conduct. Yet he knew he should not be surprised. In the past, he had had to smooth over several mishaps. The worst had been Sophie's pregnancy with a much younger lover. She had been devastated, both for the requisite abortion of the child and her betrayal to her husband.

Joseph calmed himself as much as he could. "Sophie, darling, you have been very incautious and self-centered in your dealings with your Dr. Christopher. You have proved yourself weak once again. While in the past your weakness has been tolerated, this time it is inexcusable for you to have involved Helena."

Sophia returned to the sofa and sat like an admonished child. "Yes, Joseph. I apologize. I know I have been an inconsiderate wife and mother."

"Well, that's a start. Now about Helena, how does she feel about this young man?"

"Oh dear," Sophia started.

"What?"

"He's not a young man, Joseph."

"Well, O.K." He had expected as much. "So how old is he?"

"Forty-eight."

"Good Christ above!" Joseph threw his arms in the air. "He's older than I am! Oh no. No. That will not do. Is she in love with him?"

"I think she is fond of him."

"Fond? Fond?" He raked his fingers through his hair. "Go get her. I want to talk to her. Now."

Sophia complied immediately.

Helena burst through the door of the morning room and ran into her father's arms. "Papa! How wonderful to see you! I didn't expect you back for quite some time."

Joseph kissed his daughter on the forehead. "My sweet dove. I was summoned by news of your engagement."

"Oh." Helena sat down on the couch, her hands folded primly, mirroring the pose once again assumed by her mother.

"Helena," Joseph began, pacing before her, "what do you think of this man to whom you are engaged?"

"Well," she began haltingly, "Dr. Christopher is intelligent, polite, and, I suppose, fine-looking."

"Hmm." Joseph recognized the traits as rather generic and his daughter's enthusiasm as rather dull. "Are you worried that he might be a bit old for you?"

"Well, he is much, much older than all the other men I've been dancing with this Season. I don't suppose it is very odd for a young girl to marry an older man, though. Why, one of the Roxton twins is engaged to a man her father's age."

"Your Dr. Christopher, as you call him, is older than your mother and myself."

"Oh. Yes, I see. I had thought perhaps that might be the case," she said diffidently.

Good God. She knows nothing about the man.

Joseph sat on the couch next to his daughter and took her hand in his. "Darling Helena, I must ask this, are you in love with him?"

Helena began to cry.

It was a most unexpected response. Either she was desperately in love with him or she felt quite the opposite. Joseph handed her his handkerchief. "Sweet, please tell me why you are crying," he said gently.

"I'm so terribly confused, Papa. I thought I was to marry a duke or a marquess or an earl, and I did meet some very nice young men who would eventually hold those titles, I even got on with some of them." She gulped a mouthful of air. "And I just thought that if I had to marry a man so that I could be a duchess or countess and make you and Mama happy, then I would accept that I might not be in love with whomever you would choose for me. But then I fell in love and he was a doctor and I knew I couldn't have him and it was so unfair."

Joseph was not quite certain he understood the last part of her speech as it was said amidst screeching sobs and squawking breaths. But if what he thought she said was really what she said, then he was prepared to stand by her. "So, sweet, you are in love with Dr. Christopher, then?"

A deluge of fresh sobs fell uncontrollably. Joseph's patience with the female members of his household was wearing thin. "Helena, pull yourself together. What is going on?"

"I'm in love with Dr. Ramsay!"

Sophia gasped and covered her mouth with her hand.

As his daughter was thoroughly inconsolable, Joseph turned to his wife. "Sophie, who is Dr. Ramsay?"

"He is Dr. Christopher's colleague. They share an office."

"I see." Really he did not, but it was something to say.

"Papa," Helena's voice was thin and plaintive, "do I really have to marry Dr. Christopher?"

Joseph wrapped his arms around his daughter. "No, my sweet, you do not."

Sophia tore her fingers from her mouth thwarting the impulse to chew on her nails as she paced in the library. Joseph had sent her there while he pondered the predicament she had put them all in. She knew she deserved to be punished in some way—at the very least berated—for her unconscionable behavior. Only when Joseph had returned to London did she comprehend how misguided, how enchanted she had been. Her husband's presence had brought her back to reality and sanity.

The door opened and she quickly turned toward a bookshelf, the titles on the spines a blur from the tears pooling behind her lashes. She couldn't face him; she was too ashamed. She heard his footsteps on the carpet, steady and even, until they stopped right behind her.

She braced herself for his bitter words, balling her fists, shutting her eyes tight so she would not have to witness her own castigation.

Instead, she felt his hands, warm and strong, on her shoulders.

"Sophie," he murmured. His lips delicately brushed along the pulse in her neck.

Every nerve in her body sparked with astonishment and yearning. The tears fell to her cheeks as she trembled, her relief still tinged with despair.

His hands smoothed down her arms, one returning to the high collar of her dress. "I wonder what it is I do to you that makes you so vulnerable when I'm gone?" He released her buttons slowly, one by one. "What it is that a man can do for you that you cannot do for yourself?" He continued undressing her, taking her bodice off and dropping it on a side table.

Sophia remained still as he unfastened her skirt and petticoats and pushed them to the floor. His touch was gentle, allaying her remaining fears.

He wrapped a strong arm around her waist, pulled her hip back against his thigh, and slowly rubbed in a circular motion on her butt.

She tensed in glorious anticipation.

"Chastisement and discipline." He rubbed more powerfully. "That is properly the realm of the husband."

His swat stung even through the layers of underclothes.

"No one else may do that," he murmured against her ear. "It is my privilege."

The next blow produced a delicious burn that warmed the wetness welling between her legs.

He urged her around until she faced him, then lifted her chin and kissed her lips.

He hadn't kissed her yet since he had returned. He hadn't kissed her for months. Her desperate hunger for his touch, his attention, surged forth. She devoured all he offered, her fears melting into joy at his own fervor for their reunion. Tears streamed down her face as she encircled his neck with her arms. He pulled her more closely to him, deepening the kiss, plumbing her depths with his tongue.

"A kiss. A difficult task when alone," he said when they parted. "Let's find another."

He undid her corset slowly, worrying his lower lip at first, his expression softening in wonderment as the separation of each hook and eye freed her. He pulled the garment off and let it fall to the ground with a thud, then loosened the top of her chemise, drawing it down over her shoulders.

"A suck, that's another." He uncovered a breast, bent down and took the nipple in his mouth.

His hot, moist tongue surprised her, awakening her once again to his lust, quickening her need for him as if she were the libidinous virgin of her youth. She arched for him, cradling his head in her hands as he sought the other breast. He kissed the pale flesh before licking her hardened tip, unrelenting, determined, expertly driving her to a culmination he had first discovered so many years ago. A sharp nip sent her over the edge with an ecstatic yelp.

"Yes, yes, let me pleasure you, my love."

He continued his torment of her sensitive peaks as he pulled down her chemise and untied her drawers. She complied with his actions willingly, letting him take control, letting him expose her, letting him excite her. He lifted her in his arms and carried her to the large library table in the center of the room, then placed her on the edge gently. He parted her legs as he knelt on the floor before her.

"I suppose it is rather difficult to lick yourself."

She gasped when his tongue caressed her clitoris, lapping enthusiastically at first, then tickling the sensitive nub with practiced precision. She writhed on the polished table, his strong hands holding her steady at her thighs, his fingers indenting her flesh. She pressed herself into him, wrapped her stocking-clad legs around his neck wanting more. He gave her everything she wanted, everything she needed.

Her cries of pleasure mingled with his moans of satisfaction.

He moved up her body, kissing every inch of her with wet, slick lips, until he reached her mouth. Her hands cupped his face, the stubble masculine and thrilling, rough on her sensitive skin. He explored the depths of her mouth as he had explored her sex, all the while frantically removing what he could reach of his own clothing, parting from her only briefly to tear off his shirt. She watched as he stripped, enthralled at his enthusiasm, enamored at his eagerness, enticed by his excitement. He was rampant, his eyes and face revealing his devoted desire.

"And you certainly cannot do this on your own."

He entered her slowly, holding her gaze with raw intensity, his lust-darkened eyes marking her reactions, sighing his approbation and gratification as she succumbed.

When he was embedded fully, he held himself there, unmoving, then clasped her body to his.

"I love you so very much," he murmured, his breath hot on her skin. "Nothing will change that."

"I'm so sorry—"

"Shh, love. I know. I know. I've been far too neglectful of late. Let me make up for it."

He kissed her lips tenderly, then plunged in, his tongue mirroring his thrusts below. His hands roamed impatiently, frantically, touching her everywhere, making up for lost time. He rapidly reached a steady rhythm, driving them both to the edge of finality.

"Joseph…darling…stay inside me when you have your crisis."

"Yes, my love." He slammed inside her one last time, growling his release amidst her cries of ecstasy.

He held her sobbing, shaking form closely, his own tears dampening her neck and back.

"Darling, Sophie, I've no more need to go to America quite so frequently. I've put a man in charge. He's far better with guns than I am, and a damn good engineer. He'll send me reports." He caressed her back, then trailed his fingers gently up her spine. "It's time we acted like a proper husband and wife. No more affairs, Sophie. Not for a while, anyway."

"Yes, Joseph." It was what she had wanted for a very long time.

"We'll not let any machines come between us ever again."

Helena could not believe her eyes. The moment she had opened the library door just a crack, she knew she should not have been in the doorway. The scene before her was riveting, like the illustrations from the naughty books come to life. Seeing her mother and father joined in an intimate act of lovemaking was jolting at first, but after less than a second, rather intriguing. They were the both of them in the prime of life, their bodies perfect paradigms of the male and the female, their intercourse the acme of physical ecstasy and emotional joy.

She did not watch to the end; that was an intimacy for them to experience only. But when she silently closed the door and walked away she wondered if she would ever share such a perfect union with another soul, and rejoiced that she would not have to take part in such acts with Dr. Julius Christopher.

CHAPTER SEVENTEEN

Julius read the note over and over until he could no longer decipher the words. Sophia's handwriting was as precise as her meaning. Mr. Joseph Phillips had disallowed the marriage of his daughter to Julius. The engagement was rendered null and void as the consent of both parents was required for the marriage of a young woman under twenty-one years of age. Sophia warned against Julius pursuing the matter and reminded him the promise to marry was obtained by fraud.

It was, of course, one possible outcome, but as Mr. Phillips had been overseas for an uncertain amount of time, one that Julius had hoped to avoid.

What the hell compelled the man to return all the way across the Atlantic back to England anyway? With their damn democracy and republicanism and egalitarianism, Americans couldn't tell a baronet from the Prince of Wales. Someone must have told him.

Lavinia.

Julius cursed the woman.

She couldn't stand that her former lover could find happiness without her. That was it, wasn't it? Surely her latest fancy-man was not enough of a distraction that she had to meddle into his life as well. Clearly, Dr. Nicholas Ramsay needed to learn a thing or two about women and one was that they could not be relied upon for promoting a man's career.

"Out!" Julius yelled as he stormed into Ramsay's office.

Grace clutched the tea tray for dear life, her face twisted in anxious surprise.

The young doctor rose slowly from his desk, a pen still poised in his hand. "Dr. Christopher, what is the matter?" he asked in a voice imbued with a mixture of assurance and distress.

"You are the matter. I want you out of here. Now. You are not needed back."

"I don't understand, sir," he said far too coolly. "What is it I am supposed to have done?" The sod should have been whining.

"Please, Dr. Christopher, Dr. Ramsay is a good doctor. The patients love him—"

"Grace, stay out of this. Go to my examination room at once and wait for me there."

"Yes, sir." She curtsied before leaving.

Julius strutted before his colleague who, it appeared, was finally feeling some measure of agitation. Good. Let him wonder what the future held for him.

"I offered to mentor you and allowed you to share my office based on the recommendation of a certain woman. Due to current circumstances that woman is no longer in my favor."

"Lavinia? What has she done?"

The use of the familiar name only highlighted the fact that the young man was bedding her. "Lady Foxley-Graham has convinced my fiancée's father to not consent to the marriage."

Ramsay paled. "I'm certain she did no such thing, Dr. Christopher." The hesitation of his words betrayed his knowledge of the scheme.

"Obviously she did it for your benefit. But why Helena would marry a dolt like you is beyond comprehension, really."

Ramsay just stared at the floor pursing his lips in strained emotion.

"I will give you five minutes to gather your personal effects, then I want you out of here. Truthfully, I hope to never see you again. Do you understand me, boy?"

"Yes, sir, Dr. Christopher."

Julius strode out and into his own examination room where Grace sat primly on a chair waiting for his instructions. She was far too nervous, as if she had been part of the plot all along. He eyed her intently.

"You haven't been sleeping with him as well, have you?"

"What! Who?"

"Your Dr. Ramsay."

"Dr. Ramsay!" As if the idea had never crossed her mind. "Oh no, sir. I would never. Please, you have to believe me!"

She remained seated during her protest, staring up at him, her golden brown eyes wide and helpless. He absently took off her cap, pulling the pins from her hair until it fell to her shoulders in soft brown waves.

Like it used to.

Her hair was still the same color it had been twenty years ago, chocolate brown mixed with streaks of gold and ebony, always a welcome sight against the crisp white of his bed pillows. Julius grabbed a handful of her tresses and pressed it to his lips, then drew the strands through his fingers, slowly, until he reached the ends. He pulled upward, evoking a squeak of complaint.

He laughed derisively. "Don't pretend you don't enjoy it."

He wrapped her hair around his fist and pulled her out of the chair, yanking back until her face was in full view. She cringed in pain. Then he did the one thing he had been waiting decades to do.

He slapped her.

"Julius?" Tears streamed from her frightened eyes.

But he didn't want to hear it. He didn't want to hear her explanations or her protests or her promises. She had nearly destroyed him back then. She needed to learn her place now.

One hand pressed against her mouth, he dragged her by her lovely brown hair to the examination table and bent her over, securing her arms with the restraints meant for an uncooperative patient. Her dress was certainly an impediment to her lessons, so he grabbed his medical shears and cut down the back, back up through the lacings of her corset, back down through the sheer fabric of her chemise, careful not to nick her smooth, creamy flesh, nor slice her luxurious locks. His cock livened as he pulled aside the rent clothing, disappointment sputtering through him at the sight of her cambric drawers. Those too he cut, right through at the crotch, admiring the sight of the lacy fabric slipping down to her ankles.

"I cannot tolerate such behavior, my dear. It is most unbecoming for a lady to betray her lover. You have been very wicked."

He grabbed his ebony-handled vectis, never realizing until that moment that the obstetric instrument was well-shaped as a tool of chastisement. He drew in a long breath as his hand caressed the coolness of the looped metal end, the feel of the sensuous curve under his fingertips sending a lascivious thrill to pulse within him. He lifted his arm and struck the vectis against the perfect white skin of his lover's behind.

She cried out at the impact. He lovingly touched the now pink flesh, soothing her, priming her for the next swat.

He mirrored the strike on the other fleshy cheek and cooed honeyed words to ease her fears.

By the fourth blow, she was no longer crying. She lay unmoving, subdued.

Julius fingered her cunt. She was wet, deliciously so. He chuckled to himself. Pain did always result in pleasure. He kicked her legs open as he unbuttoned his fly. Entering her was a bit of a nuisance as she was not totally primed. It wasn't his problem though. His only concern was his relief and her reprimand.

He slammed into her with such force the table moved. He grabbed her hair once again, holding it like the reins of a horse, while he plowed into her over and over, this time with the needed leverage. She endured her discipline silently. Her submission was most appreciated, her cunt even fluttered around him. As quick as his anger with his old lover was to flare, it was just as quick to assuage. His crisis was upon him rapidly.

He pulled out and spewed his semen onto her naked back and thighs. As he let his breathing calm, he watched rivulets of the milky fluid course down and drip onto the floor.

Disgusted, Julius left the room and closed the door.

Nicholas was overjoyed with the news. Helena was free of Julius Christopher and his debauchery.

Helena was his.

Well, he hoped at least. Mr. Phillips' arrival on the scene certainly shook up one man's plans, he would have no idea how the American would react to his own offer of marriage.

Lavinia's butler should have been used to his rather boorish way of bursting into her terrace house and demanding to see her wherever she was. She was, as usual, in her morning room reading the afternoon paper.

"Darling, the most wonderful news," he said as she smiled at him in surprise.

"Nicky! Sit down." She patted the couch next to her.

Instead he pulled her up out of her seat and whirled her about. "Vinny, I've been shelved by your former lover."

"Julius? Whatever for?" She looked so charming with tendrils of loosened hair framing her inquisitive face.

"Because of you." He gave her a squeeze of victory. "It seems you were the author of a great plot to bring Mr. Phillips back to England and refuse consent to his daughter's marriage."

"Yes, I suppose I was." She freed herself from his zealous embrace. "How did Julius come to find out?"

"He's not daft, darling." He grabbed her hands. "Vinny, she's free. Helena's free!" He felt possibility all around him.

She beamed, his own happiness reflected in her expression. "Nicky, come with me upstairs. I've something for you, for precisely this occasion."

They quickly climbed the stairs to her bedroom. Nicholas lay on the familiar bed and watched her root around in her jewelry cases.

"It's been a few years, but I know it's here somewhere." She kept looking. "Aha!"

She sat on the bed next to him and opened her hand. In her palm were three rings.

"This one's yours," she said handing him a masculine band of gold. "Your family signet ring, remember?"

He did remember. He had put it on the nightstand in his bedroom at the estate the day he left.

"Your mother found it, and kept it. She wore it around her neck."

"Oh, God. I never knew that." Old emotions of sorrow and regret swelled in him.

"And this was her engagement ring. It's been the property of the Earls of St. Albans for generations. And this," she held up a simple but elegant gold band, "was her wedding ring. It was made expressly for her by your father." She placed both in his outstretched palm.

Nicholas stared at the precious rings remembering how tiny his mother's hands were, how delicate her fingers. How small she was against the brutality of his father. He could no longer hold back the tears.

"Shh, shh, love," Lavinia consoled. "I took them from her room after her death. She always meant for you to have them. She actually predicted Jack would not survive your father. She hoped you would come back and return honor to the family."

He put his own ring on his pinkie finger. It felt heavy, its weight not just from the gold but from the memories of his painful past. He knew he would grow accustomed to the feeling of it on his hand, just as he would eventually grow accustomed to the responsibilities of his position.

"It still fits you, darling." Lavinia traced the circumference.

"Yes." Nicholas held the engagement ring to the sunlight streaming through the window. "Emerald," he said. "It will look lovely on Helena with her coloring."

"Yes, darling, it will."

"But Vinny, what do I do? Mr. Phillips will think it odd an earl has simply come out of the woodwork to marry his daughter. Especially since Helena has absolutely no idea."

"Yes, you may be right." Lavinia pressed a finger to her lips in thought. "I have a plan, Nicky, darling. Tonight is the Raeburn ball. I'll send a message to Charlotte to make sure the entire Phillips family is in attendance."

"But surely Helena will not be in any mood to go to a ball."

"The girl must not appear to be too distraught over a broken engagement, otherwise no other man will think there is room in her heart. She will be there. And so will you. I know Lord and Lady Raeburn intimately. I'll make sure your entrance is most memorable."

Grace remained in her position bent over the examination table long after Julius had left. His mood was a new one. She wasn't sure what the consequences would be if he found her attempting to free herself.

The once-warm ejaculate had turned cold long ago, its wetness now dried globules cool on her back, uncovered and exposed to the chilly air. She had been utterly terrified during the whole ordeal. Dr. Christopher had never hit her before, had never before threatened her with any implement, sharp or otherwise. As he cut her clothes in his agitated state, she had braced herself against a nick. Her bum still ached where he had struck her.

While she knew him to be eccentric, she had never thought him dangerous. Her only consolation was that she knew he relied upon her for his experiments, perhaps even enjoyed their times together. She'd been faithful, loyal in her desire to serve him. He couldn't possibly have been angry with her.

No it was someone else.

A woman.

Deep in the recesses of his past a woman still tormented him, still tortured him. Whoever she was, Julius needed to forget her.

It was dusk when Grace decided she had waited long enough. She worried at the buckles of the restraints, loosening them until she could get her hands through. Her clothing sagged on her body. She took off what was left of her drawers and turned her dress around. She was about to leave, to go to her room, have a bath, attempt to salvage what she could of her dress, when she was stopped by an idea. She looked at the doors of the cabinets lining one corner of the room, knowing what existed behind them. She had watched Dr. Ramsay make tinctures of opium for mothers and for children, so she knew the proper proportions. Well, at least, how not to kill a man.

After all, she didn't want to hurt her Julius. She just wanted to prove her worth to him and help him forget.

CHAPTER EIGHTEEN

Nicholas had been rather nervous while Lavinia had primped and preened him in preparation for the ball at Lord and Lady Raeburn's Mayfair house. He had to look especially well-dressed that night, so he borrowed diamond shirt studs, a pair of buff kid gloves, and a silk mourning armband from her dead husband's wardrobe. But she also wanted him to stand out in the crowd.

"What have you got from your travels? Waistcoat? Tie?" she had asked.

He had smiled at that. She never allowed him to wear such garish attire when he was in her presence. "I've a waistcoat I absolutely adore. Embroidered Persian silk velveteen in the most beautiful crimson."

On any other day Lavinia would have cringed at such a notion. "Right. Let's see."

And when he put it on, she was visibly impressed. "Hmm, not so much out of fashion as terribly exotic, really," she had mused, turning him around. "It suits you. Very handsome." She raised a brow. "If that girl doesn't marry you, Nicky, I will."

Lavinia herself wore a pale-olive dress subdued and elegant so as not to distract from her companion's daring display.

As they waited their turn to be announced by the Raeburn's footman, Nicholas' attire was already becoming the topic of whispers amongst the young ladies. Of course, most recognized him from previous events, some had even danced with him, but none had really taken much note of him beyond his particular good looks. Somehow he was turning heads that night.

"You're looking rather confident, I must say, my lord," Lavinia confided.

"Thank you, my dear lady." It wasn't just the dashing clothes, it was his hope, the promise of a future with the woman he loved.

From the lobby he watched as Lavinia motioned to Lady Banbury, who waved back with a nod and a smile.

"Everything is in place, Nicky."

By the time Nicholas and Lavinia were before the footman to be announced, the room had quieted to murmurs. Nicholas spied Sophia and Helena Phillips with a rather attractive graying man who, he could only assume, was Mr. Phillips.

"Pay attention, Nicky," Lavinia said under her breath.

"The Earl of St. Albans and the Viscountess Foxley-Graham."

The footman's voice seemed to boom more loudly with their introduction than those previous. From the corner of his eye, Nicholas saw Helena flush and stare at him incredulously.

"How do you do, my lord?" Lady Raeburn smiled with a curtsy.

"Very well, thank you, madam," Nicholas replied. He was far too distracted to remember proper etiquette at that moment.

"St. Albans, eh?" queried Lord Raeburn. "We read about your father's death. So sorry, my good man." He patted Nicholas' shoulder above his armband. "Your return to England is most opportune." He raised an eyebrow at Nicholas' waistcoat.

"Yes, my travels did bring me home at the right time, sir."

Lavinia took his arm as they entered the crush of the ballroom. She looked quite dismayed when the first to approach was Penelope Hardcastle.

"Dr. Ramsay," she greeted. "Or shall I say Lord St. Albans?" She curtsied.

"Good evening, Miss Hardcastle." Nicholas really liked Penelope. She was politeness wrapped around a powder keg of sensuality. But she was his second choice and Lavinia had counseled him to discourage her.

"My lord," interjected Lavinia, "we really must make our compliments to Lady Banbury."

He smiled and gave a slight bow to Penelope as Lavinia led him away.

"Charlotte." Lavinia greeted her co-conspirator with a kiss.

"My dear St. Albans, you look absolutely splendid," Lady Banbury said as she gave Nicholas the once-over. "May I borrow his left arm, Lavinia? I need an escort to the other side of the ballroom."

As the three strolled through the crowd, Nicholas bowed and smiled to awestruck young ladies and their dumbfounded mothers who, once he had passed, proceeded to whisper about what possibly could have happened to elevate the young doctor.

And then he saw her. Helena looked beautiful as always, but more so that night. Her pale pink dress hugged every curve on her body, the bodice cut so low he had to remind himself to stare at the glittering rubies and garnets encircling her lovely neck, a neck, he inappropriately reminded himself, he had kissed more than once.

It was Lady Banbury who broke the spell. "Mr. Phillips, I would like to introduce a young man I have had the pleasure of knowing this Season, the Earl of St. Albans." She turned to Nicholas. "My lord, Mr. Joseph Phillips."

The uncommonly attractive middle-aged man Nicholas had noticed earlier stuck out his hand. "Albans, pleased to meet you, I'm sure."

His American accent was disconcerting. "Mr. Phillips," Nicholas said with a bow.

"May I introduce my wife, Sophia, and my daughter, Helena." His gray eyes flashed with pride.

The two women stared at Nicholas, their utter stillness an obvious attempt to subvert their astonishment.

"We have already met, sir," Nicholas said over the loud thumping of his heart.

Clinging to her husband, Mrs. Phillips curtsied with a touch of embarrassment. "My lord."

As a properly trained young lady, Helena kept her composure as she curtsied her introduction. "My lord."

"Already met, eh? And how is that?"

Mortification oozed through every pore of Nicholas' body. How the hell was he supposed to respond? *Because I've been working alongside the man who fucked your wife and almost defiled your daughter?*

"They met through me, Joseph," offered Lady Banbury. "I know Doc—er, the earl through Lady Foxley-Graham who is a longtime friend of the family."

"Ah, very good, very good," Mr. Phillips declared. "And what sort of thing do you do as an earl?"

Nicholas shot a glance at Lavinia, but she merely smiled sweetly at the Phillipses. "I, uh, have an estate in Hertfordshire." Mr. Phillips seemed impressed at that so Nicholas continued. "I was just there recently, in fact." He flashed a glance at Helena. "There are some badly needed renovations, that sort of thing."

Mr. Phillips slapped Nicholas on the back as if they were long-lost mates. "Good! Keeps you out of trouble!"

Nicholas smiled at the man's easy-going nature, hoping he would be as cheery when it came to the subject of his daughter. The music struck up and couples began sauntering toward the dance floor. "Sir, if I may, I would like to ask your daughter to dance. Please." He stammered like an awkward youth at his first ball.

"Helena?" Mr. Phillips responded as if it were a completely extraordinary notion. He turned to her. "What say you, love?"

"Yes, Papa. I would very much like to dance with the earl."

Nicholas' heart was now banging so loudly he feared everybody could hear. He held out his right arm. When Helena took it, his head spun as if he were in a dream.

The whispers became murmurs as he escorted her to the ballroom floor. Helena blushed at the attention, a color so very like her dress the thought of her utterly nude flashed in his mind. Placing his hand above her waist agitated his senses even more. He was uncomfortably hard, a state he prayed Mr. Phillips would not notice.

Once safely ensconced in his arms during the waltz, Helena gazed up at him, her eyes reflecting both curiosity and understanding. She deserved an explanation.

"Helena," he began.

"Please, my lord," she said in a voice just above a whisper. "I just want to be with you at this moment. To feel you holding me."

A thrill shot through him, flushing his skin, enlivening his senses. He spread his fingers on her back and pressed her a little more closely to him. She sucked in air and blushed again, turning her head off to the side as if embarrassed by a wicked thought. When she regained her composure, her lips curled in a smile all at once sultry and innocent.

He wanted desperately to take her outside and find a quiet corner of the garden where he could make passionate love to her, introducing her to the delights of the flesh. In the intimacy of afterglow, he would confess all about his family and his past. But Nicholas knew he could not act with such impropriety tonight. Most in attendance knew his scandalous family history, but lacked familiarity with his own disposition and behavior. He would hate to despoil his uncertain reputation. All eyes were on him. They were on Helena as well, as news of her broken engagement was also the topic of whispers and murmurs.

He leaned down against her ear. "Helena, I would like to dance as many dances as possible with you tonight."

She looked up at him knowing exactly what that implied. "Yes, Nicholas," she murmured. "I would very much like that."

Helena had never danced so elegantly in her life. Nicholas' energy and desire flowed through her, uniting them as the most perfect couple in the ballroom. All eyes watched as they continued to partner dance after dance, the utter happiness of the pair turning disbelieving whispers into hums of acceptance and shocked expressions into genuine smiles.

The excitement and attention were draining. "I feel I need a bit of air, my lord."

"Yes, Miss Phillips, of course," Nicholas responded with concern.

He took her arm to weave their way through the overly interested crush and out onto the only slightly less crowded terrace. Nicholas took her to an unoccupied space at the railing, nodding and greeting polite, smiling faces along the way.

The cool night air was refreshing. Helena drew in a long breath and exhaled slowly. It seemed a long time ago when she had felt contented enough to take enjoyment from the simple act of breathing.

Nicholas sighed. "So many eyes on us. It's disconcerting."

Helena laughed. "Well, there's my broken engagement. And your marvelous waistcoat. Then the fact that you're suddenly an earl. Plus, you danced with me three times. Everyone knows what that means."

He brightened at that. "Do you?"

"I think so, my lord."

"Ugh, please don't call me that, Helena. That's just not who I am."

"Then am I still allowed to call you 'Nicholas'?" she teased.

"Yes, oh, yes. I love hearing you say my name." He glanced around restlessly at the couples milling about on the terrace. "Damn and blast, I wish we could be alone. If there weren't so many people, I would sneak you off into the garden—"

"And ravish me against a tree?" she offered playfully.

A pleased grin spread across his astonished face. "Your disheveled appearance would draw even more attention, Miss Phillips." He grabbed her arm as soon as he spied a newly vacated bench.

He paced a bit before he sat down next to her. "Darling," he began softly, "it was all quite unexpected. I was never meant to be in this position."

"You mean about being an earl."

"Uh, yes. Sorry. I feel a bit like a frightened schoolboy at the moment." He flexed his fingers against his thighs, gathering his thoughts. "You see, I'm the youngest son of my father. My brother Jack was his heir." He inhaled deeply. "Jack was a violent wastrel, an attribute he inherited from my father. I hated being a part of that family. So I went away."

"Is that when you went to Turkey?"

That brought another grin to his face. "I very much wish I could hold your hand right now," he murmured. "Damned social conventions." He sighed. "Yes, that's when I traveled. I studied medicine abroad. I had to do something with my life. I was twenty-one, I had a small income, and I was a second son."

The moon was behind him, providing her with of view of his profile, serious and pensive, in need of solace. She suppressed the urge to reach out with a gentle caress of his cheek and damned social conventions as well.

He toyed with the fingers of his gloves. "But then my mother was killed. At the time I thought both my father and brother played a part in her death." His voice trembled. "I only just learned the truth. Jack killed her. My father shouldered part of the blame to protect an innocent who had been regrettably caught up in the affair."

Her heart clenched at his pain. She slid her hand across the bench toward him. Nicholas surreptitiously glanced around before placing his palm over her offer of comfort.

"I never wanted to come back after that. I changed my name to distance myself even more. Ramsay was my mother's surname."

"But you did come back."

"Yes. Lavinia insisted. And I suppose I grew tired of aimlessly wandering. I needed to put what I had learned into practice. And I started to have thoughts of having my own family." He gazed at her. "A proper family."

A flush of heat rose in her cheeks. "Did you make amends with your father?"

"Just before he died. I'm glad of that." He let out a grunt. "I suppose that's why he chose me over Bertie—my cousin."

The pieces were beginning to fall into place. Somewhere, deep inside, Helena had known to trust Nicholas, to not second-guess why he suddenly appeared before her as a titled bachelor. "You thought me engaged already when you went to see your father."

"Yes," he admitted sullenly. "There was no incentive for me to be the earl. Just a lot of bother, really. And I was rather enjoying my new life." His expression softened into a mischievous smile. "I probably would have been quite content with doctoring and having you as my mistress."

Her pulse quickened.

He leaned toward her, his breath hot on her skin. "We would not be in this frustrating position at the moment. Instead we'd be satisfying our desires against a tree."

Her heart pounded in her ears as a flush of excitement tormented her privates.

"But I don't want any of that now."

"You don't?" Helena panicked at what he could possibly mean.

"No, darling, I don't, because I want you to be my wife."

Helena stifled a squeal of joy, emitting a clipped squeak instead. The horrid noise turned heads on the terrace.

Which made her giggle.

"How can I possibly ask you to marry me when you are laughing?" Nicholas asked, clearly trying to quash his own mirth.

She wanted to scream and shout, twirl about in uninhibited joy. Instead, she sucked her lips between her teeth struggling to contain a grin.

"You might want to take a breath soon."

It was true, she was holding her breath. "Nicholas," she puffed, "you'll need to—"

"Ask your father?" He chuckled. "Don't worry. After your last suitor, I plan to do this correctly."

Hope and possibility flurried about in her head. "He cannot refuse you. He simply cannot. You're an earl. It's what they want for me."

He was what she wanted for her as well.

Julius had quite forgotten how exhausting a full day of dealing with frightened mothers and their ill children could be. Perhaps he had been rash in dismissing the young Ramsay. The lad was certainly well-liked from the inquiries after his health posed by his patients. But Julius had to remind himself, Ramsay knew far too much and meddled in his affairs rather excessively. He exhaled a long breath in exasperation.

Grace knocked before entering with the tea tray.

"Thank you, Grace." Julius eyed her. She also knew too much, but she was useful and, he had to admit, not just as a servant. He watched her, certain she was moving her hips in an exaggerated manner.

When she was finished with preparing his cup, she went around the office straightening up without a word. She had been very subdued since the incident after he had dismissed Ramsay. As he drank his tea—a bit too strong for his liking—he wondered if he should apologize.

"Grace?"

She looked at him with a strained expression. "Yes, Dr. Christopher?"

"Since you've been in my employ I have come to rely upon you." He took another sip of tea. This time it seemed not just strong, but oddly bitter. He never used sugar, but even a lump of that did not help. He winced and put the cup down.

Grace stepped forward. "Thank you, sir." She seemed keen to observe his expression. He liked that, he supposed.

"I just wanted to say that I hope you understand that if I have mistreated you in the past, it was a mistake."

"Yes, Doctor."

Julius stood to leave. A rush of dizziness made him somewhat unsteady. Exhaustion probably. He got as far as the office door.

Grace was by his side when he fell to one knee. "Doctor!" She grabbed his arm and wrapped it around her shoulder.

"Thank you," he murmured, stupefied. "If you could help me upstairs to the study—"

"No," she said firmly. "We'll just go in here." She led him into the opposite office, and bent him over the examination table. The padded table felt oddly comfortable under his enervated torso. He watched as she set to busying about, with what, he wasn't quite sure.

His limbs felt heavy and weak. He tried to lift his head but it could only loll against the padding. His eyes grew drowsy watching Grace. She was doing something with the leather bindings on the sides of the table. He raised his head with great effort and found his upper body had been strapped down. "Grace?" he queried meekly.

But she said nothing as she closed and locked the office door.

A sudden rush of anxiety burst into fear. Grace would never do anything to harm him, would she?

He heard her move the metal cart closer to the examination table, heard her set up the electro-mechanical vibrating machine as she had been taught to do. But she was taking too long, doing something that he didn't always do to the machine, something they did infrequently, only with certain patients. He tried to think, but his mind was growing murkier by the minute.

She went to the cabinets, took something out, and came back. Her movements were matter-of-fact, as if he were an actual patient and not a...

Captive.

She was behind him, unbuttoning his braces, unbuttoning his trousers, untucking his shirt.

She paused only a moment to snap open a pair of shears.

The blades were cold against his back as she cut right through his trousers and drawers from the waistband to the fly. Alarm lifted him momentarily from his delirious state when the blades passed between his buttocks and under his stones. However, she was very careful. She had learned such delicacy from his lessons in dressing wounds and cutting bandages.

"Now, Julius," she said with the blades still poised between his thighs, "you will spread your legs wide. It should be so much easier now that I've cut your trousers."

He did so with difficulty, his legs as heavy as lead.

She reached under him and grabbed his cock. He jolted up.

"Ah, the locus of pleasure," she said.

As if a trained courtesan, Grace masturbated him to full stand, coaxing and giggling in his ear. The stimulation was confusing and arousing, his mind somehow disconnected yet all at once immersed in the intense feelings.

She released him, engorged and unsatisfied. Behind him she moved the machine once again. He heard the familiar click and buzzing of the motor.

Suddenly her insistent and oily fingers separated his butt cheeks to massage his anus, twisting inside him and pulling out, first one finger, then two. Julius sighed.

"I think we're ready."

Something nudged against his lubricated buttocks, something oscillating with a rapid rhythm.

Julius lurched when the rubber tip of the vibrator pushed into the tight puckered hole of his arse. Grace consoled him with encouraging words while she slowly drove the device deeper and deeper. He wanted it, he didn't want it, his mind vacillating until the pain dissolved into an unknown ecstasy.

Of course he knew intellectually that a man could be stimulated physically in such a way as to achieve a sort of orgasm, knew from his research that the ecstasy was more intense if effected along with genital stimulation. He had, however, never himself actually experienced any such thing.

Until now.

Grace grabbed his cock and massaged slowly, pumping steadily, gripping resolutely. Inside him, the vibrations matched her rhythm, the insistent pulsing intensifying her ministrations. She cooed over him, assuring him she would take care of him, exhorting him to simply give in and let go.

Julius flinched in reaction. He never let go. Grace most definitely should not be in control.

But his body fought his intellect, mired in the most wondrous sensations it had ever experienced. Grace, he convinced himself, was simply taking him on a journey he had always been curious about.

He closed his eyes and relaxed on the padding to let Grace do her will.

He spun into the depths where sensation became oblivion.

His culmination was unexpected, explosive, the most astounding he had ever experienced.

Grace milked him seemingly endlessly, murmuring praises as his emission spattered on the floor.

His body utterly spent, his mind retook control with a nagging thought.

How had he ever lived without Grace?

CHAPTER NINETEEN

It was a bold move, to be sure, but Nicholas did not want to miss his chance, did not want to let Helena get away. He called on Mr. Phillips at the Phillips' Belgravia mansion at the earliest possible moment the very next day after the Raeburn ball, determined to make Helena his bride.

Left to his own devices to wait in the morning room, he paced around, surveying the décor. From the sleek geometric pottery displayed on the hand-joined side table, to the Whistler landscape hanging against the block-printed floral wallpaper, everything was new and modern, as if the objects had jumped from the pages of one of Lavinia's radical interior design magazines. By lacking any sort of history, the room and its contents revealed inhabitants who were defiantly forward-looking. Even the house itself was new, the Phillipses probably the very first occupants.

It made Nicholas potently aware that, with Helena at his side, he would start a new life, free from the entanglements of his own past, his own heritage.

He was kept waiting longer than he had hoped, giving him time to practice what he would say, yet also giving his stomach time to clench with doubt and fear. Permission was not a certainty especially after the disaster with Dr. Christopher.

Nicholas desperately wished Helena were there with him. Her presence would buoy him; her love would give him strength.

The door opened and Mr. Phillips entered, the almost imperceptible dishevelment of his morning suit hinting at his already having attended to a great deal of business that day. He raised his brows in surprise.

"Albans, correct?"

"Actually, St. Albans, sir."

Mr. Phillips snorted at the correction. "What are you doing here, son?"

American directness was quite disarming. "Yes, to get to the point, sir, I would like to ask your permission for your daughter's hand in marriage."

"You, too?" he exclaimed. He threw up his hands and shook his head in irritation.

Had the floodgates restraining the legions of Helena's suitors suddenly been opened? "Sir?"

Mr. Phillips' countenance grew stern. "After that blasted Christopher affair I'm not sure Helena's ready to marry anyone."

Nicholas' heart sank. He had been prepared to plead his case, but was not prepared for such a vehement reaction. "Sir, if I may say so," he began quietly, "I've known your daughter all Season. We get on quite well."

"That may well be, young man, but she claims to be in love with someone else."

Helena in love? Of course it was with him. "Pardon me for asking, sir, but who might that be?"

"Some fellow named Ramsay."

"Dr. Nicholas Ramsay?"

Mr. Phillips brightened only slightly. "Why yes. Do you know him?"

"Yes, sir. Well, what I mean to say, sir, is that I am Dr. Nicholas Ramsay." *Blast!* The man was making him far too nervous.

Mr. Phillips frowned. "What the devil do you mean by that? Is this a joke?"

"No, sir. You can ask Miss Phillips to confirm, if you like."

Mr. Phillips paced before Nicholas, staring at him warily, like a lion ready to strike its prey. "Is this one of those English aristocratic quirks where the nobility have all sorts of names?"

Nicholas did not know how precisely to respond to that. The question was partly an insult, partly in earnest. "It may very well be, sir. I was born Nicholas Atherley, the second son of my father, the Earl of St. Albans. My older brother, Jonathan, was in line to inherit from my father. But he died before my father, and so I became the heir."

"So where does 'Ramsay' come in? And the part about being a doctor?"

"Ramsay is my mother's surname. And it is traditional for second sons to take on a profession of sorts, so I became a doctor."

Despite his weak attempt at cluttering subterfuge, Nicholas could tell his omissions were not missed by Mr. Phillips. "Why do you not use the name Atherley?"

Nicholas drew in a bolstering breath. Honesty worked with Helena, so it might be the best course of action with her father. "My father was cruel to my mother, sir, as was my brother. When I reached my majority and received an income, I left my family and went abroad. I decided to study to become a doctor. A few years ago, I received word that my mother had been killed by my brother. In her honor and to distance myself from my father, I took the name Ramsay."

"And how much of this story does my daughter know?"

Nicholas started at that, slightly abashed. "I've only just told her, sir."

"What do you mean by that—'only just'?"

"Last night, sir. I told her everything last night."

"Last night?" He slammed his fist on a table dulling the polish. "Last night? You've known her for how long—two months?—and you only told her last night?"

"I was only just recently made earl, sir."

"But you thought nothing of harboring secrets from the woman you supposedly love?"

"Until I was made earl I was not considered worthy of your daughter's hand. We were merely friends, sir. The truth did not seem important."

The second the words came out Nicholas wanted to take them back.

"Truth not important?" Mr. Phillips hissed. "Well, tell me the truth now Ramsay. When you say your father and brother were cruel to your mother, what do you mean by that?"

Nicholas swallowed hard. "My father beat her and cheated on her, my brother was cruel with his words," he admitted ashamedly.

Mr. Phillips eyed him. "And how did your brother die?"

It was as if he knew, and knew the answer would be damning to Nicholas' suit. "My brother shot himself, sir."

"And your father?"

"My brother shot my father. The wound was not treated properly. He died a short while later."

Mr. Phillips clenched his fists and paced slowly but determinedly. "Guns," he muttered. He stopped and rounded on Nicholas. "So, Nicholas Ramsay, doctor and earl, what you are saying to me is that you come from a family of a murderous and violent disposition, and you have been hiding this from my daughter for most of the time you've known her. Now I should ask you, if you were in my position would you allow your daughter to marry such a man?"

Nicholas was stunned at the question and all it implied. "Sir, it is not like that at all. I love Helena—"

"Do you know what love is, young man? I have been married for eighteen years to the woman I love. I have never been deceitful to her. There are no secrets between us. I have been nothing but honest with her. And I expect no less for my daughter. Do you understand?"

Nicholas fought back every angry riposte, desperately tamping the rage welling within. Before he could respond the door to the morning room opened.

Helena. The enmity melted at the very sight of her.

She looked at both men, wide-eyed, realizing she had just interrupted something rather grave.

"Papa?" Her brow twisted in anguish.

"Helena, sweet, do you know this man?" Her presence had softened him somewhat.

"Of course, Papa," she intoned with quiet incredulity. "We danced at the Raeburns' last night."

"Yes, of course you did. What I mean is, do you know his name?"

"His name?" Helena looked questioningly at Nicholas, but all he could do was nod. "His name is Nicholas," she responded.

"Do you know the name given him at birth?"

Alarm flitted across her face. "Papa?"

"Do you know who he is?"

"He is a doctor," she responded meekly, "and I suppose he is now Earl of St. Albans."

"Do you know how his mother died?"

"His mother?" Helena turned to Nicholas again, fear in her eyes. "She was killed by his brother, Papa," she said helplessly.

"And do you wish the same fate to befall you?" Mr. Phillips bellowed. "Helena, this man has asked for your hand in marriage and I have forbidden it. He has won your love through deceit, concealing his family's murderous past. I cannot allow such a union. It is almost as preposterous as marriage to that Dr. Christopher."

Helena paled, gaping at her father, wavering as if she were going to faint. She turned to Nicholas, tears in her eyes. He reached for her, but she ran from the room.

Nicholas' heart tightened, the loss of his love leaving him bereft, debilitated, the same overwhelming bleakness he had felt after reading the news of his mother's death.

He turned on his heel and left.

Alone in her room, Helena sobbed into her pillow.

She had no idea what had just transpired between Papa and Nicholas. All she knew was that she loved Nicholas enough to spend the rest of her life with him. But she also loved Papa and had to respect his decision.

Except in this instance Papa was wrong. She was sure of it. Nicholas would never hurt her. Never.

She gulped air and cried until her head hurt, until she could cry no more. Until she fell asleep from exhaustion.

The memory of Nicholas' pained and defeated expression before her father ripped her from her dreams. Nicholas wanted to be with her as much as she wanted to be with him. She had to do something.

It was late afternoon, still an acceptable time of day for a young lady to visit a friend. If she took the back stairs and left the house from the servants' hall, no one would think anything of it. Busy servants certainly wouldn't inquire as to where she was going and if she had permission to go.

Helena had only been past Lady Foxley-Graham's house, and in a carriage, but she was certain she knew where it was and how to get there. She knocked on the wrong door at first, and was directed to the right one.

Lady Foxley-Graham was certainly very surprised to see her.

"Miss Phillips, this is quite unexpected."

But Helena was tired of formalities and let loose with a deluge of emotions. Lavinia, as she requested to be called, listened to her every word, consoling her.

"Lavinia, why would my father forbid us to be together?" she asked through sniffles and tears.

"He's worried for your safety, I suppose," she replied, stroking Helena's hair as her mother would. "He must have been shocked to hear of Nicholas' past. Your father cares for you very much."

"But Nicholas is nothing like his family! He's sweet and kind and ever such a gentleman."

"You must prove that to your father."

"How can I?"

"We'll think of something, dear."

Lavinia told her butler to cancel all her engagements for that evening, that she was to be undisturbed "by anyone".

Helena giggled. "You're expecting him tonight, aren't you?"

Lavinia blushed. "Helena—"

"I don't mind. It makes him ever so much more appealing having a longtime special friend like you. That's a point in his favor, don't you think?"

Lavinia laughed. "Well, I don't think your father wants to know that Nicky has a mistress. We'll keep that part out."

Nicky. It was so personal, so intimate.

"Lavinia, tell me everything about him. Please."

And for the rest of the evening, Helena was enthralled with stories about Nicholas Ramsay.

Morning light streamed into the library as Helena searched Lavinia's collection for something diverting. Lavinia had decided Helena should avail herself of her books while "this whole horrible business" was being settled. She had said she would send word later that morning to Mama and Papa about her whereabouts.

"Helena, I think I've found the novels," Lavinia called from the other side of the room. "Ah, yes, here they are."

Lavinia held out a volume of Jane Austen.

"*Persuasion*. Ironic, isn't it?" Helena took the book and settled on the window seat.

The door to the library crashed open.

"Vinny, what do you mean by canceling last night! I've been in a complete funk. I needed you—"

It was Nicholas. He stopped the moment their eyes met.

"Helena," he greeted with strained emotion. "Lavinia, I apologize, I had no idea you had company."

Lavinia went to him, caressing his shoulders tenderly. "Darling, Helena has run away from home." She took his hands in hers and led him to the window seat. "She came here, of all places. Her parents do not know where she is yet."

Helena knew she should feel a pang of envy, but she did not. It was exciting to see Nicholas and his lover acting so comfortably familiar with each other.

Nicholas looked at her with concern. "Helena, is this true?"

"Nicholas, my father was beastly to you. And to me, as well." She looked up at him. "You came to ask for my hand and I want to marry you. Why does he want to keep us apart?"

Nicholas perched on the edge of the window seat. "I completely understand his motives. He's trying to protect you from a wretched life which, I am sure, far too many wives must endure."

There was a tap on the door before the butler, Mr. Sims, entered. He shot Nicholas a withering look as he handed Lavinia a calling card on his silver tray.

"Oh! It appears I have a visitor. I must excuse myself." Lavinia gave both Helena and Nicholas the once-over. "You two behave yourselves. I will only be downstairs. Wait here and I will return."

When she left, Helena giggled.

"Why so amused?"

"I think Lavinia is afraid I will ravish you in the library."

Nicholas flushed crimson. He sat back on the seat and gazed at her. "You should behave yourself, young lady. For both our sakes. You've done a very bad thing and your parents will think I'm to blame."

Helena pouted. "I'm sorry. You're right. I was just so upset." She reached for his hand and almost fainted from joy when their fingers touched, interlacing. "But Papa was so unreasonable."

Nicholas exhaled and leaned against the side of the niche. "I think part of it is that I wasn't completely honest with you about my past, but really I had no need to be. I was never going to be considered a potential suitor for you. I was only a doctor." There was a twinkle in his eye. "Then everything happened so fast, and I wanted you to be mine as soon as possible. It was really my mistake for thinking I could suddenly ask for your hand without a proper courtship." He toyed with her fingers. "I suppose I was emboldened by my love for you."

Helena's heart skipped a beat. "You love me?"

He grinned. "I love you, Helena. I really do."

It tormented her that they had to comport themselves properly even in the absence of others. "I love you too, Nicky."

He chuckled.

"What is it?"

"You called me 'Nicky'. Only Lavinia and my family ever call me that."

"Well," she began honestly, "I would like to be considered as such an intimate one day." She tugged at his fingers. "Nicky, tell me about your family."

He told his story, some of it the same as what Lavinia had told her the previous night, but more revealing of his own deeply held feelings surrounding all the events of his past. She listened intently as he confessed the violence of his family history to her, watched the emotion twisting on his face, wanting so much to comfort him as the memories were still so painful, and wishing she could have been there for him—which, she realized, was nonsense as she would have been only a child. When he was finished, he looked exhausted and yet somehow relieved that it was all out of him.

There was one thing he hadn't told her, something she knew was so very important to him and dear to his heart. "What was your mother like?"

His face brightened. "She was beautiful, not just because she was a lovely woman, but because she was also such a gentle, kind person." He looked around the library. "She liked novels quite a bit, but sometimes I think it was because stories helped her escape from the truth of her own life." He noticed the Jane Austen in Helena's hand. "She liked *Persuasion*, it was her favorite. It's a tale of fearing one has made an incredibly bad decision in life, only to find there is still hope."

Out of frustration from wanting to wrap her arms around him and kiss him, Helena played with his fingers, pulling and tugging. Nicholas stilled her hand.

"Did I forget anything?"

A wicked notion took hold of her. "I want to know about your first time."

"My first time?" He raised his brow in astonishment. "You mean with a woman?"

"Yes."

"I really don't think I should tell you."

"I want to know." She lowered her voice. "If I am to give you my first time, I want to know about yours."

"All right," he agreed. "It was the summer before I went to university. There had been quite a drunken row between my father and myself, so I left on horseback. I really had no idea where I was going, I just rode on for hours." His palm caressed the top of her hand. "Eventually my poor horse started to complain. I stopped at a tavern and had some supper. There was a serving girl there who struck my fancy and, I suppose, I struck hers. She was older than I, not by much, but certainly more experienced. I decided to stay there for the night and she came to my room and didn't leave until morning."

Helena was mesmerized. "Was it nice?'

"It was nothing and yet everything like I had imagined. Yes," he chuckled, "it was quite nice."

"Did you think yourself in love with her?"

"Maybe at one point I wondered if I could love her, but it just seemed like such a natural thing to do, that one didn't really need love to perform the physical act."

Helena looked up at him. "Nicholas, I'll run away with you."

He stood up, dropping her hand. "Oh, no, you will not! I'm not running away any more." He paced nervously, then noticed something on Lavinia's library desk. He picked it up and brought it to her. "I had a present for you yesterday. I came to Lavinia's straight away after seeing your father, but she chastised me for visiting my lover so soon after proposing marriage. I guess I left it here."

Helena took the small package from him.

"Open it."

She pulled away the wrapping to reveal a small leather volume. She touched the smooth binding, then gently turned the gilded pages. "Nicholas, this is wonderful! Will you tell me all about it?"

Lavinia had to prepare herself for the guest waiting for her in the morning room. She drew in a deep breath and squared her shoulders before opening the door.

Mr. Phillips had not bothered to sit. When she entered, he stood glaring at her.

"Where is my daughter? I've just been to Charlotte's and she said Helena might be here."

Obviously there were to be no pleasantries. "She is, Mr. Phillips."

"I want to see her. Now." His voice was steady, but perhaps overly controlled.

"No. Not until you explain yourself."

"Explain myself? Who the hell do you think you are?" The control cracked just a little.

"Whoever I am, Helena came to me for refuge, for understanding, for safety." Lavinia was surprised at how incensed she was becoming.

"You are this man's lover, are you not?"

"Nicholas? Yes. I won't deny that and neither will he. It is my understanding you have such arrangements in America as well."

Mr. Phillips grunted at that. "Why should I let him marry my daughter?"

"Besides the fact that they are in love with each other?"

"What is love to an eighteen-year-old girl?"

"I could ask you that very same question, Mr. Phillips. I believe Sophia was the same age as Helena when she fell in love with you."

"That was different!"

"How so?"

He stood and paced. "O.K. You got me. But it was different. I'm different. I mean from that young man. He's from a violent family. A family that uses guns to solve their problems. I have seen what that can do to people. I will not have my daughter involved with that."

Lavinia sat on the couch. "Mr. Phillips, I understand completely how you feel. I, too, despise violence. It is a form of cowardice, really, if you ask me. Nicholas hated being in such an environment so much he gave up his inheritance and forsook his family. He even went so far as to change his name, his identity."

"Changing one's name does not alter one's inherent nature. If he's from a violent family, he will have violence in him."

"Nicholas ran far away from the violence, and not just with distance. He became a doctor so he could help people, heal people. I've known him since he was a child. He's never been like his father or his brother. Perhaps more like his mother, but really quite different from the rest of the family. He's always had a keen interest in how things work, in science. Such curiosity lends itself to creation, not destruction."

A glimmer in Mr. Phillips' eye indicated he was coming around, ever so slightly. Still, he would not give in. "How is it that you know him?"

"I knew his mother, Louisa, for years. We were very close. She was like an older sister to me. When the earl and Louisa came to town, we two girls were quite inseparable. She used to stay here with my husband and me sometimes, despite the fact that at that time there was still a London property owned by the family. Unfortunately, when she was at the estate with the earl and Jack, there was no one there to protect her. I knew all of this was going on, and I counseled her she should seek divorce."

Mr. Phillips' shock at the notion was unexpected.

"But her devotion to her family meant she would never do such a thing even if it meant enduring physical and emotional pain. Mr. Phillips, you should know she adored Nicholas, and he her. It hurt him terribly to leave her, he even asked that she go with him, but she would not leave her husband. He took her maiden name of Ramsay after she died." Painful memories swelled inside her. She drew in a deep breath and squeezed her eyes shut against the tears.

He sat down on the couch next to her, elbows on his knees, his hands flailing, as if at a loss what to do. "Helena is my life. You must understand this."

"I do, truly, I very much understand. As Nicholas' wife she will be his life. He will adore her and protect her and keep her happy. Trust me. He is a wonderful companion." Lavinia steadied her breathing to further calm her emotions, enabling her to see more clearly an unexpected aspect of a father's apprehension. "And, in case you are concerned about her physical satisfaction, he is a wonderful lover, as well."

Mr. Phillips blushed. "I don't think I need to know that, Lady Foxley-Graham."

"Oh yes you do. It is important to you and Sophia, I know." She squeezed his hand. "Shall we go see them?"

"Them?" He looked at her hopefully.

"Nicholas is here. They are in the library together."

Mr. Phillips seemed somehow cheered by the notion. "Yes, yes. I think I would like that."

Nicholas grabbed another volume from the shelves and put it on the pile next to Helena on the window seat. "That one too."

"Oh, Nicky, this is going to be so much fun." Helena clapped her hands in excitement.

Mr. Phillips cleared his throat.

Engrossed in the task at hand, and with Helena, Nicholas had not heard Lavinia and Mr. Phillips enter the library. Alarm coursed through him. He glanced at Lavinia, who simply raised a brow and smirked.

"Papa!" Helena exclaimed with a twinge of fear in her voice.

Mr. Phillips' face lit up as he approached his daughter. "I'm relieved that you are safe, sweet. Your mother and I have worried so." He held out his arms.

Helena gave him a quick hug. "I am safe, Papa."

"It appears that you are." He studied her. "It appears you are also very happy."

Helena blushed. "I am very happy when I am with Nicholas, Papa."

"I see."

It was clear that Mr. Phillips did not want to give in too readily.

"Look, Papa. He gave me a present."

Helena held out the book he had given her. Her father turned the small leather-bound volume over in his hands before opening it to the title page. He proceeded to review it, turning the pages carefully. He looked at his daughter, then at Nicholas.

"It's Pliny's *Historia Naturalis*, sir," Nicholas offered.

"Goodness. Does Helena read Latin?"

Nicholas quashed a grin. "A little, it appears. I'm happy to help her learn more, sir, as you can see." He pointed to the stack of books, which were mostly Latin grammars and dictionaries.

"Yes, I see." Mr. Phillips seemed a bit overwhelmed. "Helena, I would like to have a private word with the earl."

Nicholas wasn't sure if he should be worried or hopeful.

"Helena," Lavinia said gently. "Let's go to the garden, shall we? I've some lovely flowers."

Helena glanced at Nicholas who nodded. Still, she hesitated. It was obvious she did not want to leave him alone with her father.

Nicholas took her hands in his. "Helena, I'll be down shortly. Go with Lavinia. She has her very own rose named for her." His voice was calm, concealing the anxiety that tore through him. He watched as the two women left, then stared down at his feet as he shifted uncomfortably.

"May I call you Nicholas?"

It was the most disarming thing Mr. Phillips could have said. "Yes." Nicholas met his eyes, now slightly less afraid to look at the man. "I've never used a title. I fear it will take some getting used to being called 'my lord' and such."

"What will Helena be called if she marries you?"

"She would be the Countess of St. Albans or Lady St. Albans." Nicholas did not want to appear too enthusiastic about the prospect, but his voice betrayed him.

Mr. Phillips chuckled. "That's a mouthful."

"Yes, sir." Nicholas hardly knew what to say in response.

"I expect it will please Sophia, though. Did you know she was once Lady Sophia Harwell? The daughter of a marquess, no less. She could still be called the Lady Sophia Phillips, but I thought all that was balderdash. We fought a revolution so we could be rid of your aristocratic nonsense." Mr. Phillips sat on the window seat and peered down at the garden. "It looks as if I've been beaten in this war, though."

Nicholas hoped he had heard correctly. "Sir?"

Mr. Phillips smiled at him. "Do you have a ring, son?"

His heart jumped. "Yes, sir. In my pocket." Nicholas brought out the delicate gold band set with the greenest of emeralds flanked by two tiny diamonds.

"That is beautiful," Mr. Phillips said with genuine awe. He quickly looked at Nicholas. "You didn't have this made for her, did you?"

"No, sir. It was my mother's. Lavinia had been safekeeping it and my mother's wedding ring since her death."

"It will look stunning on Helena's hand."

"Sir?" Nicholas could barely conceal his jubilance. "Do you mean, sir—"

"Yes, yes, you have my permission to marry my daughter."

"Thank you, sir." Nicholas grabbed Mr. Phillips' hands and shook them vigorously. "I promise I will put her happiness before my own."

Mr. Phillips chuckled. "We all say that, Nicholas. Let me offer you some advice, son, as someone who's been married for as long as Helena has been alive." He noticed Nicholas' smile. "Yes, and now you know my little secret. Sophie and I couldn't wait until we were married."

"Sir," Nicholas said nervously, "please know there has been nothing improper between Helena and me."

"No, no, I'm sure there has not been. I trust my daughter in that regard." Mr. Phillips sighed. "When I met Sophie, I thought her the most beautiful girl in the world. We were both of us very young, neither knowing anything about being married. But I realized I had been attracted to her not just because of her beauty, but because of who she was, how we got on with each other, made each other laugh, trusted each other. We are best friends, really, and I simply could not live without her. I want that for my Helena. I want her to be with her best friend, a man she can talk to about anything, a man she can trust with her life, her heart, her happiness."

Nicholas feared his heart would burst from overwhelming joy. "Sir, I am very much looking forward to being Helena's best friend."

"Good, good, that's what I want to hear. Go along now son. She's waiting for you."

With a grin on his face and a skip in his step, Nicholas left the library to ask for his beloved's hand in marriage.

Joseph watched from the library window as Nicholas met the two women in the garden. Lady Foxley-Graham retreated deftly, handing Nicholas a rose, which he promptly gave to a delighted Helena. The besotted couple walked over to a garden bench and sat, Nicholas speaking rapidly, in earnest, Helena listening just as ardently.

And then it happened, the moment every daughter's father worries about and yet hopes for.

Nicholas got down on bended knee and took the ring from his coat pocket. Joseph grinned, knowing Helena let out a little gasp, knowing there were tears of joy glittering at the corners of her lovely hazely eyes as the ring was slipped onto her finger. He chortled at her enthusiastic reaction, looking at her hand as if she had never seen it before.

And then he sighed when Helena stood and pulled her betrothed into her arms. He had to turn away at the sight of their passionate affirming kiss.

Lady Foxley-Graham came in and joined him on the window seat. "I've sent a carriage around for Sophia. And told Sims to retrieve some champagne. We'll have a private celebration."

"Thank you." He would apologize later for being such a fool.

EPILOGUE

London, September 1879

Julius turned the page of his afternoon newspaper and happened upon the society column. He hadn't been out much since the whole business with Helena, so his curiosity was piqued. There was much discussion of who was attending whose hunting party and with whom, but rather than being mere gossip it was somewhat more like a list of which debutante had been engaged to which fine gentleman. He recognized several of the names, was surprised by some of the pairings, and found two in particular of utmost interest. It appeared that, in a ceremony swarming with marquesses and earls, Miss Helena Phillips had been married to the Earl of St. Albans, previously known by many that Season as Dr. Nicholas Ramsay.

"The couple will honeymoon in Exeter at the rustic cottage of the Viscountess Foxley-Graham," concluded the announcement. Rustic, indeed, Julius snorted. More like well-appointed and supremely comfortable, albeit perhaps a little cozy. Perfect for a pair of lovebirds—or a tryst with the married owner.

He looked up from his paper to watch Grace as she busied about his study organizing his notebooks, clearing away the tea things, and generally just keeping his space in tip-top shape.

Observing her drove him to a conclusion—Grace Danby was a marvelous specimen of the female sex.

The more Julius thought about it, the more he realized Helena just would not have done for him. She might have ended up like her mother—wanton and willing but with the drawback of being weak and submissive. Besides, she was still so young and unformed, the possibility existed that she would have grown to be appalled and disgusted at his desires.

Grace, on the other hand, reveled in his proclivities and discovered new desires within him he never thought he had. In her he found more than just an assistant, she was a willing partner, an abettor. They were of like minds.

It wasn't as if they were in love or anything so overly-sentimental and saccharine as that. Helena would have insisted on such an arrangement, and he would have eventually had to let her have her romantic affairs to alleviate that need in her. But Grace was very different. Julius often wondered what sort of bond it was he and Grace really shared. Truly it did not matter. Whatever she did with him, for him, or let him do to her, it was with absolute determination and enthusiasm.

Indeed it was she who had suggested the installation of a private electro-mechanical vibrating device in his bedroom—really their bedroom now. It was a stroke of brilliance. And as they became more inventive with the device, just the sound of the motor could make him hard.

"Julius, it's time."

Her soothing tone shook him from his thoughts. "Grace?"

"Dr. Christopher, your patient will be here shortly. I think you should get ready."

"Yes, yes, quite." He followed her downstairs.

It had also been her idea to renovate the little room under the stairs. They had cleared away some of the ill-used equipment and had made a comfortable space near the peephole. The latter they enlarged but obscured on the other side of the wall so as not to be detected even by the most anxious and cautious patient. An ingenious arrangement of screens amplified the sounds in the examination room for the listening pleasure of the occupant of the little chamber.

Julius sat in the easy chair before what was now a small observation window. He unbuttoned his flies as he watched Grace lead in their patient.

It had also been her idea to have him be the consulting doctor nervous women would see first. He would examine them to see the nature of their anxiety. If they were married, or mothers, or widows, he would teach them the skills to alleviate their own sufferings. But if they were found to be virgins, they were asked to return for a series of appointments with the nurse. Grace, as nurse, would introduce these invariably young women to the wonders of the vibrating machine.

And Julius would sit in the little room and watch.

The patient for that afternoon happened to be one of Julius' favorites. She was quite young—she had just turned eighteen when he first touched her—had the most gorgeous fiery auburn hair, and the most alluring unaffected manner. Grace always made the girls undress down to their chemise and stockings, and when their ginger-haired patient was finished, Julius saw before him the most magnificent body he had ever seen in his decades of being a doctor.

As if to tantalize him further, her chemise was of the sheerest fabric. Her nipples, hardened by the cool air of the room, puckered the thin cloth.

Julius grabbed his rampant cock and stroked himself.

Grace was masterful in her direction of patients. In a moment the ginger-haired girl was on the examination table, her legs spread wide, secured with the straps, and open to Julius' view. He watched Grace gently touch the girl's sex, separating her labia to find and oil her tender clitoris. As usual, Grace assuaged the patient, explaining what she was about to experience and to not hold any emotion back. "It is the release of pent-up feelings that leads to the cure of hysteria," she would always tell them. "You must cry out as much as you need."

Grace certainly knew his letches very well.

He frigged himself more assiduously when she clicked on the machine and the familiar whirring began.

He almost came when the wand touched the clit fringed with ginger hair, but he held on. When the girl yelped with a new understanding of ecstasy, he shivered in expectation again.

But her reaction was simply surprise, not awareness. She hadn't yet discovered her climax. She writhed on the table, at times lifting her hips to further feel the pressure of the wand on her body's most sensitive spot, crying out in abandon. Julius licked his lips fantasizing about the tightness of the girl's cunt, his hand firmly gripping his erection to simulate the sensations of her unused passage surrounding him. Grace had said one day he could teach such a patient the wonders of penetrative massage. God, could this be the one?

She was panting now, barking moans with her frantic breaths, her fingers clutching at the padding on the sides of the table. Julius rubbed his cock savagely knowing she was approaching her peak.

And when she thrust her hips up in one final reach for satisfaction and howled in orgiastic joy, Julius spewed his semen onto the floor, shuddering as he milked himself dry and listened to the ginger-haired girl exclaim in wonder at her newfound delight.

Helena inhaled deeply then let out a sigh, her tremulous exhale doing nothing to dispel the fluttering in her stomach or the heat prickling her face.

Ugh. She hadn't been so anxious since her wedding day.

That day had been terribly nerve-racking, mostly because Mama and Lavinia had fretted over her so much, as well as fretted over the presence of the Marquess and Marchioness of Richmond. Everything about the day had to be perfect—her dress, her veil, her flowers, the breakfast. And as she walked down the aisle, her heart pounding in her ears, her cheeks flushed in excitement, Nicholas watching with a satisfied grin, everything *was* perfect.

But the months leading up to the wedding had been somewhat agitating. While she and Nicholas had spent their engagement sharing a deep emotional intimacy, they had refrained from—or, rather, *he* had refrained from—exploring anything physical beyond a few furtive kisses. She felt an intense freedom when in his presence, giving her leave to be the fiery, passionate young woman she discovered she truly was, free to touch, to suggest, to attempt seduction. But Nicholas, out of a sudden sense of chivalry, had insisted she remain a virgin until their wedding night.

Or, it turned out, the night after their wedding night, as they spent most of that time traveling to Lavinia's cottage in the outskirts of Exeter. Even in the private railway car, Nicholas had kept his hands to himself, except to fend off Helena's ardent advances to give herself up to him on the moving train.

But now in the peace and quiet of the rather luxurious, if small, house, Helena felt the nervousness she was sure all brides felt. After a light supper, husband and wife had retreated to the sitting room off the bedroom. They relaxed in silence on an overstuffed couch before a stone hearth, Nicholas' arm draped languidly around her shoulders, the occasional popping of the dying fire uncomfortably marking the passage of time before Helena would give herself completely to him.

She no longer felt her usual confidence, her giddy curiosity to explore. She was no longer an enchanted girl with a dizzying infatuation, but a new wife with a perfect husband she wanted to be absolutely perfect for, worrying inexperience would lead her astray, to do something embarrassing, or, even worse, stupid. As they sat together, his closeness, his heat, his scent overwhelmed her senses. She nuzzled deeper into the crook of his arm and reached for his hand, seeking assurance. Wordlessly, they watched the glowing embers, their bodies melting, until the pop of a log brought her anxieties back to the fore.

He stroked her fingers, idly tracing the wedding band that still felt so very present on her fourth finger, his gentle steady caress sparking a warmth to smolder in her belly.

He leaned in. "Darling, do you know what fire is?" His breath was hot and moist against her forehead.

She lifted her face. "Fire?" Her lips brushed against his. The smoldering warmth flared within.

"Fire," he replied in his deep, sultry baritone. "Combustion that creates light and heat." His tongue drew a cooling path down her neck as his thumb smoothed her ring. "Temperatures so hot, gold becomes molten liquid."

Like the scorching lava flowing slowly within her. "I think so," she choked.

His hand blazed a path from her wedding band to her bodice, searching for the fastenings constricting her. "The fire needs to be fanned." One by one, he loosed the buttons, exposing her burning skin to the chilly night, then pulled the garment off. "It needs air to live."

She gulped a breath against her trepidation as his hands feverishly grabbed her corset, unhooking rapidly, untying her chemise, baring her, liberating her. She surrendered to his relentless mouth cooling her heated flesh, his lips pressed against her heart, moving lower to her naked breast.

"A fire needs tending." He caught a nipple between his teeth.

Helena yelped with a jolt, but Nicholas held her firmly as he sucked the excited peak, his wet tongue searing her tender skin, tempering her anxieties.

She let out a shivering exhale. She had so longed for him, and now that she had him, her body demanded more.

She arched her back, offering herself, willing him to tend to the other breast, letting him lay her back onto the couch to lick and nip at her belly. He moved lower, opening the tie of her drawers, loosening the tapes of her petticoats, laying kisses achingly slowly along the way.

At the hairline of her mound, he tugged down her underthings, his mouth moving toward a place that was wholly unexpected.

She grabbed his hair and pulled him up to face her. "Nicky, I'm scared."

He smiled. "I know, love." He pecked her heated brow.

He hovered above her, completely dressed, she vulnerable in her half-nudity.

"I want to see you. All of you."

He chuckled and stood up. He held her gaze as he removed his waistcoat and shoes, trousers and drawers. Still covered by his draping linen shirt, he sat and removed his collar and tie, socks and suspenders.

"All right, my blushing bride, now we're even."

"No we are not, sir!" she exclaimed. "I can't see a thing!" Her mouth watered at the tenting at his crotch.

"I feel equally deprived, madam." In one swift move, he reached down and jerked off her skirt, petticoat, and drawers. She screamed with giddy glee as he pulled off her shoes and stockings, mercilessly tickling her amidst her kicks.

Utterly nude, she lay panting on the couch and watched as he tore off his shirt.

He was magnificent.

Like a Greek god carved from marble, his pale flesh was exquisitely sculpted, the chiseled ridges and dusky hair forming shadows in the dancing firelight, his jutting cock and shallow breathing evidence of the aroused, vibrant man within.

She reached for him, wanting to touch everything at once, to feel his nakedness against her, and hers against him. He squeezed her hand before extending himself on top of her, nestling between her legs.

She grabbed his hair, slightly damp from his playful exertions, and tugged down. His mouth devoured hers, his tongue insistent, forcing her to open fully to his demands.

He pulled back. "Remember that."

She gazed at him quizzically. He cupped her cheek with a grin then once again trailed kisses down her neck. He paused at her breasts, nipping and licking, before continuing to her belly, his warm, wet tongue tantalizing the delicate skin above the curls at the apex of her thighs. Helena rocked beneath him, moaning her approbation, her invitation.

This time he didn't stop. He proceeded lower, kissing lazily until he reached the tender flesh between her legs. He bit his lip, watching with eyes widened in eager wonder as he spread her open at the knees, exposing her intimately before him. And then he dipped his head and licked her wetness.

"Oh, God!" Her hips flinched against him.

She had never imagined such a delight. It was too exquisite. His hot tongue lapped languidly, teasing her, thrilling her with new sensations. He tentatively thrust the velvety tip into her virginal passage, twisting inside, toying with her, offering an idea of what was to come, before tormenting her clit. She writhed, moaning beneath him, exhausting herself in uncontrollable throes of ecstasy, tensing at the familiar building, reaching the pinnacle in a new, wondrous way. She cried out for mercy and grabbed his hair, pulling him up to meet her face.

He gazed down at her in awe as he settled himself against her body, his lips glistening invitingly. She lifted her head to taste herself. Nicholas growled approvingly against her mouth.

"Shall I take you to bed and ravish you now?"

Helena giggled. She opened her mouth farther at the insistence of his tongue. "Why not right here?"

He raised an eyebrow at her daring suggestion. Realizing she was in earnest, he grew serious. "Darling, are you ready?"

"Yes, love," she assured him, flattening her hands against his chest. "I want you now, Nicky."

He reached down and positioned himself, holding her eyes with his own as he hovered above her, his forehead crinkled in concern above his enraptured gaze. She nodded her assent and he pushed in.

Helena gasped at what felt like a pinch, a momentary distraction of pain before the most astonishing shock wave of pleasure. A tingling flush of sensuality rippled across her entire body.

As he pulled out, she clutched at his shoulders.

Nicholas hesitated. "Helena, am I hurting you?"

"No," she choked, her voice quivering with every emotion tearing through her. "Nicky, please don't stop. Please."

He proceeded slowly, resolutely, making sure of her before quickening his pace. She looked between their bodies to watch their joining, seeing his length when he pulled out, feeling its strength when he pushed in. She smoothed her palms over the straining muscles of his back, saw the tension on his face, knowing what he felt was a mirror to the deluge of voluptuousness engulfing her. He bent down and kissed her, desperately, fervidly, his tongue tangling with hers as if he would never let her go.

He increased his rhythm, forcing her to bend acutely at the hips, and enveloped her body firmly in his arms, enabling him to drive into her more deeply. They were as one, undulating to an instinctive rhythm. She felt every inch of him, her passage clenching around him tightly, striving for some innate pleasure, one very much different from what she experienced under her own hand. A pleasure made more exciting by the presence of Nicholas, her Nicholas, her husband, his flesh, his determined desire mingling with her own.

The pleasure shattered, in her mind or in her body she was not sure. She cried out, needing more, needing solace. But Nicholas was lost to her, his head bent down in concentration, seeking his own gratification. He drove into her heedlessly, his eyes screwed shut, grunting, groaning. Unbelievably her orgasm built again, peaked, then sent her crashing over the precipice. She thrust up at the very moment he slammed into her one last time, his head tossed back, letting loose a wailing howl. He held himself steady as his hips jerked fitfully, melting her with his molten emission.

With a satiated sigh he loosened his hold and collapsed his weight onto her, his heart pounding against her breast, his breaths slowing steadily in her ear.

Her senses still reeled from the sensual satisfaction suffusing her body. Involuntarily she contracted around his still-hard cock. He twitched against her with a clipped cry, then nuzzled his face into her neck.

"Darling, thank you," he murmured. "Thank you. That was wonderful."

He was in awe of her, and she of him, of them. It had been wonderful. "Nicky, is it like that every time?"

He chuckled softly. "Only when you're with someone you love."

The Harwell Heirs

Victorian aristocracy has very strict rules concerning marital connections and familial obligations. But the Harwell heirs—Helena, Sophia, and Arthur—discover love doesn't always follow the rules. Scandalous affairs force these scions of society to choose between duty and desire, deference and destiny.

Book 1: *The Pleasure Device*
Helena and Nicholas's story

Book 2: *Disobedience By Design*
Sophia and Joseph's – and Arthur and Joseph's – story

Book 3: *Where Destiny Plays*
Arthur and Lavinia's story

Book 4: *A Delicate Seduction*
Percival and Bertram's story

Book 5: *Discovering Her Delight*
William and Beatrice's story

Book 6: *Their Noble Deceit*
Percival, Bertram, Penelope, and Viola's story

More historical romance by Regina

Victorian
The Westerman Affair (Art & Discipline Book 1)
The Invitation (Art & Discipline Book 1.5)
Disputed Boundaries (Stories from the San Juan Islands)

American Revolution
The General's Wife: An American Revolutionary Tale
Winter Interlude: An American Revolutionary Novelette

About the Author

Regina Kammer is a librarian, an art historian, and a multi-published writer of provocative historical romance and contemporary romance with a touch of history. Her short stories and novels make history sexier, whether the era is Roman, Byzantine, Viking, American Revolution, or Victorian. She's even sexed up contemporary settings, Steampunk, and Greco-Roman mythology. She has been published by Cleis Press, Go Deeper Press, Ellora's Cave, House of Erotica, Story Ink, Loose Id, The Naughty Literati, and her own imprint, Viridium Press. She began writing historical fiction with romantic elements during National Novel Writing Month 2006, switching to erotica when all her characters suddenly demanded to have sex.

Keep up with Regina
Check out her website: https://reginakammer.com/
Never miss a new release! Subscribe to *Kammerotica News*:
   https://reginakammer.com/newsletter/

www.ingramcontent.com/pod-product-compliance
Lightning Source LLC
Chambersburg PA
CBHW070441120726
47910CB00003B/885